Brigid said, "We've seen this effect before."

Shizuka fumbled with the underjaw lock-guard on Grant's helmet, and finally managed to pull it off. The top half of his face was its normal deep brown complexion while the lower part was as jet-black as his mustache. The ends of it were scorched.

Swiftly, she looked around the chamber and asked, "Where is the woman—Quavell?"

Lakesh, in a strained, hoarse voice said, "She has been taken."

Shizuka swung her head up and around. "By whom?" she demanded.

Before Lakesh could answer, Brigid interposed, "There's only one possibility. We've been expecting a move from him for months."

Horrified comprehension suddenly gleamed in Shizuka's eyes. "The Imperator?"

Lakesh passed a trembling hand over his forehead. "Yes. The Imperator has taken her."

"Why?" Shizuka's voice trembled with the effort to keep her emotions in check.

Brigid glanced toward her. Her one-word answer chilled the blood of both Shizuka and Lakesh. "Bait."

Other titles in this series:

James Axler
Outlanders

FAR EMPIRE

A GOLD EAGLE BOOK FROM
WORLDWIDE.

TORONTO • NEW YORK • LONDON
AMSTERDAM • PARIS • SYDNEY • HAMBURG
STOCKHOLM • ATHENS • TOKYO • MILAN
MADRID • WARSAW • BUDAPEST • AUCKLAND

First edition November 2002

ISBN 0-373-63836-1

FAR EMPIRE

Special thanks to Mark Ellis for his contribution to the
Outlanders concept, developed for Gold Eagle.

To sit in darkness here
Hatching vain empires.
　　　　　　—John Milton, 1608–1674

The Road to Outlands—
From Secret Government Files to the Future

Almost two hundred years after the global holocaust, Kane, a former Magistrate of Cobaltville, often thought the world had been lucky to survive at all after a nuclear device detonated in the Russian embassy in Washington, D.C. The aftermath—forever known as skydark—reshaped continents and turned civilization into ashes.

Nearly depopulated, America became the Deathlands—poisoned by radiation, home to chaos and mutated life forms. Feudal rule reappeared in the form of baronies, while remote outposts clung to a brutish existence.

What eventually helped shape this wasteland were the redoubts, the secret preholocaust military installations with stores of weapons, and the home of gateways, the locational matter-transfer facilities. Some of the redoubts hid clues that had once fed wild theories of government cover-ups and alien visitations.

Rearmed from redoubt stockpiles, the barons consolidated their power and reclaimed technology for the villes. Their power, supported by some invisible authority, extended beyond their fortified walls to what was now called the Outlands. It was here that the rootstock of humanity survived, living with hellzones and chemical storms, hounded by Magistrates.

In the villes, rigid laws were enforced—to atone for the sins of the past and prepare the way for a better future. That was the barons' public credo and their right-to-rule.

Kane, along with friend and fellow Magistrate Grant, had upheld that claim until a fateful Outlands expedition. A displaced piece of technology…a question to a keeper of the archives…a vague clue about alien masters—and their world shifted radically. Suddenly, Brigid Baptiste, the archivist, faced summary execution, and Grant a quick termination. For Kane there was forgiveness if he pledged his unquestioning allegiance to Baron Cobalt and his unknown masters and abandoned his friends.

But that allegiance would make him support a mysterious and alien power and deny loyalty and friends. Then what else was there?

Kane had been brought up solely to serve the ville. Brigid's only link with her family was her mother's red-gold hair, green eyes and supple form. Grant's clues to his lineage were his ebony skin and powerful physique. But Domi, she of the white hair, was an Outlander pressed into sexual servitude in Cobaltville. She at least knew her roots and was a reminder to the exiles that the outcasts belonged in the human family.

Parents, friends, community—the very rootedness of humanity was denied. With no continuity, there was no forward momentum to the future. And that was the crux—when Kane began to wonder if there *was* a future.

For Kane, it wouldn't do. So the only way was out—way, way out.

After their escape, they found shelter at the forgotten Cerberus redoubt headed by Lakesh, a scientist, Cobaltville's head archivist, and secret opponent of the barons.

With their past turned into a lie, their future threatened, only one thing was left to give meaning to the outcasts. The hunger for freedom, the will to resist the hostile influences. And perhaps, by opposing, end them.

Prologue

Imperial Guard Corporal McCloy raised the visor of his helmet and lifted the binoculars to his eyes. He adjusted a knurled knob on the binoculars to compensate for the fast-fading light. The glaring yellow orb of the sun had already dropped halfway below the horizon, while the other half was draped by a thick stratum of fleecy clouds.

Squinting through the eyepieces, McCloy slowly swept the ruby-coated lenses of the binoculars from left to right. The image enhancers presented a sharp image of the undulating plain. There was nothing to see but a vast expanse of coarse-grained, red-hued sand. He saw small depressions and prints made by snakes, thorny devils, dingoes, lizards and goannas, but nothing else. He bit back a curse, all too aware of his superior officer standing beside him.

"I swear I saw something moving out there, sir." McCloy lowered the binoculars and gave Lieutenant Yan a deferential smile.

Yan didn't return it. He was nearly half a head shorter than McCloy, and his features, masked by the smoke-tinted visor of his black helmet, were Asiatic. Although the two men were very different in height and build, they both wore high black boots, ebony leggings and tailored tunics of a satiny fabric. Emblazoned on the left sleeve was a red, thick-walled pyramid enclosing three elongated but reversed triangles. Small disks topped each one, lending them a resemblance to round-hilted daggers. Both men had slender SIG-AMT autorifles slung over their shoulders.

"Don't get nervous," Yan said flatly. "There's nothing out there but vermin. And they don't come close because of the construction."

McCloy didn't need reminding. From deep within the triangular slash of the cave opening behind him, he heard the clank of metal, the whining buzz of power tools and the steady pounding of hammers. Faintly, he could also hear the obscenities uttered by a garrison of soldiers forced to act as a construction crew.

Above Yan and McCloy a massive dome of rust-red rock shouldered the sky. The formation was gargantuan, almost as mind-staggeringly immense as the Xian pyramid in China, which had been the corporal's post for three months. For the past two weeks McCloy's station had been at the base of the monolith of stone so huge that he could see only a small portion of its vast proportions.

He still didn't know why he and twenty other men had been reassigned from Xian to the Australian outback, the ass end of nowhere, but he assumed it was the will of the woman known as the Imperial Mother.

McCloy had glimpsed her only a time or two within the labyrinth of caves and tunnels, as she inspected the work being done. She was the kind of woman men noticed—tall, very shapely and always poised. Her hair was very dark, her glance direct and appraising, like a commander viewing a new recruit for the first time.

But McCloy wasn't part of her staff. She was always in the company of a pair of Baronial Guardsmen, whose overdeveloped physiques were accentuated by the neat white uniform jackets they invariably wore. McCloy had heard of the Baronial Guardsmen, but never before seen one, much less two.

He was fresh to the forces of the imperator, a recent transplant from the barony of Thulia's Magistrate Division. His low scores at the academy had left him with two miserable alternatives—a clerk, or permanent sentry duty, marching around in the heavy polycarbonate black armor. Since he detested paperwork marginally more than the armor, he chose the sentry duty.

Fortunately, he had pulled guard duty only once in Thuliaville before he was ordered to trade in the hated black body armor for the much more comfortable black uniform of the imperator.

Feeling uncomfortable in the company of Lieutenant Yan, McCloy put the binoculars to his eyes again. He had seen a flicker of motion out there in the sand, behind the tangled thickets. The only movement he ever glimpsed during his previous tours of guard duty had been high in the sky, bat-winged creatures soaring and circling at the onset of dusk. One of his fellow troopers had identified them as flying foxes, but he hadn't sounded certain. Not that it mattered, since they never flapped close enough for McCloy to get a good look at them. He had on occasion received the uncomfortable but distinct impression the winged creatures were spying on them even though there was very little to see of their camp.

A handful of supply tents and the skeleton of a watchtower comprised the garrison's perimeter. A scattering of boulders and jagged outcroppings led up to the cave mouth. McCloy wasn't an imaginative man, but he was all too aware of the encampment's isolation, set into the horizon-reaching plains of desolation.

"I told you there's nothing to see out there," Yan said, an edge to his voice.

McCloy swiftly lowered the binoculars, worried that Yan misinterpreted his actions as a covert form of insubordination.

Yan pointed to the watchtower and the outline of a man standing within the enclosed platform. "If there was, don't you think Lydecker would've reported it?"

"Yes, sir," McCloy replied. "I just thought—I mean, people lived here at one time."

"Why do you say that, Corporal?"

McCloy jerked his head back toward the cave. "There were paintings and things on the walls."

Yan snorted derisively. "Those were made thousands of years ago."

"Yes, sir," McCloy said again.

The wind suddenly lifted, and dust rose thick about the perimeter. It swirled and billowed. McCloy hastily lowered the visor of his helmet, then stiffened in surprise when he heard the distant wailing note. For a few seconds he assumed the sound was caused by the wind, singing over the sand.

But the dust began to settle, shifting like streamers of filthy lace, and the wailing sound continued. Yan and McCloy jerked, both men unable to stifle wordless outcries of shock.

A long line of dark, slender figures stood inside the perimeter. All of them were naked to the waist, wearing only beaded loincloths and feathered headbands. White strips of paint decorated their broad-nosed, heavy-jawed faces. Some were bearded, others clean shaved. Their eyes were lost in the shadows cast by their jutting brows. All of them carried oval shields made of cured animal hide, stretched tight over wooden frameworks and long-shafted lances. McCloy stood motionless, held fast by the savage pageantry arrayed before him.

"What the hell?" Yan snarled out the words. "Why didn't Lydecker—?"

His words clogged in his throat when he noticed that the silhouette of the guard in the watchtower was different. A spear transfixed his torso, pinning him to the wall of the platform like a butterfly to a board.

Without waiting for an order, McCloy snatched the trans-comm unit from his belt and depressed the red button, the "chicken switch" on its molded plastic surface. From deep within the cave, an alarm siren began to hoot.

For a long moment it was all confusion as men shouted curses, dropped tools to grab weapons and pounded out side passages. Before the first man reached the mouth of the cave, the dark men swept across the plain like a wave. They didn't shout or scream or voice war cries. They simply rushed forward, shoulder to shoulder, moving in unison, as if each one were a three-dimensional reflection of the other.

Lances arced overhead, sticking quivering in the loose sand mere yards from where McCloy and Yan stood. The two hastily stepped back, unslinging and shouldering their AMTs. They squeezed the triggers, and the staccato jackhammering of full-auto fire drowned out the alarm. Spent shell casings fell in a tinkling rain at their feet. Against the swiftly moving targets, Yan and McCloy could only lay down their fire ahead of the onrushing line, hoping that they judged close enough so the savages would run into the hailstorm of lead.

The range closed with alarming speed. The dark men leading the charge clutched at themselves and staggered, but the attackers behind them kept coming, pushing them headlong. They fell, dashed against the bulwarks of stone leading up to the cavern mouth. A volley of spears clattered against the cave mouth. Yan fell back, a hand clamped over a wooden shaft protruding from his right thigh. Even running full tilt and in the fading light, the savages' aim was excellent.

A group of black-uniformed imperial soldiers raced out of the cave, firing as they came. The blended autofire gave rise to a deafening, prolonged drum roll. Their fire was disorganized and too rapid, but it had some effect—a few of the warriors toppled and fell, but the main body wasn't stopped. A trooper went down at McCloy's feet, writhing around the spear lodged in his guts. At that instant, McCoy would have traded all of his possessions—which were few and of poor quality—for even a partial suit of the despised Mag armor.

Another imperial soldier went down, snatching at a spear embedded in his breastbone. McCloy caught a glimpse of the warrior who had hurled the lance spinning, clutching at himself as the bullets clawed open his chest, sending fragments of clavicle and rib bones spinning off in all directions, propelled by crimson sprays.

The rain of spears stopped. Then, as quickly as they struck, the savages vanished, seeming to be swallowed by the encroaching shadows cast by the giant monolith of rock. In the stunned silence that followed, the moans of the wounded were frighteningly loud.

''Who the fuck are they?'' a man demanded in between gasps.

His question wasn't answered. A PRB 424 mortar

launcher was rushed up and loaded with a 60 mm, high-ex round. A trooper shouted, "Here they come again!"

McCloy looked out past the boulders and saw the dark mass of warriors gathering once more, at the same place they had begun their first charge.

Yan yelled with wild anger and fear, "Mortar, fire! Hit 'em hard!"

The mortar launcher gouted thunder and smoke, but the projectile passed over the heads of the warriors, bursting behind them with no other effect than to shower them with sand.

As another round was loaded, the SIG-AMT rifles in the hands of the soldiers roared in a stuttering rhythm, tracer rounds cutting threads of phosphorescence through the twilight. The mortar spit another shell, and this time it landed in the center of the warriors. Dark bodies flew up, out and apart amid a mushroom of yellow flame.

The near naked, spear-wielding savages came on with fanatical courage, still fighting with a silence that was more unnerving than bloodcurdling shrieks. Their bullet-slashed bodies dropped atop their dead or crippled brothers, but more appeared to clamber over the red shambles of maimed flesh and broken bone.

The mortar launcher belched more rounds, just as fast as the soldiers could load them. Shell after shell detonated, until the smoke and dust boiled high and the explosions rolled like a thunderstorm. McCloy, all but blinded, kept the trigger of his SIG-AMT depressed until the bolt snapped open on the empty chamber.

As more soldiers fired their weapons dry, a man began shouting, "Cease fire, cease fire!"

After a few seconds, the soldiers obeyed, but one trooper kept snapping his empty autorifle until Mc-Cloy took it away from him. Yan, limping because of his spear-pierced leg, shambled around in apparent shock, but when a soldier offered to pull out the lance, Yan shoved him away with a curse.

The men reloaded hastily, peering into billows of eye-stinging, astringent vapor. As it thinned, all of the troopers looked for moving targets. When they saw none, they looked on the ground for casualties. They expected to see an open-air slaughterhouse, the perimeter littered with corpses and the wounded. They saw nothing, not even a spattering of blood, but the mortar rounds had destroyed the supply tents and knocked the watchtower off its support stilts. For a long, stretched-out tick of time, nobody spoke or so much as moved.

Then Yan snarled, "This can't be! We killed dozens of those bastards! This is fucking crazy!"

He started to say more, but he coughed rackingly, pink foam flecking his lips.

Trembling, keeping his jaws clamped tight so his teeth wouldn't chatter, McCloy slid up his dust-filmed visor and lifted the binoculars to his face. He squinted through the eyepieces, making adjustments so he could see through the shifting clouds of grit and gathering twilight.

Focusing on a point beyond the perimeter, he looked for signs of the warriors' retreat, of marks in the sand where they had dragged away their dead and wounded. He saw nothing, then a dark shape suddenly arose, as if disgorged from the shadows. For a shaved sliver of an instant he thought he glimpsed one of the bat creatures flapping over the figure's head.

McCloy's heart spasmed painfully in his chest, and his breath seemed to seize in his lungs. The man stood as motionless as a statue. Around his hips was a loincloth bearing a complex design of intertwining curves and arcs. He saw those clearly, far more clearly than anything else about the figure.

The man's otherwise naked body was painted with alternating strips of bright yellow and red on his chest, midriff and arms. McCloy couldn't see his face. For some reason, the electronics of the binoculars refused to bring it into focus. Before he could stop himself, he blurted, "Oh, my God."

Yan's voice growled, "What is it now?"

"That man out there, sir."

After a moment, Yan said in disgust, "There's nobody out there. Not anymore."

McCloy didn't bother to dispute or correct him. He continued to gaze at the shadowy figure. The man slowly raised his right arm. Gripped within his hand and attached to his wrist by a leather thong was a sharpened length of bone about two feet long. It was inscribed with symbols identical to those decorating the man's body.

The bone pointed directly at McCloy, then slid to the right, where Yan stood beside him, then to the left and back to the right, as if the man were using it to count the number of soldiers assembled at the mouth of the cave.

McCloy shivered violently and lowered the binoculars. He turned to Lieutenant Yan. "You don't see him?"

Yan's face twisted in pain. McCloy started to speak again, then felt the warm tickle of liquid sliding over his lips and tasted the salty tang of blood. Murmuring wordlessly in surprise, McCloy dabbed at his nose and stared in confusion at the crimson wetness shining on his fingertips.

Yan stared at it, too, and McCloy saw blood flowing from the lieutenant's nostrils, too. "Sir—"

The lieutenant pitched into McCloy's arms as slack-limbed as a corpse. His lips writhed and he croaked, "We're all dead here."

A torrent of blood spilled from his mouth and splashed onto the ground, turning the rust-red sand into deep vermilion sludge. McCloy eased Lieutenant Yan down, chill fingers of terror knotting in his chest, squeezing his heart. He knew without knowing how he knew that Yan's wound hadn't killed him—just as he knew that he and every man in the garrison were dying.

They just hadn't realized it yet.

Chapter 1

Scavenging trips eastward were by and large unprofitable, dangerous and a complete waste of time. Although Mammoth Mare McSween fancied herself a champion salvager, she didn't like to take risks. Most of the old predark villes in her central Nevada territory had been looted of their valuables long, long before, and so she rarely considered it worth the effort to pick through them.

What Mare usually looked for were items the manufacturing divisions of the baronies didn't make or didn't widely distribute. However, the southwestern Outlands were pretty well cleaned out, so she and her crew of ten men almost never came across anything worthwhile.

The problem was that most of the places where tradeable items might be found were more than likely slap-square in the middle of hellzones, in the center of nuke craters surrounded by acres and acres of radioactive wasteland. Or, like Frisco or Lost Angeles, under several fathoms of the Cific. Mammoth Mare McSween had neither the resources nor the inclination to seek out those possible treasure troves. Therefore, she suffered through one lean time after another.

Looting the abandoned ruins of predark villes was not only an Outland tradition; it was also Mammoth Mare's family business. Her mother, her mother's father and his father before him, had made a career from ferreting out and plundering the secret stockpiles the beforetime government had hidden in anticipation of a nation-wide catastrophe.

After the world burned in nuclear flames, debris settled into the lower atmosphere to very nearly create another ice age. The remnants of humankind had waited until the Earth got a little warmer to venture forth again. Most of the early survivors had been scavengers. They really had no choice. They banded together, found predark wags and recruited men and women strong enough to defend those armored vehicles. They raided villes of the dead where the radiation had finally weakened enough to allow limited access. They traded among the settlements, swapping equipment for supplies, supplies for gas, gas for ammo, and the ammo was used to blast the hell out of whatever muties or competitors stood in the way of their scavenging.

Finding a well-stocked redoubt, one of the many underground military installations seemingly scattered all over the nuke-ravaged face of America, assured a trader of wealth and security, presupposing he or she didn't intersect with the trajectory of a bullet that had their name on it. Most of the redoubts had been found and raided decades ago, but occasionally one hitherto untouched would be located.

Although Mare's mother, Big Ma McSween, had discovered some fine hauls in the past—crates of blasters, ammunition, even clothes—by the time she died after meeting up with a bullet, most of the easy pickings and higher quality items had become as rare as a smiling Magistrate.

In the southwestern Outlands—what used to be New Mexico, Arizona and Nevada—small, impoverished settlements were isolated by hundreds of square miles of barren wasteland. Although they were prey for marauders, Mammoth Mare didn't care to turn her mother's operation into that of a wolf pack. Her reluctance had little to do with morals or ethics. Most of the outlanders who lived in the settlements rarely agreed to give up their possessions without a fight—even if they were possessions they would have had difficulty giving away.

Outlanders, anyone who chose to live outside baronial society or had that fate chosen for them, were a different sort from those bred within the walls of the nine villes. Born into a raw, wild world, they were accustomed to living on the edge of death. Grim necessity had taught them the skills to survive, even thrive, in the postnuke environment. They may have been the great-great-great grandchildren of civilized men and women, but they had no choice but to embrace lives of semibarbarism. They were tough and vicious, and protected even their low-quality goods with their lives. As far as Mare was concerned, it wasn't worth risking life and limb to raze a settlement to the ground and then find out all they had were some old boots, or maybe some home-forged black-powder firearms.

So when she caught word that there was a brisk, burgeoning trade in human beings out around the Timpahute mountains, Mare began to seriously consider expanding the focus of her operation. Humans were legitimate commodities, and though there was no longer a thriving market for slave labor, due in the main to the Magistrates, people were easier to find than usable engine parts.

Mare's philosophy, handed down to her from Big Ma, was to always follow the path of least resistance. A number of her employees subscribed to the same "when the going gets tough, the tough get going" philosophy. The tougher the going got, the more they got themselves going, leaving her operation for greener pastures—not that there were many pastures, green or otherwise, around the Big Smoke Valley she used as winter quarters.

Mammoth Mare McSween's crew didn't have a permanent headquarters. They had to be able to travel with the trade, as nomadic as any group that made its living from mobility. New markets often opened up when other scavenger groups made new strikes, digging through rubble down into the predark villes. Supplies had to be gotten to the other scavengers that joined them, as well as transport arranged for all the things they found. A permanent location would have been detrimental to profit.

Despite having inherited two heavy-duty wags from Big Ma, not to mention a network of bolt-holes, food caches and supply depots, Mammoth Mare found it increasingly difficult to keep employees, particularly those with an IQ greater than his or her shoe size. She was never sure why they kept running off. It was true, being a scavenger had become almost intolerably risky since her mother had been picked off by a Roamer sniper four years before. In the interim, Roamer gangs had become bolder. As a general rule, Roamers were dangerous only to isolated Outland settlements.

Outlaw nomads, Roamers used resistance to ville authority as a justification for their raids, murders and rapes. Inasmuch as they stayed as far away as possible from the villes, she often wondered whom they thought they were fooling by paying lip service to a political cause.

But lately Roamers had been attacking armed convoys closer and closer to the villes, as if they no longer feared apprehension by the Magistrates. Rumors had filtered into the Outland territories about an internecine war raging among the nine barons, so she assumed the Mags were too busy dealing with that to track down Roamers. So far, she had seen no evidence of a baronial power struggle, but then she tended to stay far away from the nearest barony, that of Snakefish.

Muties weren't much of a threat any longer, either. The worst of the bunch, the stickies, had long ago been all but exterminated. They were one of the most common of the mutie strains spawned by the nuke-caust of two centuries ago, and no one really knew where they came from, or even theorized on what monstrous combination of genetic malfunctions had created them in the first place.

Supposedly, none had even been seen until the first couple of years of the previous century, then like floodgates opening, sightings were reported from all over. Mare had never seen one, but she knew that about a hundred years before, the stickies had been terrors of the nuke-scarred country, because of their psychotic love of mutilating norms and torching settlements.

Legend had it that nearly a century ago a charismatic leader had united the mutie marauders to wage a holy war against the norms. As far as Mare recollected from the campfire tales she had heard, the war had not quite come off, but the memory of the threat was burned deep into the collective minds of the baronial hierarchies. It had burned so brightly that a major early aspect of the Program of Unification had been a campaign of genocide against mutie settlements in ville territories. Therefore she doubted the likelihood of members of her crew having fallen prey to stickies.

Granted, Mammoth Mare knew very little about the situation outside her territory, and she couldn't spare the resources or manpower to mount a dubious adventure east to find out.

The possibility that her men were deserting her organization to join a Farer group was also so remote that she didn't even seriously consider it. Farers were nomads, a loosely knit conglomeration of wanderers, scavengers and self-styled salvage experts and traders. Their ranging territory was the Midwest, so they couldn't have offered any personal inducements to her crew. Lately, she had begun to suspect the desertions were due more to her gender than poor pickings.

Although she had been christened Mary Lou, somewhere in her teens the Mammoth Mare sobriquet had been applied to her, probably after she topped six feet tall and began weighing in at two-hundred-plus pounds. Now she was three inches over six feet and she had no real idea of her weight, but she guessed it was in the vicinity of 250. She took a secret pride in the fact that none of it was flab.

Mare usually kept her dark-blond hair cut exceptionally short, and her normal mode of attire was a one-piece zippered coverall. To detract further from her femininity, she had adopted Big Ma's habit of chewing tobacco. But still the men continued to quit on her, a few of them offering feeble excuses, but most of them simply wandering away when she was asleep or otherwise occupied.

But she was never so preoccupied as to be deaf—she had heard whispered references to her as "Mammoth Mare McSwine." A scrawny, sun-browned rodent of a man who went by the name of Squint had been the first to coin the name, and she overlooked the disrespect the first time. She liked the man personally. He was her most seasoned scavenger and served with Big Ma for a number of years, so his mockery had been like a blowtorch applied to her heart.

The second time she warned him privately about it and went on at profane length about how she didn't find the nickname amusing. Squint pretended not to understand her anger and met her warning with a torrent of words. He was a yakker, not a conversationalist. Opinion poured out of him like water from a spigot, and Mare doubted he even heard her words over his own defensive yapping.

The third time she heard him utter the name, Mare didn't even bother with a confrontation. She ordered him spread-eagled to the rear of a wag and peeled the flesh off his back with a horsewhip, her late mother's emblem of office and authority.

Squint didn't die, but he was permanently disfigured and as soon as he had healed sufficiently, he slunk off one night with a week's supply of MREs and water. As much as she wanted to, Mammoth Mare didn't track him down. Squint had enjoyed a certain popularity among her crew, and publicly scourging him hadn't raised her esteem in the eyes of the men. From that point on, they rarely spoke to her, and then only when she directly addressed them. She pretended that was the way she wanted it.

Her mother had told her many times that the female chief of a scavenger crew couldn't afford to get lonely or vulnerable. "You get too close to one them slag-jackers," she had said, "and some night he slits your throat and takes what's yours."

Big Ma had a very low opinion of men, although Mare figured it had to have been fairly high at one time; otherwise she herself would have never been born. She often wished for a mate so she could have a child, but most of the men in her crew had spent their lives scrounging around the edges of hellzones and hot spots. Her mother had warned that such men could shoot nothing but strange, twisted seed that produced offspring fit only to be drowned as soon as they drew their first breath.

Therefore, the female of the species was vastly superior, and it did no good to wish for companionship. Mare never sought it out, but she couldn't help but admit to herself she missed Squint. At about the same time, the rumors of a trade in human beings reached her through a couple of her scouts. They were third hand reports, and her first inclination was to dismiss them.

As a child, she had heard similar stories of cannibals running wild in the deserts, eating everybody and anybody they saw. She assumed the people-trade tale was nothing but an updated version of that old fable. But the bizarre rumors persisted, and as puzzling as the situation seemed, she seriously considered sending a scouting party to check it out.

Before Mare made up her mind, Squint came sauntering into the camp one sunset about five weeks after he had disappeared. He made no apologies, nor did he offer a single word of explanation. Instead he began yapping in his characteristic staccato, full-auto fashion about the profitable trade in human beings out in the old dry basin of Groom Lake. He claimed that for the past two weeks he had been staying with an isolated group of that very same commodity.

Squint claimed that he had been living with a band of people in a collection of shanties near old 376, just outside of Big Creek. He assured her they weren't any kind of mutie; they were genuine, bona fide human beings, about as healthy as could be expected, so they definitely weren't Dregs.

Dregs were the outlanders shunned even by other outlanders. One of the legacies of the nukecaust was a fixation on genetic purity, and an important aspect of the unification program had been the extermination of all human deviates, particularly muties. Although Dregs weren't muties, they had been classified as such a hundred or so years before. Therefore, they hadn't been spared the genocidal purges that virtually exterminated all the mutie strains, except for a few isolated pockets in dark territories.

The Dregs were diseased, genetically ruined human beings who had lived too long near hellzones and rad hot spots. They were the lepers of the postskydark world.

Squint's story sounded convincing, although he couldn't offer much in the way of intelligence regarding the identity of the people, who the buyers were or what they wanted the merchandise for. Mare couldn't help but wonder briefly if the cannibals were at it again, but now buying their food of choice instead of hunting for it.

"Whoever the buyers are," Squint concluded, "they're offerin' contracts. So why don't we let bygones be bygones and get in on this afore we're outbid by small-time Farer trash? All I want is a little extra skimmed off the top—sort of a finder's fee."

Mammoth Mare preferred to kill him, but the man was so persuasive she decided to check out his story. If it wasn't true, she could always put a bullet in his brain later. Or, she reminded herself, maybe even it was true.

She agreed for Squint to lead them to the encampment, and he made no attempt to conceal his smirk of triumph. The next day at dawn, Mare and her crew set off in her biggest, most heavily armored transport wag, a converted dump truck. With large rusting patches, dents and the missing front bumper, the wag looked like a wired-together rattletrap, but it was a true behemoth. Big Ma McSween had killed any number of men who had coveted it and proposed to take it from her by force.

The trip wasn't a long one, but it was rough. The wag, with its huge knobby tires, rolled over the rotten asphalt of the highway. Mare, Squint and Levitz, the wheelman, sat in comparative comfort in the cab. The rest of the crew rode in the back, where they were jolted, jounced and bounced. All of them were armed, although Mare had warned them the objective was take the people alive.

She tried to make herself comfortable, but it was almost impossible with the constant jouncing of the truck and the hard seats with their broken springs. The asphalt had a peculiar ripple pattern to it, and weeds sprouted from splits in the surface. The rippling effect was a characteristic result of earthquakes triggered by nuclear-bomb shock waves.

The wag bounced and groaned onward, pushing through billows of alkali dust. After a couple of hours of being pummeled, Squint directed the driver to turn northward, and the roadbed abruptly and mercifully became smooth. After another half hour's travel, Squint told Levitz to cut across a median strip and leave the highway altogether.

The truck crossed the shoulder of the road and plowed through a high hedgerow of mesquite and sagebrush. An old, almost completely overgrown gravel path cut through the tangle of underbrush. Mare figured it was an ancient maintenance road. Levitz downshifted and proceeded slowly.

As the vehicle rolled farther down the path, the brush became sparser. Squint leaned forward, peering through the dust-filmed windshield. He said suddenly, "Stop."

The wheelman braked the big wag to a groaning stop. He sat with his hands gripping the steering wheel and glanced questioningly toward Mare. She in turn glanced at Squint. The little man met her gaze with a twisting of his lips she interpreted as a smile. "They're a little ways ahead," he told her.

Mare instructed Levitz to turn off the engine and she climbed out of the cab, dragging her Mossberg 5100 rifle from beneath the seat. Squint stayed put, watching her with inscrutable eyes. "I told you…they ain't armed."

"I remember," she replied, working the bolt action to chamber a .243-caliber round. "What I don't remember is telling you to sit on your ass. You're leading the way."

Squint hesitated for a second, then shrugged and climbed out. Mare's crew clambered down from the bed of the truck and stood around it uncertainly. She told them not to wander off, then she and Squint pushed through a copse of shrubbery.

They hadn't walked far before the settlement, if it could be called that, came into view. It looked like the rough sketch of a shantytown someone intended to build one day. Mare and Squint cautiously approached the outer perimeter, not that one was clearly defined. A square wooden sign hung crookedly on a tall post. The words painted on it were nearly indecipherable due to long exposure to the harsh elements, but Mare was able to read it. The sign read Road Runner Station Members Of Kiwanis And Rotary Clubs. We Don't Rent Coyotes. Beep-Beep.

Mare was perplexed by the legend, particularly the last few words, but she knew there were plenty of crazy people in the Outlands. Anybody who lived in the Outlands had seen enough terrible things to push sanity right out of their heads, so she figured the people of Road Runner Station were as fused-out as some of the other lunatics she had met.

A half-dozen shelters made of splintering wooden siding and rotted canvas formed a squared U shape around a spacious central area. At the apex of the U, three of the ramshackle structures converged, leaning into one another. The suggestion of a stockade fence was barely identifiable, rising from the sandy soil. On the far side of the settlement, down a short embankment, a thin stream of water trickled, curving around the farthest outbuilding. In the center of the settlement, Mare saw the residents.

There were four men, three white, one black, two black women, one white girl barely out of her teens and four little kids. They sat around a collection of wagons cobbled together out of bicycle wheels and wheelbarrows. They were singing. Mare could catch only half the lyrics—some nonsense about having faith in the Lord and His angelic host. But still the song affected her strangely. It made her think of how lonely and barren her life had been, and she nearly burst into tears. She quickly got control and sneered at herself.

What impressed, and stunned, Mammoth Mare most was the fact there wasn't one blaster among them—not a single home-forged muzzle loader, not one pistol or a rifle. The people just sat and sang, as if they weren't straddling the thin line between life and death. She found herself envying their ease, their foolish sense of safety. Even though they seemed too stupid to live, she envied them.

"Do they trust you?" she whispered in Squint's ear.

The man lifted his knobby shoulders in a shrug. "I reckon."

"Then go out there and say something to them, get them off guard."

Squint nodded and stepped out into full view. Loudly he announced, "Hello again, folks. Guess what? You're all goin' on a trip!"

Chapter 2

When Mare moved out into the open and showed them her rifle, the people's reaction wasn't what she expected. One of the children burst into tears. Two of them ran behind the women. The men started shaking. All of their faces twisted into expressions of horror, but not because of the gun. They looked as if they knew where Squint and Mare intended to take them—and the reasons why.

They didn't resist, even though the children sobbed uncontrollably when Mare herded them out of the settlement at blaster point. As she and Squint marched them down the path to the truck, she contemplated briefly taking the crying child as her own to raise, but she didn't give the notion serious consideration. Once they reached the truck, her men forced all of the captives into the back.

Mare and Squint climbed back into the cab with Levitz, who keyed the engine to life. When the wag shuddered and began to move slowly back toward the highway, the prisoners screamed and a couple of them tried to leap over the side, but they were clubbed down. Mare ordered Levtiz to stop so the prisoners could be subdued.

Rather than waste time, rope and effort tying them up, Mammoth Mare sent Elroy among them, forcing ladlefuls of dark liquid down their throats. It was a simple sleep potion, and within minutes all of them were slumped unconscious across the truck bed. Mare saw no reason to bruise and batter them after going to such lengths to acquire them in the first place. Putting them to sleep until they reached their destination was much more efficient than keeping them bound. She hoped that by the time they awoke, the transaction would be over.

One of the black women was the most difficult to subdue. She didn't submit meekly to having the potion poured down her gullet, and she managed to bite Elroy's fingers and kick him in the groin. Mare then sat on her, held her nose and dumped a measure of the liquid into her open mouth.

Within a few minutes she was slumbering and the wag got under way again. The Groom Lake basin area was less than 180 miles away, and Mare figured if they maintained a steady rate they could reach it before sunset. On a flat straightaway like 376, the dump truck quickly built up a good head of speed, averaging forty-five miles per hour.

The wag covered twenty miles in a little more than half an hour. The highway was in fairly good condition, despite such obstacles as small boulders scattered across it and clumps of brush sprouting from the cracks in the tarmac.

The terrain on either side of the road was bleak and

dark, as if it had been exposed to open flames. The few trees they saw were leached of all color, a mono-chromatic shade of gray. It was like looking at the world through a set of night-vision goggles. Although the sun overhead was bright, the countryside was various shades of gray. Dead brush crunched under the tires, falling apart like sculptures made of ash.

Powdery sand and ash floated up in the wake of the truck's passage, coating Mare's throat so thickly that she nearly succumbed to a coughing fit. Drinking deeply from a canteen, she washed out her mouth. She had seen rad-blasted landscapes like this before, hellzones where invisible poisons had leached all life away.

As Mare absently clocked the miles on the odometer, a queasiness, then a cold nausea crawled into the pit of her stomach. At first she assumed it was due to motion sickness, but when a lump seemed to form in her throat and made breathing difficult, she realized with a distant astonishment the sensation of sickness was actually guilt.

She tried to ignore it, to push it into a dark corner of her mind, but she found herself glancing through the rear window of the cab at the bodies huddled on the floor of the bed. She told herself that the people were just commodities, simply statistics. Life in the Outlands was never easy, and it was bound to grind up some folks. Morality had nothing to do with it. It was a matter of survival.

Mare had no choice but to be hard-hearted, since

the baronies hired their own traders, who in turn controlled the supply routes and made a profit that was plowed back into getting more vehicles onto the supply routes. Now the various traders were organizing, forming a consortium, and independent operations like hers were in danger of becoming extinct, just like the stickies. She couldn't afford to feel sentiment over statistics.

But the trouble was that these people weren't just a group of statistics. They had faces, they had voices, they had names. They hadn't crossed her path; she had gone out of her way to cross theirs.

As the miles rolled by and the sun climbed to its noonday apex, Mare's sense of foreboding grew, until it was one baby step below a full-fledged anxiety attack. When Squint commented, "Getting' closer," the sound of his reedy voice made her jump.

Levitz cast him a quizzical glance. "Why do you say that?"

With a dry chuckle, Squint pointed through the dirty windshield. "Look up. About eleven o'clock."

Mare and Levitz leaned forward, gazing in the direction of the small man's index finger. For a moment, Mare saw nothing but a deep-blue sky, with only the wispy suggestions of clouds. Then she glimpsed a tiny fleck of jet black against the vast tapestry of azure. She managed to bite back a curse, but she wasn't quite able to suppress a groan.

Levitz saw it, too. "Oh, shit," he husked out.

Both he and Mare instantly identified the waspish

configuration of a Deathbird. The black choppers were the primary form of air transportation to make a comeback after the nukecaust, and they were the sole property of the Magistrate Divisions. Levitz instinctively lessened the pressure of his foot on the wag's accelerator.

"What the hell is a Deathbird doing out here?" he demanded in angry fright. "We must be four or five hundred miles from Snakefish!"

Mare turned her head to apprise Squint with a slit-eyed stare. "Mags have a base out here, don't they? They're the people buyers, ain't they?"

Squint raised a pair of conciliatory hands, but didn't make eye contact with her. "All I know is that there's a base out in Groom Lake. I don't know who operates it, but they got Mags runnin' security for it."

Mare bared her teeth and clutched the man around his wattled throat. "If Mags are out here, then so are the fuckin' barons!"

"Mebbe we can just turn around afore we're spotted," Levitz blurted.

Mare continued to glare at Squint while she thought over the wheelman's suggestion.

Squint's lips writhed, either in a grin or grimace. "Too late for that. They know we're here." He sounded almost happy about it.

Mare's heart skipped a beat and then began to thud frantically. She released the scrawny man and glanced out the windshield again. Although she knew the Deathbird was a predark helicopter, the distant sight of it awakened in her a superstitious dread, rekindling old folk tales told around campfires, about sky monsters, giant bats that haunted the ruins of nuke-scorched cities. The notion of cannibals bartering for her wares now seemed almost quaint.

The Deathbird rotated in the air, banked, then arrowed straight toward them. It circled, hovering for a long moment. Mare could barely hear the droning chop of the blades over the rattle and roar of the wag's engine. She figured the crew of the Bird was examining her cargo in the vehicle's bed.

The black chopper made a low, slow pass, flying alongside the truck, pacing it. Even through the smoke-hued foreport, Mare saw a dark figure making an unmistakable gesture that they should continue down the road.

Levitz licked his pale, dry lips. "What should I do?"

"Keep going," Squint retorted sharply. "Ain't no chance in hell of outrunnin' 'em."

Mare cuffed the man on the side of his head. "I give the orders here, pissant!"

Levitz turned his terrified, wide eyes toward her. "Then give some, for God's sake!"

Mare looked past him at the Deathbird pacing them like a hungry vulture. Painted a matte, nonreflective black, the chopper's sleek, streamlined contours were interrupted by only the two ventral stub wings. Each wing carried a pod of missiles. The perforated barrel of the forward-mounted chain gun in its swivel turret winked dully in the sunlight.

She sighed heavily. "Squint's right. We can't out-run them. Let's keep going."

Levitz nodded grimly and said nothing more. He gripped the steering wheel so tightly his knuckles were white, looking almost as if the skin would split. The road inclined slightly to the top of a knoll. Ahead of them loomed the jagged battlements of the rugged Timpahute mountain range. Mineral deposits glittered with the reflected radiance of the sun. The jagged peaks, much eroded by the ages, resembled the fangs of an unbelievably huge, fossilized predator.

The wag followed the chopper along the road, down a narrow pass twisting between ridges of barren rock. At the bottom of the pass, in a vast bowl of desolation, the sere basin of Groom Lake was spread out. It was basically flatland, with no sign of desert scrub to relieve the monotony of the dry, sunken lake bed. There was nothing resembling a lake, not even a few puddles. The basin was sunk well below the foothills of the mountain range.

Far in the distance, on the other side of the lake bed, a scattered collection of structures rose from the ground. They reminded Mare of the broken-off stumps of teeth. There looked to be at least a mile's worth of ruins. The line of structures was completely dwarfed by a building so tremendous in size, it was easily seen without the aid of the binoculars. She estimated it was more than three-quarters of a mile long and a quarter-mile wide, and at the very least a hundred feet tall. Two dark bug shapes hovered above it, and she guessed they were two more Deathbirds.

A few yards beyond the mouth of the pass, a pair of small concrete-block cupolas bracketed the road. Protruding from rectangular ports were the long barrels of big, multibored automatic weapons. Mare figured they were miniguns, capable of firing 5.56 mm ammo at the rate of 6000 rounds per minute. If her wag was caught in a cross fire between the two blasters, it would be reduced to scrap metal in less than half a minute. She saw no movements from within the ports and wondered if the minigun emplacements were remote controlled.

Past the blockhouses, pyramid-shaped ''dragon's teeth'' obstacles made of reinforced concrete lined both sides of the path. Weighing a thousand pounds each and five feet tall, they were designed to break the tracks or wheels of any assault vehicle trying to cross them.

Levitz braked the wag and put the gears into neutral. ''Now what?'' he asked hoarsely.

Mare looked past the obstacles toward the ruins and saw a vehicle cutting a swath across the tableland. She knew what it was and set her teeth on another groan. A Sandcat churned its way over the lake bed, twin plumes of grit curving up from the clattering metal tracks. The controlled roar of the 750-horsepower engine was easily audible, even though the Cat was nearly half a mile away.

A pair of flat, retractable tracks supported the Sandcat's low-slung, blunt-lined chassis. An armored topside gun turret concealed a pair of USMG-73 heavy machine guns. The wag's armor was composed of a ceramic-armaglass bond, shielded against both intense and ambient radiation—or at least that's what Mare had been told by her father. He had also told her that only Magistrates traveled in Sandcats, just as Deathbirds only carried Magistrates.

The Sandcat clanked to a halt between the pair of blockhouses, and its gull-wing doors popped open. Two men climbed out, both of them wearing the Magistrate-issue black, polycarbonate body armor. A small, disk-shaped badge of office was emblazoned on the left pectoral. It depicted a crimson, stylized, balanced scales of justice, superimposed over a nine-spoked wheel, which symbolized the Magistrate oath to keep the wheels of justice turning in the nine baronies.

The helmets were also of black polycarbonate, conforming to the shape of the men's heads and exposing only a portion of mouth and chin. The red-tinted visor was slightly concave. The design of the Magistrate armor was for more than functional, practical reasons. The two men were symbols of awe, of fear. They looked strong, fierce, implacable and not altogether human.

Mare's heart spasmed painfully within her rib cage, and she felt her bowels loosen. She had never seen a Magistrate before and more importantly, she had undertaken a great deal of effort never to be seen by them. Big Ma had warned her many times that to earn a swift death, known in Outland vernacular as a ''Mag's mercy,'' all she had to do was come to their attention.

The pair of black-armored men stared at the truck steadily, expressionlessly. Neither one of them made a move to unleather his Sin Eater from his forearm holster.

''I think you'd better go talk to them, Mare.'' Levitz said.

Dabbing at the film of cold sweat beading on her upper lip, Mare nodded, then carefully opened the door of the cab. She stepped out and walked slowly to the front of the truck, moving as deliberately as if she were treading on eggshells. She made certain to hold her hands well away from her body. The Deathbird hovered over the lake bed, a few yards behind the Sandcat. The rotor wash sent dust devils spinning and whirling like miniature cyclones. The bore of the chain gun seemed to fix on her like a hollow, cyclopean eye.

The taller of the pair of Magistrates stepped around one of the pyramid-shaped obstacles. ''Tell your driver to kill the engine.''

His loud, aggressive voice punched Mare's eardrums and she flinched. She turned toward the cab and drew her finger across her throat. Levitz obligingly keyed off the truck's engine.

"You've brought us merchandise." The Mag wasn't asking a question; he was making a statement.

For an instant, Mare wondered how he knew, then she realized the Deathbird's crew had radioed in a description of the wag's contents. She nodded, doing her best to keep her face a blank mask.

"Answer me when I speak to you, you Outland slag-jacker!" the Magistrate snarled.

"Y-yes sir," Mare stammered. "We have merchandise. Found 'em this morning and brought 'em here straightaway." Her words nearly tumbled over one another in their haste to leave her mouth.

A cold, stitched-on grin creased the armored man's face. "Tell your crew to throw out their blasters and climb down."

Mare turned her head and shouted, "Throw down your guns, then come out!"

Far in the distance, she saw a pair of tiny specks, looking like newborn tadpoles swimming through a clear azure pool. She paid them no attention at first, but as she began to face the Mags again, she absently noted how the specks appeared to grow larger between one eye blink and another. She thought again of the legendary sky monsters, but knew the black helicopter was far more dangerous than any creature out of folklore.

Her crew complied with the order, and a flurry of weapons flew over the sides of the truck's bed and clattered noisily against the ground. The men followed their weapons, taking up position in a ragged line at the rear of the wag. The silent Magistrate moved forward, extending his right arm toward them. Mare caught only a blurred fragment of motion, then the man's Sin Eater slapped solidly into his open hand.

Mare had heard about the Sin Eaters, of course. The big-bored handblasters were part of the Magistrate mystique, the official side arms that were as much of a badge of office as the ones they wore on their chests. Stripped down to skeletal frames, the Sin Eaters were barely fourteen inches long. The extended magazines held twenty rounds of 9 mm ammo. There was no trigger guard, no fripperies, not a wasted inch of design. The Sin Eaters looked exactly like what they were supposed to be—the most wickedly efficient blasters ever made.

"Hands behind your heads!" the Mag barked.

Their faces pale with fright, Mare's crew did as commanded. Her temples throbbed with tension. At any instant she expected both Magistrates to let loose with a full-auto salvo, kill them all where they stood and appropriate her wag and cargo. Her only consolation was that Squint would die, too, but it was a small comfort, under the circumstances. At the far edge of audibility, she heard a faint, keening whine. She wondered briefly if, in her terror, she was unconsciously making the noise.

Then she saw the two Magistrates glancing around in wonder, and tilting their heads back, mouths gaping open in astonishment. Mare started to look up, too, but at that moment the *real* sky monsters struck.

Chapter 3

Grant saw the other two Deathbirds making a high and wide circling pattern over the giant hangar—or rather, the heads-up display in his faceplate registered their radar signatures.

"Two more players on the field," he said, his lion-like growl of a voice echoing within his helmet.

"I'm figuring they're about three minutes away at top speed," Kane's voice responded crisply in his ear. "Once they see us, anyway."

Although they were flying low, the two Manta ships had their atmospheric cruising throttles opened three-quarters of the way as they streaked across the sky at five hundred miles per hour. Within seconds, the men aboard the hovering Deathbirds would realize that the strangely shaped dark objects in the sky were aircraft, but neither Kane nor Grant was worried about engaging the Birds—one of the reasons they had flown the TAVs—Transatmospheric Vehicles—from Montana to Nevada was to test their air-to-air and air-to-ground combat capabilities.

The craft were little more than wedges with curves, flattened javelin heads equipped with two different kinds of engines—a ramjet and solid-fuel pulse detonation rockets—that worked in tandem to enable the craft to fly in a vacuum and in an atmosphere.

They called the ships Mantas for a simple reason— the resemblance to seagoing manta rays was more than superficial, particularly when the ribbed, incurving wings were at full extension. The vehicles had fifteen-yard-long fuselages, twenty-yard wingspans with five-yard tails, tipped by spade-shaped rudders.

They appeared to be made of a burnished bronze alloy, but in reality the composition of the outer armor most closely resembled armaglass, the plasticized metal created in zero-G conditions and overlaid by a pyroceramic hull finish. Intricate geometric designs covered almost the entire hull surface, deeply inscribed into the metal itself. Interlocking swirling glyphs, graceful cup and spiral symbols, even elaborate cuneiform markings decorated the ships from stem to stern.

The cockpits were almost invisible, little more than elongated oval humps in the exact center of the sleek topside fuselages. The hulls were smooth, with barely perceptible seams where the metal plates joined. The craft had no external apparatus at all, no fins, no exhaust ports.

In the pilot's seat of his Manta, Grant wore a bronze-colored helmet with an opaque full-face visor. The back of the helmet was attached to the headrest of the chair, and a pair of tubes stretched from the rear to an oxygen tank at the back of the seat. The chair and helmet were of one piece, a self-contained unit.

The interior curve of the helmet's visor swarmed with CGI icons of sensor scopes, range finders and various indicators. Seeming to float in the air between his eyes and the visor, a column of numbers appeared, glowing red against the pale bronze. When he focused on a distant object, the visor magnified it and provided a readout as to distance and dimension. Now he focused on the Deathbird hovering above the Sandcat at the leading edge of the dry lake bed.

Even though he was intimately familiar with them, the Deathbird attack helicopters were frightening pieces of machinery. They were modified AH-64 Apache attack gunships, and most of the ones in the Magistrate Division fleets had been reengineered and retrofitted dozens of times.

Thirty feet long, fifteen feet high, the maximum speed of the insectlike choppers was 185 miles per hour. In the hands of an experienced pilot, they could maneuver like hummingbirds, up, down, sideways, backward, all very swiftly and fairly quietly.

"You ready?" Kane asked.

Grant glanced out the cockpit canopy and saw Kane's ship nosing ahead of his. He wasn't surprised, but he was annoyed. Kane was a born and bred point man. During his Mag days, because of his uncanny ability to sniff danger in the offing, he was always chosen to act as the advance scout. Kane claimed that when he took point, he felt electrically alive, sharply attuned to every nuance of his surroundings and what he was doing.

"How about dropping back?" Grant didn't bother to disguise the irritation in his tone.

A somewhat contrite laugh sounded in his ear. "Sorry," Kane said. "Old habits and all that."

Grant replied, "Yeah, I know all about your old habits. They've nearly gotten me killed a few times. Let's do this together."

"Hit the Bird at the same time?"

"Why not?"

"Why not indeed," Kane responded in a sardonic drawl. "Let's do it."

Kane's Manta ship tipped up on the starboard wing and banked away, arrowing in on the Deathbird from the left. Grant's fingers squeezed the triggers on the control stick just as rockets flamed from the wings of Kane's craft. Grant fired off two mini-Sidewinders.

The combined missile barrage hit the Deathbird amidships. To Grant's surprise, the chopper split in two a second before its fuel tank exploded. The craft side-slipped to starboard and plummeted straight down, as if it had been dangling from a string that had been cut. The rotor blades fanned the air sluggishly, even as it plunged toward the ground.

Grant pulled back on the stick to avoid colliding with the spray of flaming debris. He and Kane's Manta ships roared by on either side of the thick column of smoke, leaving such a whirlwind in their wakes that plumes of vapor followed them like accusatory fingers.

As he reduced his ship's speed to 100 mph, Grant's ears started buzzing. He recognized the sound as the radar lock-on warning, piped from the forward sensor array into his helmet.

"Hear that?" Kane asked.

"Very clearly," Grant answered gruffly. He punched a series of numbers into flight control computer, trying to achieve a fix on the radar emitters.

"Uh-oh," Kane commented mildly.

"What?" demanded Grant.

"We should've known they'd beef up the perimeter defenses after the last time we were here."

A red square of light suddenly appeared on Grant's HUD, superimposed over a small, grid-enclosed area of the terrain. Simultaneously, the warning chime sounded. Then another red glowing square appeared and the chime bonged again.

From the lake bed, two cylindrical ten-foot-tall towers arose, sand and pebbles cascading down from their domed tops. The towers rotated, the laser targeters mounted on top of them popping on, following the Mantas' flight path. Protruding from four oblong slits on each side of the towers were multiple blaster barrels.

Grant stared at the image of the Vulcan-Phalanx gun housings on his helmet display. The rotating, multibarreled weapons fired uranium-tipped explosive shells at 6600 rounds per minute. The Vulcan-Phalanx system was a standard defense of the network of villes stretching across the length and breadth of the country. The housings were automated, containing tracking and firing control radars. He and Kane had seen similarly camouflaged emplacements before.

Flickering spear points of flame erupted from the slits of the housings. Kane's Manta lurched to port as a shell exploded in a flaring shower of metal and flame against the tip of its starboard wing. The fragments rattled noisily against the fuselage of Grant's own ship.

"Climb!" Kane shouted.

Applying full throttle, Grant pulled the TAV into a steep climb, the Manta rising so swiftly and sharply that it appeared to be standing on its tail. The maneuver created a force equivalent to three times that of gravity, but the pilot seats instantly compensated for the increased pressure.

At the apex of the ascent, with the airspeed decreased to thirty knots, Grant pushed the stick forward and nosed the Manta into a steep dive. The cockpit resonated with the high-pitched whine of the stressed ramjets and the slipstream of air sliding around the hull.

He dropped the TAV rapidly to an altitude of barely fifty feet, while increasing its airspeed to a 120 mph. Absently he saw Kane expertly duplicating the maneuver. Both men leveled off their crafts, and the Mantas hurtled forward, skimming the rocky ground, leaving streams of grit swirling in their wake.

The thudding hammer of the Vulcan-Phalanx guns continued, and Grant knew the few seconds' respite from the radar could be counted on the fingers of one hand. The tracking controls would reestablish their lock at any second. His fingers hovered over the nose-mounted cannon trigger, and his HUD automatically adjusted the CGI crosshairs, superimposing them over the image of the gun turret. The warheads of the cannon shells contained incendiary properties and the immediate result of an impact was a flash fire. If the projectiles struck a flammable target such as a fuel tank or ammunition, it would cause them to instantly explode.

Grant achieved target acquisition and squeezed the trigger. A stream of armor-piercing steel and tungsten carbide shells punched a cross-stitch pattern in the dirt in front of the housing. The lines of impact scampered across the lake bed, flinging divots and tongues of flame in all directions. They intersected with the base of the tower, penetrated the metal and the explosive warheads detonated.

The Vulcan-Phalanx gun tower was swallowed by a billowing, red-orange fireball. The staccato hammering of the gun ceased abruptly as the circuitry within the turret was smashed, scorched and melted.

"You want to take the other one?" Grant asked casually, "or should I give you the Birds?"

"All things being equal," retorted Kane, "I'll give the Birds my undivided attention."

ALTHOUGH HE WAS sorely tempted, Kane didn't fly toward the gargantuan hangar or the scattering of ruins. He knew ninety-nine percent of the Area 51 installation lay deep beneath Groom Lake, shielded by hundreds of feet of steel-reinforced bedrock. The base extended even into the foothills of the mountain range, so there was little point in staging an attack against the surface structures. They were exactly what they looked like—ruins dating back to the nukecaust.

He jockeyed his TAV toward the swiftly approaching Deathbirds, pulled the Manta into a climb and performed a swift loop that sent the little space plane arrowing toward choppers from behind. The Bird on his right veered around in a fast curve, a Shrike missile flaring from its port-side stub wing. It streaked beneath the Manta and impacted against the lake bed amid a spray of gravel, sand and a yellow-orange fireball.

Kane pulled back on the joystick controls again and went up over the Deathbirds, banked in the opposite direction, then dived again.

Opening full throttle, he sent the Manta skating beneath the helicopters and turned sharply into a barrel roll. Through the canopy Kane saw the horizon wheeling crazily. When it straightened out, he brought the closer of the choppers into target acquisition and squeezed the cannon's trigger.

He glimpsed a ragged series of holes appearing in the black hull of the Bird, then a shaved sliver of a second later, he was all but blinded by a hell-hued blossom of light as the Deathbird's fuel tank ruptured, ignited and exploded. Flying pieces of machinery rang reverberating chimes on the Manta's hull. Fragments of the main rotor blade, pinwheeling at incredible velocities, smashed into the TAV's frontal armor and bounced away.

Cursing, Kane pushed the control stick forward and put the craft into a sharp dive, then he pulled up equally sharply. A missile smoked from the surviving Deathbird's launcher, arcing well below him.

The Deathbird climbed in wind-screaming pursuit, little spear points of orange flame flickering from the chain gun. Kane winced at the series of ear-knocking clangs as .50-caliber rounds struck the Manta's hull. Kane didn't know if the TAV's armor would withstand a prolonged pounding of .50-caliber blockbusters, but he was certain a high-ex missile scoring a direct hit would certainly disable the ship. Most of the Shrikes carried incend and high-ex warheads, so a solid strike had the capacity of piercing armor plate to a depth of twelve inches.

Kane pulled back on the stick, dropping both the Manta's speed and altitude. The Deathbird overshot him, roaring directly overhead. It fought to turn to face him, performing a straining, clumsy pirouette, until the tinted Plexiglas port faced the Manta.

Missiles burst from both the Bird's wings, streaking and flaming all around. For a moment, all Kane could see were yellow-red tongues of fire and spark-shot vapor trails. He banked sharply ninety degrees to starboard. A hail of steel-jacketed hornets stung and splattered against the wings of the TAV, as the Deathbird unleashed its full arsenal of machine-gun fire and missiles. Craters of varied size and shape burst open in the lake bed.

Kane pulled back on the control stick, and the acceleration of the vertical thrust slammed down on him, pushing him hard against the back of his chair. The HUD's speed gauge icon scrolled with numbers. He disengaged the throttle until the Manta lost speed. Then he ruddered the craft around sharply, shoving the joystick forward. Kane dropped the ship in a sharp dive and came rushing up on the Deathbird from below and behind. The sensor scope targeted the chopper and he launched two missiles.

The missiles flamed from their pod sheaths on the TAV's wings. He felt the craft shudder slightly with the explosive release of the projectiles. The missiles inscribed fiery trails toward the Deathbird. The chopper banked around, and the flare of return fire spit from its missile launchers. Kane sent the Manta straight up, engines at full thrust and over on its back in a half roll. The rockets sketched a wavering track well below him.

The Sidewinders impacted against the Deathbird and detonated in eruptions of fiery smoke. Shards of metal spun out in flashing, flaming sprays. The Bird's control cables were sheared away, locking out the horizontal and vertical stabilizers. An oil line burst amid a squirting of black fluid, and the engine stopped.

Kane caught a fragmented glimpse of an orange mushroom of fire ballooning outward from the Deathbird's fuselage. The black chopper slid sideways in the air at a swiftly decreasing angle and plowed into the ground. The whirling blades struck the hard-packed earth and shattered into gleaming shards. The entire body of the aircraft exploded a moment later, a sheet of flame interwoven with boiling coils of red and orange, leaping in all directions like the blossoming petals of a huge flower. A funnel of gray smoke billowed skyward. Flickering sparks corkscrewed into the air, like a swarm of fireflies just released from a jar.

Kane saw another flower of flame blooming in the lake bed, and through the canopy he saw the second gun housing engulfed in a lapping cocoon of fire. Grant's Manta soared over it.

"Took you long enough to attend to that damn thing," Kane grunted.

"I held back in case you needed help with the Birds."

"Thanks," Kane retorted sarcastically. "You want my help with the Cat?"

"Sure," Grant said breezily. "Why the hell not?"

The Sandcat had begun chugging at top speed away from the blockhouses, cutting a straight swath across the basin toward the distant collection of ruined buildings.

The snout of the MG in the turret swiveled and spit flame toward them. Kane swerved as a few stray bullets sparked off the Manta's hull. "You know," he remarked, "I think we've made our point. We could just let them go."

There was a moment of silence as though Grant were pondering the merits of the suggestion. Then he said, "Nah."

He dived in toward the fleeing vehicle, a missile bursting from his TAV's wings. The Sidewinder vectored in and exploded in a flaring fireball on the Sandcat's rear armor, spreading a blanket of flame up over the ob ports and the gun turret. The warhead punched a deep cavity into the back of the Cat. The concussion shook the vehicle violently, and fragments of metal spun away from the chassis.

The left-side treads sheared away from the rollers, the entire track thrashing in a long flapping strip, crashing against the hull. Sparks showered and metal screamed as the tread slashed deep scars into the armor. The vehicle rocked to a shuddering, clanking halt. Smoke boiled from the gun ports and the seams, but the doors weren't flung open. Circling the disabled vehicle, Kane assumed the Mags inside the Sandcat had either been incinerated or suffocated. Neither possibility made him feel happy.

"I'm taking out the gun emplacements next," Grant said as calmly as if he were announcing his intent to take off his shoes.

"All by yourself?"

"All by myself."

"For all we know," Kane said, "there may be Mags in them."

"True enough."

Grant's Manta came screaming around in a fast, flat crescent. He expended two missiles apiece on the blockhouses, and all four struck dead on target. The cupolas vanished in eruptions of billowing orange-yellow flame. The quadruple detonations hurled chunks of concrete upward like a reversed hailstorm.

A Magistrate lunged away from the right-hand blockhouse, sprinting madly toward the burning Sandcat. Grant triggered the nose cannon, the jack-hammering roar sounding like stuttering thunderclaps. The short burst of tungsten-carbide shells spun the Mag in a spray of blood, flinders of black polycarbonate armor flying away from his body. Fountains of dust exploded all around him as he hurtled backward, his chest seeming to burst open in tatters.

"And that," announced Grant with a great deal of satisfaction, "is pretty much that."

"You know," Kane commented offhandedly, "I can remember a time when you went out of your way *not* to kill Mags."

"That was before." Grant's voice held an ominous note, silently warning Kane not to pursue the subject.

Kane ignored the warning. "Before what?"

"Before they attacked New Edo."

Even though Grant couldn't see him, Kane nodded in understanding. *A Magistrate is virtuous in the per-*

formance of his duty. The panegyric phrase drifted through his mind. The duties and obligations that came with the badge and blaster were drilled into him—all Magistrates, for that matter—from the day he first entered the academy. The oath was a part of a Mag's every action and reaction—a justification and a reason to live at once, a moral sword and a shield for the work he performed in service to maintain order, in service to the baron. And as Kane and Grant learned, in service to a lie, a conspiracy to manipulate that was hatched hundreds of years before any of them were born.

Kane banked his Manta, looking toward the line of buildings and ruins. His HUD registered no signatures of any sort, no motion, mass or thermal. "It doesn't seem like they're scrambling another interception committee."

"Under the circumstances," Grant inquired, "would you?"

Assuming the question was rhetorical, Kane didn't bother with an answer beyond a mirthless chuckle. The security forces of Dreamland were more than equipped to contend with interlopers of the kind who had arrived by truck, but he was certain none of the planners had anticipated an assault from above—particularly not of the kind of craft he and Grant piloted. He wondered briefly if the irony was lost on the people who occupied the vast installation.

Two hundred years before, the Dreamland complex was where America's most advanced weaponry and aircraft were developed. Most of America's top-secret aircraft were rolled from the hidden hangars of the Area 51 complex.

"What do you want to do about the slaggers?" Grant asked.

Kane made a slow, low pass, glancing down at the wag below him—and the people huddling around and beneath it. He counted at least eleven people in the bed of the truck, several of them children.

"Not all of them are slaggers," he said. "Let's set down and put on our act for the ones who are."

Chapter 4

Engaging the vectored-thrust ramjets, Kane and Grant dropped their Mantas straight down and gracefully brought them to rest on the extended tripod landing gear. Fine clouds of dust puffed up all around.

The two men opened the seals of their helmets and unlatched the cockpit canopies. Sliding them back, they climbed out of the TAVs and shoulder to shoulder they marched toward the wag. Kane arranged his expression into a grim, foreboding scowl, knowing the image he and Grant presented was likely to be far more frightening than that of the Magistrates.

A very tall, very broad-shouldered man, Grant's heavy brows were drawn, shadowing his dark eyes. A fierce, down-sweeping mustache showed jet black against his coffee-brown skin. Gray showed at the temples of his short hair, as if sprinkled there by a diffident hand. His heavy-jawed face was set in a threatening scowl.

At an inch over six feet, Kane was not as tall or as broad as Grant, but every line of his supple, compact body was hard and stripped of excess flesh. He looked like a warrior—from the hawklike set of his head on his corded neck, to the square shoulders and the lean hips and long legs. Kane was built with the savage economy of a gray wolf, with most of his muscle mass in his upper body.

His high-planed face held a grim expression, as did his narrowed, gray-blue eyes. A faint scar showed like a white thread against the sun-bronzed skin of his left cheek.

As different as Grant and Kane were physically, they were clad identically. From throat to fingertip to heel they wore one-piece black leathery garments that fit as tightly as doeskin gloves.

Kane had christened the garments shadow suits, and though they didn't appear as if they could offer protection from a mosquito bite, he had learned they were impervious to most wavelengths of radiation. The suits were climate-controlled for environments up to highs of 150 degrees and as cold as minus ten degrees Fahrenheit. Microfilaments controlled the internal temperature.

The manufacturing technique known in predark days as electrospin lacing electrically charged the polymer particles, weaving a dense web of form fitting fibers. Composed of a compilated weave of spider silk, Monocrys and Spectra fabrics, the garments were essentially a single-crystal metallic microfiber with a very dense molecular structure. The outer Monocrys sheathing went opaque when exposed to radiation, and the Kevlar and Spectra layers provided protection against blunt trauma. The fibers were embedded with enzymes and other catalysts that broke down all toxic and infectious agents on contact. The spider silk allowed flexibility, but it traded protection from firearms for freedom of movement.

Grant still preferred the polycarbonate Magistrate body armor to the shadow suits, but he had stopped arguing about it. Ever since they absconded with the suits from Sindri's stronghold on Thunder Isle, the garments had proved their worth and their superiority to the Mag armor, if for nothing else than their internal subsystems.

Built around nanotechnologies, the microelectromechanical systems combined computers with tiny semiconductor chips. The nanotechnology reduced the size of the electronic components to one-millionth of a meter, roughly ten times the size of an atom. The inner layer was lined by carbon nanotubes only a nanometer wide, rolled-up sheets of graphite with a tensile strength greater than steel. The suits were almost impossible to tear, but a heavy-enough bullet could penetrate them, and unlike the Mag exoskeletons, wouldn't redistribute the kinetic shock.

Although they rarely wore the armor any longer, they still carried their Sin Eaters, strapped to holsters on their right arms. Sensitive actuators attached to the weapons popped the Sin Eaters down into their waiting hands when they flexed their wrist tendons in the right sequence, putting the pistols there in an eye blink. There was no trigger guard, and when the firing stud came in contact with their crooked trigger fingers, the pistols fired immediately.

They unleathered their weapons, keeping their index fingers straight. The Sin Eaters slapped solidly into their palms as they approached the wag, walking on either side of the dragon's-teeth obstacles. Kane looked at the truck with an appraising, critical eye. Despite the dented, rusted-out bodywork, it appeared to be in reasonably good condition, at least compared to some of the other wired-together rattletraps he had seen elsewhere in the Outlands.

Ever since the long winter of skydark, motorized transport had been at a premium. The metal-working skills were still available for mechanical repairs of vehicles, but making tires and finding fuel was a lot more difficult. Gasoline that even remotely approached the quality of predark supplies was almost nonexistent anywhere but in the villes. There were a few crude processing plants down along the Gulf Coast of Texas, a few more in Oklahoma, but the product certainly wasn't cheap and just as certainly, it was barely acceptable as fuel.

He and Grant came to a halt in front of the truck, noting with amusement the number of feet visible just beneath the frame. In his best deep, lionlike rumble, Grant commanded, "All you slaggers—out here where we can see you. *Now!*"

Slowly, reluctantly, with a great deal of rustling and fumbling, people began crawling out from beneath the chassis of the dump truck. They were of a type that both Kane and Grant had no problem recognizing. Almost all of them had a scrawny, under-

nourished look, with sharp features and lank hair.
Their hands were callused, the fingers blunt and short
nailed. Most of them appeared to be around forty
years of age, which probably made them closer to
twenty-five. All in all, they looked like typical outlander trash.

In the Outlands, people were divided into small,
regional units, communications were stifled, rivalries
bred, education impeded. The people who lived outside the direct influence of the villes, who worked the
farms, toiled in the fields or simply roamed from
place to place were reviled and hated. They were the
outcasts of the new feudalism, the cheap, expendable
labor forces, even the cannon fodder when circumstances warranted. Generations of Americans were
born into serfdom, slavery in everything but name.
Whatever their parents or grandparents had been before skydark, they were now only commodities of one
sort of another.

Begrimed and wearing tattered coveralls, the scavengers stood around the wag, all of them raising their
hands without having been ordered to do so.

"Which one of you is the boss of this shit-smelling
outfit?" Kane demanded.

No one spoke, but several men shuffled away from
a tall, broadly built man, casting him surreptitious
sideways glances. A second later, Kane realized the
man was actually a singularly unprepossessing
woman, with coarse features, short, wiry hair and to-
bacco-stained teeth.

"So you're in charge?" Grant asked harshly.

The woman inclined her head forward a fraction of an inch, a motion Grant assumed was a nod.

"What's your name?" he inquired.

She tried twice before she was able to husk out faintly, "Mary Lou McSween. They call me Mare."

A wizened, sun-browned rat of a man standing near her did a poor job of repressing a snicker.

"Something amuses you, slag-ass?" Kane challenged.

The man didn't seem the least bit offended or intimidated. "We calls her other things, too."

Even as pale from fright as she was, Kane saw how a flush of anger reddened Mare's face, from the base of her neck to the roots of her hair. He wasn't inclined to enter into a dialogue with any of the scavengers, so he didn't respond to the little man's comment. In a calm, cold tone he declared, "We call all of you other things, too. Scum, traitors, turds with legs. We know what you're doing here. But do you know why?"

Nobody spoke, although a couple of them exchanged puzzled glances with one another.

"I asked you a question!" Kane's voice was as sharp as a whip crack.

"Sellin' merchandise!" Mare blurted. "That's what we do. We're salvagers!"

Grant's lips worked and he spit in the dust at Mare's booted feet. "You're scavengers. Salvagers don't sell human beings."

"That's *what* you're doing," Kane grated. "Do you know why?"

Not waiting for an answer, even if one had been forthcoming, Grant strode up to Mare and grabbed her by the back of the neck. Although she winced at the painful pressure of his grasp, she didn't cry out. He forced her ahead of him alongside the truck, using her body as a wedge to push men out of the way.

At the rear of the wag, he jerked down the tailgate. The people huddled together on the bed stared at him with glazed eyes. The glassy sheen told Grant they had been drugged by some sort of soporific, but a couple of the men looked as if their faculties were returning. They were sufficiently alert to be frightened of him, at any rate.

Grant could easily guess the kind of thoughts wheeling through the minds of the prisoners, and he couldn't blame them for being too scared to speak. His and Kane's work with the Cerberus exiles always kept them in a shadowy world of danger and eternal suspicion, of sudden crisis and alarm, where human beings died in a covert war that ranged from a subterranean lair beneath New Mexico to the utter remoteness of a forgotten colony on the Moon.

Tightening his grip on the back of Mare McSween's neck, Grant bit out between clenched teeth, "You were going to sell your fellow human beings like they were cattle, so they could be harvested— their blood drained, their bodies cut open, their guts unwound, all their organs, glands and even bone marrow removed and processed. All to keep the barons alive.''

Mare's eyes widened and her lips formed the word, ''Barons?''

''Barons,'' Grant snapped, his voice so thick with barely repressed fury it was a guttural growl. ''They need human blood and guts to survive, so they set up a processing center here in Groom Lake. That's the *why* of it.''

''I didn't know,'' she said in a faltering, hoarse whisper.

''You didn't know,'' Grant growled, ''and if you had, you wouldn't have given a shit.''

Grant dragged her away from the truck and released her, pushing her away from him. She stumbled a few paces but didn't fall. He swept her and her men with a furious glare. ''Now the barons can have *you* if they want.''

Turning toward the prisoners, he demanded, ''Do any of you know how to drive?''

For a long moment, the people just stared at him blankly as if he had addressed them in a foreign language. Then a black man with wild hair resembling lengths of tarred wire said tentatively, ''Been a long time, but I think I can manage.''

''Good.'' Grant jerked a thumb toward the cab. ''Get in and get the hell out of here. As fast as you can and don't stop for anything.''

As the man jumped down from the bed, Mare

raised her voice in a feeble protest. "You can't just take my wag and leave us out here—"

Grant whirled on her, lifting his Sin Eater and holding it out at the end of his extended arm. The bore touched the woman's forehead, and she squeezed her eyes shut. Kane tensed, unconsciously holding his breath. Grant was not putting on an act now. The big man could barely restrain himself from depressing the trigger stud and blowing the scavenger chief's brains out.

"Not another word," Grant growled, lips peeled back from his teeth in a silent snarl. "Not even a sound."

The woman opened her eyes and swallowed hard. She obeyed Grant's edict to make no sound, but Kane caught a strange flicker of emotion in her eyes—he couldn't be certain, but he received the impression the woman felt relief at having the prisoners set free.

The black man climbed up into the cab and slid behind the wheel. He turned the key and the engine caught on the first try. He ground the clutch, yanked back on the stick shift and floored the accelerator.

With a clanking roar, the wag shuddered, nearly died, then lurched backward. The man wrestled with the wheel, the foot pedals, trying to upshift without stalling. The gearbox protested, but the wag picked up speed. Sand squirted out from beneath the spinning tires. He backed it straight up along the pass, over the crest of the ridge and out of sight. Within moments, the roar of the engine and the squeak of the suspension faded away.

The little man who had snickered earlier said beseechingly, "How are we gonna get out of here?"

The corner of Kane's mouth quirked in a mirthless smile. "What makes you think we care how you do it? Or even if?"

Grant gestured to the variety of weapons scattered on the ground. "You can keep your blasters—not that they'll do you much good if more Mags and Birds come out. And I'm pretty sure they will once we're gone."

A man made a move to scoop up a fallen rifle. Kane's finger tapped the trigger of his Sin Eater. The single shot was as loud as a thunderclap. The rifle went spinning across the ground, its stock a ruin of wood. The man scuttled backward, shocked and amazed.

"You can have them after we're out of back-shooting range," Kane told him.

Grant dismissively turned his back on Mare and her crew and stalked away. As he passed Kane, he said flatly, "I'm done here."

"Me, too," replied Kane. Rather than emulate his partner's display of contemptuous confidence, Kane back stepped, keeping his pistol trained on the scavengers. He didn't really expect any of them to grab up a gun and start shooting, but he figured it was safer not to give them the option.

When the dragon's-teeth obstacles were between

them and the scavenger gang, Kane felt safe enough to start walking normally and to lower his Sin Eater. He didn't holster it. Not too long before, he had been jumped by a couple of vicious Farers, one of them armed with only a pipe. It didn't pay to underestimate the murderous impulses of Outland slaggers. Even though they'd been terrorized, humiliated, robbed and now left to fend for themselves in exceptionally hostile territory, Kane would not have been surprised if they decided to throw a few parting pieces of lead their way.

When the two men reached their Manta ships, the sharp report of a shot reached them. Grant and Kane spun, reflexively dropping into crouches, their Sin Eaters questing for targets. They heard no more shots, but a confused babble of outraged voices arose from where they had left the group of scavengers. Carefully, both men straightened.

They saw a man lying spread-eagled on his back with Mare standing over him, wielding a rifle. The man's face was awash with wet scarlet. Sounding infuriated to the point of madness, Mare screeched, ''*There's* your finder's fee, Squint!''

Offhandedly, Kane commented, ''There's more to that story than meets the eye.''

Grant lifted the broad yoke of his shoulders in a negligent shrug. ''Whatever it was, Mary Lou wrote a fini to it.'' He sighed wearily and shook his head. ''If they're a hell of a lot luckier than they deserve to be, they might make it out of here without replacing the merchandise we set loose.''

Kane glanced toward the distant structures miles across the lake bed, all laid out against the gray ribbon of an extremely long runway—the longest one in the predark world, he had been told. A line of compacted rubble still stood aboveground. The place looked the same as it did when Kane had first seen it, more than six months before—godforsaken.

He saw no sign of activity in the rubble or around the monstrous hangar, but he had no trouble imagining the panic and chaos erupting beneath the lake bed. Whether any barons were presently in the installation was immaterial—there were plenty of hybrids, and he knew all of them retained vivid memories of the last time he and Grant had visited a processing center. Or for that matter, the last time the two of them had been in Area 51.

Sweeping his gaze over the burning wreckage of the Deathbirds and the Sandcat, he felt no genuine sense of satisfaction about the relative ease of the victory. He said, ''I'm kind of surprised they haven't sent out more Birds, if nothing else.''

Grant frowned. ''They're watching us, trying to figure us out. They used their conventional security measures and got their asses kicked. They won't make the same mistake twice. And I'm just as glad.''

He nodded to the shiny, bullet-inflicted scars on the wing of Kane's Manta. ''We're low on missiles and cannon rounds. I'd rather not waste what we have left on another dogfight. We made our point."

Kane grinned wolfishly. "And then some. Not to mention we found out these ships operate in an atmosphere just as well as they do in outer space."

Heaving himself up on the wing of his TAV, he said, "Race you back home."

Grant shook his head. "Not going home—at least not right away."

Kane eyed him suspiciously. "You've got some other destination for us in mind?"

Grant levered his body atop his Manta's wing. "For me, anyhow. New Edo."

"I'm not surprised." Kane's tone was studiedly casual. "And how long do you figure you'll be gone?"

Grant dropped into the cockpit and strapped himself into the pilot's seat. "Until I come back."

Kane nodded as if Grant's deliberately cryptic reply explained everything. "I'm not sure if this has occurred to you or not, but we don't know everything there is to know about these ships. You could stall out over the Cific."

Grant's teeth flashed in a grin. "We flew these crates down from the Moon, Kane. I think that's enough of a shakedown flight, don't you?"

He paused and added, "Besides, I think the only reason you're bringing that up at all is you don't want to go back to Cerberus by yourself. Not that I really blame you, under the circumstances."

Kane's eyebrows knitted in a scowl, then he

grinned ruefully. "I could probably argue, but you're pretty much on target. Give my regards to Shizuka."

Grant smiled crookedly. "Will do." He pulled down the helmet over his head and slid shut the cockpit canopy. It sealed almost instantly with a faint pop, indicating it was now airtight.

Kane decided to stay grounded until Grant was airborne, just in case more Deathbirds were dispatched. With a droning whine, the Manta slowly rose, a small and brief hurricane of dust swirling beneath it. The landing gear retracted automatically into the TAV's belly.

Grant stopped the ship's ascent at two hundred feet, and he waggled its wings in a farewell. Then he engaged the pulse-detonation wave engines, and the Manta raced across the sky like a bullet hurtling up the barrel of a gun. The columns of smoke from the destroyed Deathbirds were sucked toward the updraft.

Within a heartbeat and a half, the Manta was the merest speck over the jagged peaks of the mountain range. The trailing sonic boom slammed its thunderclap above Groom Lake. Kane felt the concussion running through the hull of his ship.

He climbed down into the cockpit, once again surprised by the simplicity of the instrument panel. The controls consisted primarily of a joystick, altimeter and fuel gauges. He slipped on the helmet over his head and heard the buzz of its internal power source juicing up immediately. The interior curve of the helmet's visor swarmed with a squall of glowing pixels.

When they cleared a nanosecond later, he had CGI icons of sensor scopes, range finders and various indicators. The ship's real controls were all computerized, reduced to microprocessors within the helmet itself.

Kane felt a pressure shifting around the base of his neck as the helmet automatically extended a lining and a seal. He heard the hiss and cool breath of oxygen pumped from the tanks mounted on the back of the chair. Closing his hand around the joystick, he pulled it back slightly, then pushed it forward. It caught and clicked into position. The hull began to vibrate around him, in tandem with a whine that grew in pitch. On the inside of his helmet flashed the words: VTOL Launch System Enabled.

With a stomach-sinking swiftness, the Manta lifted off the ground. The humming drone changed in pitch as the aircraft rose as smoothly as if it were being raised on a giant hand made of compressed air. The helmet's HUD displays offered different vantage points of the ascent, and Kane's eyes flicked from one to another. He watched as the dry lake basin and the line of rubble receded so quickly they became mere ripples of contrasting texture and color. High mountain peaks appeared, then shrank into little snow-capped cones.

Kane pulled back on the control stick, and the inventory of all the dials, switches, gauges and fire controls flashed across the helmet's visor. He started to engage the pulse-detonation wave engines, then thought about who was waiting for him back at the Cerberus redoubt. He decided he wasn't in that much of a hurry.

Chapter 5

Maddock was less unhappy about the loss of Dreamland ordnance and personnel than he was about losing the game of rock-scissors-paper to Brodeur. That meant it fell to him to brief the current baron-in-residence.

He stood in a large room lined with two aisles of computer stations. He and Brodeur faced a huge flat-screen vid monitor that covered the far wall. The screen was divided into small square sections, each one showing different black-and-white views of the lake bed. The range of the old vid spy-eyes wasn't sufficient to transmit more than suggestions of detail, but Maddock recognized destruction when he saw it.

As a survivor of the Dulce disaster, he was intimately familiar with devastation of various sorts. And though he wasn't intimately familiar with the men who had brought on the destruction in New Mexico, he was fairly certain that both Kane and Grant piloted the strange airships that had wreaked such havoc in so short a time.

Brodeur's fingers pressed a button on the console, and images on the monitor screen sped up. Flames licked crazily from the Sandcat and the Deathbird.

The airships landed nearby, and two men in black climbed out of them. All the motions were sped up to an inhuman tempo.

"Freeze it there," Maddock instructed.

Brodeur obliged him. The quality of the image was poor, but Maddock was able to recognize Grant and Kane as they strode toward the wag parked at the edge of the lake bed. He didn't feel satisfied that his guess was correct, since the conclusion was obvious. Only the pair of renegade Magistrates from Cobaltville possessed the sheer audacity to stage a daylight attack literally at the front door of the new processing and treatment center. Besides, he was sure Kane still held more than a passing grudge because of his weeks of captivity in Dreamland.

Maddock and Brodeur had been instrumental in his escape, as well helping to displace Baron Cobalt's troops from the installation. But that didn't mean Kane or his friends would necessarily cede either one of them a special dispensation when next they met.

"Grant and Kane," Brodeur muttered. "Nervy bastards coming back here."

"Nervy, but they had a hell of an ace to play," Maddock pointed out. "All of our ordnance was completely outclassed."

Brodeur ran a trembling hand over his dark face. "Where the fuck did they get those crates? I never saw anything like them. They're not like the old fighter jets I've seen pix of."

"I don't know," Maddock replied. "They must

have resources we never heard about from Domi. But it took them long enough to trot them out.''

"They weren't trying to flash-blast this place," declared Brodeur. "They were sending the imperator and the barons a message."

Maddock nodded in agreement. "Yeah. I wonder how they'll take it."

"I don't even want to think about it." Brodeur replayed the vid record of the Sandcat exploding and made a tsking sound. "Who was in the Cat?"

Maddock shook his head. "I don't know. Probably some of Baron Sharpe's men."

Sighing, Brodeur replied, "I wish he was here instead of her. Sharpe's fused out, but there's something really—I don't know—*evil* about her."

He glanced over at Maddock with narrowed eyes. "Aren't you a little worried that she might find out what you were up to with Quavell?"

"Not a little. A lot. But it's been over a month since she left, and none of the barons has asked me anything about her."

Brodeur nodded. "Yeah. It makes me wonder if they don't already know everything there is to know."

Maddock snorted disdainfully. "I thought you'd learned that the barons aren't gods."

"That doesn't make them any less dangerous," Brodeur retorted defensively. "They're still in charge, and we still have to report to them."

Maddock swallowed hard and extended his right hand. Hopefully, he asked, "Two out of three?"

Brodeur snorted. "In your dreams. You'd better stop stalling and go tell her."

Maddock dry scrubbed his short, dark-blond hair in frustration. "Some friend you are." He squared his shoulders and left the room.

He walked down a broad corridor, lit from above by neon strips, paused at a checkpoint and used his key card to open the door that led to the monorail platform. On the other side of it lay a multileveled man-made cavern. The dimensions were so vast, the far end ran away into the dimness. The ceiling was at least three hundred feet above his head and dotted with bright stadium lights. Large containers were arranged in orderly fifty-foot-tall aisles, stretching as far as he could see.

Gently sloping ramps led from level to level, broad flat passages for lift trucks and dollies to carry their loads. The ramps were the only method of getting from level to level. As always, the vast chamber was a beehive of activity, with forklifts moving to and fro, laden with boxes, and the small shifter engines of the monorail train zipping back and forth.

The area was far, far larger than the biggest chamber beneath the Archuleta Mesa, not that Maddock had been in every chamber in the installation outside of Dulce, New Mexico. If nothing else about the assignment, he was free to go anywhere he wished in Dreamland.

A high, musical voice called out from behind him. "Maddock, may I speak with you?"

Maddock turned and saw a female hybrid standing at the mouth of a maintenance accessway. Her name was Lylana, and like all of her kind she was excessively slender and small of stature, less than five feet tall. Her compact form was encased in a silver-gray, skintight bodysuit, the duty uniform of her people. Her face showed pale as new gold, with the darker masses of her silky brown hair picking up the same tint and turning it to bronze. Above prominent cheekbones, huge, up-slanting eyes of tawny gold-brown regarded him in a silent appraisal.

Aware of the vid spy-eye clamped to the ceiling, Maddock kept his expression neutral as he walked toward the accessway. Once he was inside, Lylana threw herself into his arms. She stood on tiptoe, and he bent at the knees so their lips could meet. Her tongue darted into his mouth and after a moment, Maddock pushed her away. In such a small space, the only trap deadlier than a cross fire was a compromising position.

"Not now," he whispered into her tiny ear. "I've got to report to the baron."

Lylana gazed up at him, her dark gaze unfathomable yet somehow reproachful. "It's been days since we were together."

"And we've just been attacked."

It was impossible for a hybrid's eyes to widen, so

they did the exact opposite, narrowing to suspicious slits. "I heard no alarms."

"Because it was a sneak attack. We had no warning. They're gone now. No point in sounding a general alert."

"Who attacked us?"

"I can't be sure," he replied quietly, "but I think the perpetrators were Grant and Kane."

Lylana's face didn't lose its masklike placidity, but Maddock knew the mention of Kane would instantly bring unpleasant memories to the forefront of her mind. He didn't want to cause her pain by reminding her of the man who had killed her former lover, but he wanted her to focus her wits on something other than a repetition of their clandestine meeting in the same place three days before.

"Kane..." she echoed in a breathy, contemplative whisper. "Always Kane."

"Do you want revenge?" he asked bluntly.

She looked up at him, a corner of her mouth quirking in a scornful smile. "Revenge indeed. He killed Hank before my eyes. Then only two hours later, Baron Cobalt forced me to copulate with him. No, not revenge against Kane. Retribution, a reckoning. But if Baron Cobalt was still here, I might consider exacting vengeance against him."

Cocking her head at a quizzical angle, Lylana asked, "And do you not wish retribution of some sort? Your beloved Quavell left you to be with Kane...or so it is believed."

Maddock's jaw muscles bunched. "I wouldn't call her my beloved. She carries Kane's child, as you and all the females here were intended to. I don't want revenge or retribution. I just hope she's safe."

He made a move to leave the accessway, but Lylana caught him by the hand. "You are not offended?"

Maddock smiled down at her wryly. "No, but I am in a hurry."

Lylana matched his wry smile. "No more so than I, my beautiful apeling."

Forcing a chuckle, he disengaged himself and returned to the monorail platform just as the engine pulled up with a soft electric hum. Maddock climbed into the passenger car and fished out his comm from a pocket of his zippered coverall. The monorail system was the only way to move efficiently around the many and widely separated sections of the Area 51 installation.

Into the comm unit he said, "Green. Go." Without the proper code recognition words, the controllers would not feed power to the rail.

The engine's hum rose in pitch, and with a slight lurch, the train slid almost silently along the rail. It swiftly built up speed. Overhead light fixtures flicked by so rapidly that they combined with the intervals of darkness between them to acquire a strobing pattern.

Thinking of Quavell, Maddock repressed a sigh. Quavell had performed excellently as a spy within the complex during Baron Cobalt's brief occupation of Area 51. If not for the intelligence she provided to Barons Sharpe and Samarium and her organization of a fifth column among the installation's personnel, Dreamland would have never been wrested away from Baron Cobalt and his forces.

Betraying a baron was something he never expected from either a hybrid or himself. But, he reminded himself sourly, he never expected to fall in love with a hybrid, either. He hadn't even known such a people had existed until a year ago.

Back then, he was the newest member of the Archuleta Mesa security force, recruited from the ranks of freshly badged Magistrates in Cobaltville. At the time, he wasn't certain if the assignment was superior to walking pedestrian patrol in the Tartarus Pits.

At least, in the Pits he had known what to expect, understood the kind of people he would be dealing with. Slaggers mainly, since that sector of Cobaltville was a melting pot of cheap labor, petty criminals and outlanders. The Archuleta Mesa duty was like nothing he had expected, or even imagined.

The high level of technology in use in the installation came as more than a surprise; it was profoundly shocking. Machines, wags and devices of all types far outstripped anything in Cobaltville. And if he thought some of the Pitters were strange, the permanent personnel in the subterranean complex made them seem mundane and colorless in comparison.

None of the security force dealt directly with the

slightly built, delicate-featured people. They were segregated from them, although each of the four sec squads had a designated intermediary who conveyed their orders. The people, if that's what they were, spooked Maddock, made his skin crawl and his short hair tingle on his scalp. He had only caught glimpses of them from time to time, and they struck him as more than human, but at the same time somehow other than human, too. All shared similar characteristics besides slender, almost childish builds—large, domed heads, huge, slanting eyes and faces that seemed all brow ridges and cheekbones. He had seen a couple of them walking around with plastic tube-shaped holsters strapped to their thighs.

Shortly after arriving at the mesa, he asked a fellow sec guard if the people were a breed of mutie. Since the man also hailed from Cobaltville, he figured he'd share his curiosity, especially after he pointed out to him how the small, big-headed people didn't fit any of the descriptions of stickies, scalies, swampies or scabbies he had ever heard of.

The man's response was cold and to the point: "The desert is full of the bones of stupes like you who started asking questions about this place."

Maddock immediately ceased further inquiries. Shortly thereafter, his duties ceased, too, when the installation was destroyed. Later he learned Kane, Grant and a couple of other renegades were responsible. Even at that point, the former Magistrates had become figures of inspiration to the disenfranchised, to the outlander. Their acts of sabotage triggered sporadic rebellions in the Outlands. True enough, they weren't organized uprisings, but their frequency was of a kind not seen in ninety years, since the days of the baron blasters who opposed the Program of Unification.

The monorail curved lazily to the right, plunging almost noiselessly into a side chute. Lights shone intermittently on the smooth walls, small drops of illumination that did little to alleviate the deep shadows. The train's speed dropped, and it hissed to a halt beside a broad platform. He climbed out and strode along a featureless expanse of corridor, the walls made of mortared, unpainted concrete blocks. He passed several closed, electronic-lock-equipped doors, each one bearing the circular yellow-and-black radiation-warning symbol. Beneath the symbols were plastic signs emblazoned with block red lettering: RADIATION HAZARD BEYOND THIS POINT! ENTRY FORBIDDEN TO PERSONNEL NOT WEARING ANTICONTAMINATE CLOTHING!

Maddock ignored the warning, knowing it dated back to predark days. When he reached to a T-branching intersection, Maddock walked to a door without the symbol or the warnings, although it held a small plaque that read Purity Control Orientation. He recalled what Quavell had told him about the meaning of the term.

Everyone selected for full ville citizenship in the baronies and for permission to reproduce had to meet a strict criteria. The actual, but concealed reason was simple: the purer the quality of individual genetic characteristics, the purer the quality of the hybrid. The practice was called purity control.

Even members of the baronial oligarchy, the self-proclaimed homo superior, were bred from this system. However, with the destruction of the Archuleta Mesa medical facilities, without access to the ectogenesis techniques of fetal development outside the womb, the oligarchy and the entire hybrid race were in danger of extinction. Baron Cobalt occupied Area 51 with the spoken assumption of taking responsibility to sustain his race, but only if he was elevated to a position of high authority, even above his brother barons. It wasn't a matter of making an incursion into another baron's territory, since most of Nevada was an Outland flat zone, not a part of an official baronial territory, certainly not Baron Cobalt's.

Since Area 51's history was intertwined with rumors of alien involvement, Baron Cobalt had used its medical facilities as a substitute for those destroyed in New Mexico. He reactivated the installation, turning it into a processing and treatment center, without having to rebuild from scratch. He transferred the human and hybrid personnel from the Dulce facility—those who had survived the catastrophe, at any rate. In severe cases, even damaged organs were replaced from the storage banks of organic material stockpiled there.

Still and all, the medical treatments that addressed

the congenital autoimmune system deficiencies of the
hybrids weren't enough to insure the continued survival of the race. The necessary equipment and raw
material to implement procreation had yet to be installed. Baron Cobalt had unilaterally decided that the
conventional means of conception was the only option to keep the hybrid race alive.

Cobalt's command for the female hybrids to com-
mit acts of miscegenation with human males was one
thing, perhaps even forgivable under the circumstances. When he dangled the treatments before his
fellow barons like a carrot on a string rather than sharing them freely, war was the inevitable result.

Although Area 51, Dreamland, was known in predark legends for the testing and development of advanced technology, it had also served as an international base operated by a consortium from many
countries. Over the past six months, a program had
been implemented to have its operation overseen by
a consortium of barons, which in turn would be overseen by the imperator.

The ancient Roman Empire was governed by a sen-
ate, but ruled by an emperor, sometimes known as an
imperator. This person served as the final arbiter in
matters pertaining to government. The villes acted in-
terdependently, unified in name only. Six months before, during a council of the barons in Front Royal,
Baron Cobalt put forth the proposal to establish a central ruling consortium. In effect, the barons would become viceroys, plenipotentiaries in their own territo-

ries. The barons were less in favor of the concept than Baron Cobalt's proclamation that he be recognized as the imperator. Their displeasure didn't last, since the proposal and title was appropriated by another.

The door opened into a medium-sized office suite, with six partition-enclosed desks, all of them equipped with computer terminals. Tacked on the wall, faded and yellowed with age, were large full-color illustrations, a sequence of which ran nearly the entire length of the wall. The pictures displayed images of a naked human male and female, superimposed over twisting DNA molecules.

The next illustration showed the strands of the helix separated, then moved back together in a new chain configuration. Another image showed egg cells being opened by microscalpels so their dark nuclei could be replaced with new ones.

The final picture showed the male and female holding the hands of a baby standing between them. The baby possessed a very high forehead and domed cranium, beneath pronounced brow arches overhanging big, slanting, staring eyes.

Maddock repressed a shudder as he passed the illustrations. He entered a doorway on the far side of the room, walking into a high-ceilinged chamber and past a series of cubicles adjoined by partitions. He didn't walk far before he reached the treatment area and came to a halt.

Maddock had seen pictures of ancient Egyptian sarcophagi, and the object propped up against a cross-

barred brace looked very much like one, except it
appeared to be molded from some transparent polymer. Two flexible hoses were connected to it at opposing midway points. The hoses, in turn, were connected to a metal tank with two valve wheels
projecting from the top.

Within the sarcophagus, submerged up to her neck
in a brown-hued fluid, was a naked female figure.
With her head tilted back, her perfectly formed, aquiline features composed and with her huge eyes
closed, Baron Beausoleil looked like a beautifully
crafted statue. Maddock noticed the slight rise and fall
of her lithe breasts, and he felt a stirring in his groin.
He was both astonished and not a little revolted by
his reaction.

He remembered the first time he had met a baron,
the crazy little man who ruled Sharpeville and the
suffocating sense of terror he had experienced on that
day. Now, he felt something akin to that same xenophobic cringing. He had never dreamed he would
stand in the presence of a baron who was a naked
woman.

Chapter 6

Maddock had heard stories of the barons for his entire life. Anyone serving in any division in any ville had heard of them. Part of his mind knew that maintaining a baron's mystique was contrived, a psychological gambit meant to intimidate and awe. But still, the baronial oligarchy ruling the nine villes was more than the governing body of postnukecaust America— they were god-kings, serving as a bridge between pre-dark and postdark man, the avatars of a new order.

Baron Beausoleil breathed deeply and regularly through her small nostrils. She was the only female of the oligarchy, but she also had the same wispy, duck-down-textured hair as the male barons, although hers was jet-black with dark coppery highlights and piled high on her head.

Her male attendant gave Maddock a disinterested glance, then turned two wheel valves simultaneously. Almost immediately, the sarcophagus began to drain and he stepped back, moving with a bizarrely beautiful, danceresque grace. All hybrids, male and female alike, had builds that were small, slender and gracile. Their faces were composed of sharp planes, with fine-complexioned skin stretched tight over prominent shelves of cheekbones. The craniums were very high and smooth, the ears small and set low on the head. Their back-slanting eyes were large, shadowed by sweeping supraorbital ridges. Only hair, eye color and slight differences in height differentiated them. All in all, they were a beautiful people, almost too perfect to be real.

But Maddock knew the hybrids weren't perfect, particularly the barons. Quavell had explained that although all the hybrids were extremely long-lived, cellular and metabolic deterioration was part and parcel of what they were—mixtures of human and a race called the Archons. And even though they were a biological bridge between two races, not even the barons were sure of the reasons behind the hybridization program. But they did know that in order to rule humans, they were dependent on the biological material their subjects provided.

Just like the caste system in place in the villes, the hybrids observed a similar one, although it had little to do with parentage. If the first phase of human evolution produced a package of adaptations for a particular and distinct way of life, the second phase was an effort to control that way of life by controlling the environment. The focus switched to an evolution that was cultural rather than physical.

The hybrids, at least by their way of thinking, represented the final phase of human evolution. They created wholesale, planned alterations in living organisms and were empowered to control not only their immediate environment, but also the evolution of other species. At the pinnacle of that evolutionary achievement were the barons, as high above hybrids like Lylana and the attendant as the hybrids were above mere humans.

A clear fluid sprayed from a nozzle, rinsing the residue of the chemical bath from Baron Beausoleil's body. When the cycle was completed, she opened her deep violet eyes and swept her calm gaze across Maddock, who stood with his hands clasped behind his back. She nodded to her attendant, who unlatched the lid of the sarcophagus and pulled it open. The faint reek of astringent compounds, mixed with the coppery tang of blood, entered his nostrils. He had no idea of the chemicals used in the gene therapy immersions, but he knew an equal measure of processed and liquefied human organic material composed the fluid.

The baron—he could not break a lifetime of conditioning and think of her as Baroness Beausoleil—stepped out and took the towel offered by her attendant. She dabbed at her limbs, but even in the indirect light Maddock saw few damp places on her body. It was almost as if the pores of her skin absorbed the fluid mixture. She ignored Maddock, completely at ease with her nudity.

Unlike the other unclothed female hybrids he had seen, Baron Beausoleil's body was closer to the human ideal—her skin was smooth and of a marble whiteness, but with a faint olive undertone. Her small breasts were firm, her belly flat and tautly muscled. She was nearly a half head taller than her attendant. Maddock had no idea of how old she truly was—she looked no more than twenty years of age, but she could have been as old as eighty or ninety. Quavell claimed to be on the high side of sixty herself.

Closer to a hundred, he decided as he looked at the baron's eyes. He shivered slightly when he realized there was no reflection in those eyes, as if they had been cut from slabs of onyx. But there was something about them that gave her the exotic flair of the Persian concubines he had seen pix of in old books.

She reached up behind her and unpinned her hair. It fell in a silky stream down her back, past her small, hard buttocks, like a flow of frozen India ink. The ends were cut off as square and as straight as a ruled line. Equally straight-cut bangs bisected her high forehead, sweeping down almost to the delicate brow arches above her eyes.

Maddock averted his gaze, being very careful not to stare at her. He had wondered why Beausoleil hadn't assumed the title of baroness, but he supposed it had something to do with the patriarchal tradition of the ruling class. More than likely, only her personal staff in her ville knew she was female.

The attendant stepped forward, holding out a brocade robe. He moved with a swaying motion, like a reed before a breeze. The movement was very precise, very ritualistic. Maddock had seen it before, when the servant class of hybrids faced the barons. He wondered if it was an instinctive behavior, rather than learned, perhaps encoded in their hybridized genes.

Baron Beausoleil slid her slender arms into the belled sleeves of the robe, but made no move to close it. Maddock kept his eyes cast to one side and down. In a throaty voice purring with amusement, she asked, "Why are you here?"

Maddock looked at her out of the corner of an eye. "There was an incident above, my lord."

The note of amusement left the woman's voice. "An incident? Explain."

Doing his utmost not to stammer or appear to grope for words, Maddock related everything that had happened topside, beginning with the report transcommed in from the Deathbird patrol regarding the arrival of merchandise, to the outcome of the aerial battle.

Baron Beausoleil's expression remained studiedly neutral throughout the report, as if Maddock were recounting a list of laundry yet to be washed. When he was done, he fell silent and waited. The baron remained just as silent, regarding him with her big eyes but not really looking at him.

Maddock had witnessed similar nonreactions among the hybrids in the installation, and he knew the silence and distant stare meant she was processing the information, examining the possible consequences and extrapolating on the results of all the available choices. He wasn't sure if he preferred her contemplative silence to a screaming tantrum. A violent reaction would have at least indicated she felt an emotion he could relate to, even if it were only outrage. When they experienced emotions, they only did so under in moments of stress, and then so intensely they were almost consumed by them. However, Quavell had warned him that if he were in the company of a baron who was overwhelmed by emotion, particularly a negative one, then his death would be sure to follow.

At length, Baron Beausoleil asked, "What of the people who arrived with the merchandise?"

"They are on foot, my lord."

"A contingent of our troops should be dispatched posthaste to apprehend them." Her tone was crisp. "They should be instructed to employ nonlethal force. If it becomes necessary to kill any of them, the troops should restrict their fire to head shots. We don't want the tissues or organs damaged beyond the point they are useless for recycling."

Maddock nodded. "I understand, my lord."

He turned on his heel to carry out her orders, but came to a halt when she snapped imperiously, "I did not dismiss you."

Slowly he turned to face her, this time lifting his gaze. Dread sent little cold prickles up and down his spine. She eyed him with a calm dispassion. "How are you dealing with Quavell's disappearance?"

Maddock's stomach slid sideways. He had not expected such a question, certainly not from the baron. "I don't understand."

A smile ghosted over her pale lips. "Emotionally. How are you dealing with the fact your lover deserted you for another?"

Maddock still didn't speak.

Baron Beausoleil demanded impatiently, "How do you *feel* about it?"

Discussing emotions was not a topic he had ever imagined was in a baron's repertoire. According to Quavell, the barons were bred for brilliance and therefore had emotional limitations placed upon their enormous intellects. They were captives of their shared hive-mind heritage, of a remorseless mind-set that didn't allow them to understand visceral emotions. Although the tissue of their hybridized brains was of the same organic matter as the human brain, the millions of neurons operated a bit differently in the processing of information. Therefore, their thought processes were very structured, extremely linear.

Maddock placed his hands behind his back again, not so much as a sign of deference, but to hide their sudden tremor from Baron Beausoleil. He realized denying his relationship with Quavell was pointless.

"I was upset, of course," he said quietly. "But I've come to terms with it."

"As you should," the baron replied smoothly. "Since you helped her to escape."

Maddock felt sweat spring to his hairline, and he was barely able to keep the surge of terror he experienced from showing on his face.

"You have nothing to say to that?" the baron

pressed, her haughty smile widening but not reaching her eyes.

"Was my lord asking a question," Maddock responded in a murmur, "or was she stating a fact?"

In a dry, mocking whisper, Baron Beausoleil retorted, "I will leave that up to you to decide. But I still require a response."

Maddock struggled to think clearly. He found his eyes shifting from her face to the firm, hard-tipped breasts, past them to her flat, hard belly and then to the naked juncture of her curving thighs. Despite the circumstances, he felt himself responding to the baron's nudity. His mind raced, wheeling with fears, shame and multiple choices. The baronies had not been conceived as participatory democracies, but with the advent of the imperator as the puppet master of the barons, they had come to rely more and more on human counsel—as well as direct, face-to-face interaction.

Over the past few months, Baron Beausoleil had expanded her own influence by co-opting the human personnel of the Area 51 installation who still swore allegiance to a particular baron and elevating them to positions of power. The enormous complex had originally been staffed by humans and hybrids who served Baron Cobalt. Once he had been overthrown and dispossessed, his followers were neutralized—not eliminated. Although Maddock hailed from Cobaltville, he didn't give a damn about Cobalt or any of the barons. There was little point in swearing oaths of fealty to one over another, inasmuch as he had heard rumors that several of the barons had joined forces and were building effective military operations outside of Dreamland.

They were waiting to combine their military might and take over Area 51 and defy the imperator. Then, of course, being barons, they would make their own individual snatches for that title. Maddock wasn't sure if Beausoleil was among that group who plotted and schemed or if she had her own agenda.

"I'm waiting," she snapped.

Clearing his throat, Maddock said, "Quavell did not need my help to leave the installation, my lord baron."

Baron Beausoleil smiled slyly. "You're lying."

Maddock shook his head. "She knows how to drive the vehicles in storage. Because of her standing, she had no problem requisitioning one. So she did not require any aid from me."

She uttered a low laugh and languorously stepped toward him with a feline grace. "But she required your aid in ascertaining the correct route to take to reach her destination with a minimum of danger, did she not?"

When Maddock said nothing, the baron declared, "Quavell seeks the father of her unborn child. She knows where he is—information that has never been shared with the oligarchy. Either shared by her or the imperator."

For a second, Maddock stood frozen, his breath

seizing in his lungs. The baron sidled up against him, sliding her arms around his neck and pulling his head down. She stood on tiptoes, her lips parting, her dark eyes gazing unblinkingly into his. "During Kane's captivity here, Quavell learned the location of his nest of insurrectionists."

The sweat of tension formed on Maddock's body, and he felt the physical stirring her naked proximity and sensual voice invoked in him. He tried to ignore the presence of the attendant lurking in the shadows. "What makes you so sure of that?" he asked gruffly.

The baron laughed again, her inhumanly long fingers lightly caressing his nape. She didn't answer his question. "So she went to join him, carrying a child in her womb that could easily change the balance of power. A hybrid of a hybrid. The ultimate expression of unity between old and new human. A rallying point that could one day drown the world in blood."

"Humans aren't all murderous savages," he said hoarsely. Despite himself, Maddock felt his body responding to her, to the musky scent and heat radiating from her body. He had difficulty breathing. "As more than one of your new human females have learned."

Baron Beausoleil stepped back and glanced down at the jutting evidence of his arousal straining at the crotch of his jumpsuit. Softly she said, "Savages, predators all. You have been held in check because the holocaust of two centuries ago culled the pack. Only the strongest survived. The strongest is what I and the imperator seek, so we may bring all the barons to heel. To cull *their* pack, so to speak. Such an action is imminent.''

Maddock swallowed hard. He couldn't quite believe Baron Beausoleil had confided to him the start of the long-feared clash between the disaffected barons and the forces of the imperator. He had suspected such a plan was in the works, but he realized that even when things that were expected to happen finally did, they never happened in the expected way.

''Are you one of the strongest?'' she asked coyly, lightly tracing the outline of his erection with the tip of a finger.

He jerked away from her touch. Refusing to be baited, he demanded, ''How do you know where Quavell is?''

''She can be tracked. It has been so with her since she was removed from her incubation chamber, decades before you were born.''

Blood thundered in Maddock's ears. ''If you know where she is, why hasn't a retrieval squad been sent out?''

Baron Beausoleil's laugh caused his flesh to prickle. ''Quavell is exactly where the imperator wants her to be. Both of you helped to expedite his strategy.''

Terror struck Maddock like a closed fist slammed over his heart, but he continued to stand stock-still as the baron's fingers teased him. She asked, ''Do you love her?''

Maddock had no idea of how to respond. He

doubted the barons understood the concept. Not waiting for a response, she asked, "Did she love you? Or did you simply lust for each other as you now lust for me?"

Haltingly he said, "Lust and love often seem the same. But you can have one without the other."

Baron Beausoleil shrugged as if the matter were of little importance. "So I have learned. You certainly don't love me, but you lust for me. I cannot deny I find myself intrigued by your sexual arousal. It gives me a sense of personal power. Did you experience the same sense of power when you copulated with my kind's females and learned that some of them—your precious Quavell among them—enjoyed it? Indeed, a few began to look forward to it."

Maddock finally dredged up enough angry courage to state, "It was Baron Cobalt's will. They followed his edicts."

Chuckling, Baron Beausoleil said, "Brother Cobalt turned this facility into an underground stud farm, our women into broodmares, all to find out if the conventional means of procreation between old and new human would produce offspring. Now that it *has* been proved, the only reason for the miscegenation to continue is to use the progeny born of these union—if there are any more—as raw material, to be processed and used to keep the oligarchy alive. Neither love nor lust has anything to do with it. And therefore, you no longer need console yourself with Lylana…and she no longer need corrupt herself with you."

"Lylana?" Maddock's whispered echo was like the rustle of coarse cloth.

"Has your desire for me driven all thoughts of her out of your mind?" The baron's voice was rich with mockery. She snorted. "You human males—so proud of your muscles, so proud of your strength and your organs of reproduction. But even so, only one of you could shoot the seed with sufficient potency to produce a child."

Maddock's erection began to wilt and Baron Beausoleil realized it. She began to turn away, her lips stretched in a contemptuous smirk. "Such cowards, too."

The baron's unexpected kick caught Maddock in the groin. Sickening pain exploded up through his testicles. Although he didn't give Baron Beausoleil the satisfaction of hearing him cry out, he couldn't help but clutch at his crotch and fold in the direction of the white-hot agony.

He fell to the floor and tried to huddle into himself, as his Magistrate training had taught. Baron Beausoleil kicked him again, this time in the kidneys, and as his back arched from both the pain and the impact, she hooked her toes under his chin and forced his head back. Then she planted a heel on his throat.

Through the pounding in his ears, he heard her voice, sibilant with hate and disgust. "Long, long ago, long before you were born, I decided not to rely solely on humans to protect me. I sought out the best trainers available and though I could never develop the strength in my body to match that of an apekin, I learned all of your kind's weak and vulnerable points…and how to incapacitate you with little risk to myself.''

Through pain-fogged eyes, Maddock saw Baron Beausoleil gazing down at him, her face twisted in a smile of pure, malicious triumph. He couldn't help but notice how stiffly her nipples projected. She breathed heavily, eyes glittering. Absently, he realized that Brodeur's casual description of her as evil hadn't been mere hyperbole. He glimpsed the attendant standing off to one side, his face a blank mask.

In a crooning whisper she said, ''I learned during the training period that I was aroused by watching apelings grovel and beg for their lives.''

Maddock's lips writhed, but all he could manage was a strangulated croak. ''Won't beg.''

The baron nodded as if she had expected the response. ''Then I think it's only fair for you to fulfill your Magistrate's oath—to die in the service of your baron.''

''You're not my baron,'' he gasped out. ''You bitch.''

Baron Beausoleil shrugged. ''Any will do.''

''Killing me won't help you dominate the other barons,'' Maddock husked. ''You need the apekin like me to do the dirty work. And once you kill me, you'll have a rebellion brewing here.''

''I won't deny I'm employing an old tactic,'' she replied agreeably. ''To make you an example. Kill one and frighten all the others into submission. I learned that from the Magistrate trainers, too. So your kind does have a degree of wisdom. You should be flattered that I even concede that much to humankind.''

Then Baron Beausoleil stamped down, expertly putting the proper pressure in the right place to crush Maddock's trachea with her heel.

Chapter 7

Baron Beausoleil affected a swaggering, long-legged gait as she strode purposefully and barefoot down the corridor. The open robe belled out behind her like a cloak, accentuating the startling effect. As a member of an elite group bred for physical and mental perfection, she had no inhibitions about displaying her body. But she noticed that the few human males she passed turned quickly away from her.

She wasn't sure if they averted their eyes to conceal the desire her beauty aroused in them, or if it was due to the baronial mystique. She didn't care one way or the other. She put them down as mental dwarfs, hopelessly stunted by their stupidity and fear.

The baron felt very good following the final gene-therapy session, her energy levels restored to maximum after the week-long regimen that included infusions of blood, adenine, guanine, cytosine and long-string protein molecules. All the biochemicals were absorbed through the pores of her skin and then into her cellular structure.

She would enjoy near perfect health for at least another year or so. There was a time, she reflected, in the very recent past, wherein the survival, let alone the health of the entire hybrid race was cast in serious doubt. And if the baronial oligarchy believed in sin, the death of their race would have been the ultimate crime against Creation, particularly if the destruction of such a superior species had been caused by the actions of an inferior race.

Of course, the human progenitors of the baronial oligarchy had more than once nearly destroyed themselves. In decades past, the barons had warred against one another, each struggling for control and absolute power over territory. Ten barons survived the wars of territorial expansion and clawed out enclaves of civilization.

More than ninety years before, nine of them were summoned to the ville of Front Royal to meet with a diplomatic envoy who outlined all the rewards that would be theirs if they put aside their differences, concentrated on their commonalties and united. Barons had united before, observing trade agreements and nonaggression pacts. This proposal was different. A new form of government would be institutionalized in the baronies, and all the villes would be standardized according to preexisting specifications.

The barons would be provided with all the materials needed to achieve these goals, including a vast treasure trove of long-lost predark technology, as pristine as the day it was manufactured.

Not just a few boxes of ammo or a couple of crates of guns or the odd wag, but literally tons of matériel—advanced weaponry, electronic equipment saved from electromagnetic pulses, even aircraft. All of it was in perfect operating condition. No longer would the individual barons be forced to cobble together electrical generators with spit and baling wire, or waste time with long periods of trial and error to figure out how to repair rusty engines. Moreover, they would be participating in a grand, radically new kind of social engineering.

Over the following four generations, order was indeed restored to America, and the barons themselves represented the new order, as well as a new form of humanity. Only the barons themselves knew how different they were, not only from their human progenitors, from whom they had inherited their names and territories, but also from the humans they ruled.

What made the barons so superior had little to do with the physical. The brains of the barons could absorb and process information with exceptional speed, and their cognitive abilities were little short of supernatural.

But visceral emotions did not play a large part in the psychologies of the so-called new humans, the homo superior. Complex human emotions like loyalty, self-sacrifice and anger were complete mysteries to them.

And though no one could argue that the hybrid race was as intellectually superior to humankind as the Cro-Magnon was to the Neanderthal, they paid a heavy price for their superior abilities. Compared to the "old" humans, they were fragile, their autoimmune systems at the mercy of infections and diseases that had little effect on the primitive apekin they ruled. Nor could they reproduce by intercourse. The nine barons were the products of in vitro fertilization, as were all hybrid offspring.

Once a year, the oligarchy traveled to an installation beneath the Archuleta Mesa in Dulce, New Mexico, for medical treatments. Beneath the mesa, the barons received annual transfusions of fresh blood, and a regimen of biochemical genetic therapy designed to strengthen their autoimmune systems, which granted them another year of life and power.

When the renegade Magistrates, Kane and Grant, had destroyed the critical medical facility beneath the mesa in New Mexico, it fell to the arrogant Baron Cobalt to suggest a means of reversing the floodtide of extinction lapping at the feet of the new humans. Baron Cobalt occupied Area 51 with the spoken assumption of taking responsibility to sustain his race—but only if he was elevated to a position of high authority, even above his fellow barons.

Although Baron Cobalt had learned that Area 51's history was involved with rumors of alien occupation, he wasn't sure if the aliens referred to by the predark conspiracy theorists were the Archons. More than likely they were, inasmuch as the equipment that still existed was already designed to be compatible with the hybrid metabolisms. In any event, Baron Cobalt reactivated the installation, turning it into a processing and treatment center, without having to rebuild from scratch, and transferred the surviving human and hybrid personnel from the Dulce facility.

But when Baron Cobalt dangled the medical treatments before his fellow barons, rather than share them freely, war was the inevitable result—particularly after Sam, supported by Balam—the last Archon—hijacked not only Cobalt's plan but also the title of imperator.

The baronies had been poised on the brink of civil war, sparked by one of their own. But before that happened, Baron Cobalt's forces were violently displaced from Area 51 and he had disappeared. The doctrine of unity by which the baronies were formed had been decisively shattered. Baron Beausoleil had no idea what might take its place, but she knew she had to consolidate her position by forging a stronger link with the imperator—which would, if all went according to her plans, help her establish supremacy over all the barons.

To gain control over them, Beausoleil knew she needed to strike a personal alliance with key members of the imperator's inner circle. However, the imperator seemed to have only one confidante, and she tended to wander the villes, like both a spy and a disciplinarian.

The corridor doglegged to the right, and she strode into a square room nearly twenty yards across. The overhead lighting was as dim as the hallway, but Baron Beausoleil's vision easily discerned the rows of little plastic boxes. They were like transparent cubes with no tops to them. She surveyed the make-shift nursery, noting with approval that the infants no longer lay listlessly on their foam pads, and only a couple were connected to IV drips. Most of the tiny children raised their huge, dark eyes to her, but made no noise at all.

In the recent past, the likelihood that the infants in the nursery were the last generation of hybrids was very strong. But in the intervening months, the combined resources of all the villes' medical sections provided the Area 51 medical techs with the raw organic material to reverse their deterioration. As it was, the fifteen children were the only survivors of the Archuleta Mesa catastrophe. Two thousand more had perished.

But over the past few months, new cloning tanks had been installed and a blood-purification system was up and running. Although the crisis to the hybrid race was not completely averted, it was no longer as acute or immediate.

Leaving the nursery, the baron strode through the narrow corridors, past a number of computer-locked doors. She didn't know what lay behind them, and she really didn't care overmuch. The Dreamland complex was far too huge for even its most basic layout to be depicted on a map. Beausoleil wasn't even sure how Baron Cobalt had learned about its existence in the first place. She and the other barons presumed there had been data pertaining to it in the computer banks of the Cobaltville Historical Division.

Because of the installation's sprawling size, Baron Beausoleil didn't even try to learn her way around, except for the way to and from the medical treatment section to her chambers, and even that was quite a hike, at least a mile. Unlike most of her brethren, she didn't mind a certain degree of physical exertion. After what seemed like an hour, she reached her quarters.

The chambers she had been given in Area 51 were Spartan compared to the opulent furnishings she enjoyed in her ville, but contained a direct vid-feed to the security network and a computer terminal. The lighting was dim, but perfectly comfortable for her, whose eyes functioned best in illumination only a notch above twilight. Still, she didn't see the tall figure sitting on the bed in the corner until a low, angry voice said, "You're late, Baron. I don't like to be kept waiting."

Chapter 8

For a half second, Baron Beausoleil stood frozen, until the voice touched chords of recognition within her mind. Then she pivoted swiftly, closing her robe at the same time and putting a welcoming smile on her face.

"I apologize, Imperial Mother," she said, a carefully calculated deferential note in her voice. "I was detained due to a report about a disturbance above."

Erica van Sloan stood and approached her. She was nearly a full head taller than Baron Beausoleil and equally beautiful, with a flawless complexion the hue of fine honey. Her long, straight hair, swept back from a high forehead and pronounced widow's peak, tumbled about her shoulders. It was so black as to be blue when the light caught it. The large eyes above high, regal cheekbones looked almost the same color, but glints of violet swam in them. The mark of an aristocrat showed in her delicate features, with the arch of brows and her thin-bridged nose.

A graceful, swanlike neck led to a slender body encased in a strange uniform—high black boots, jodhpurs of a shiny black fabric, with an ebony satin tunic tailored to conform to the thrust of her full breasts.

Emblazoned on the left sleeve was a symbol depicting a thick-walled pyramid worked in red thread, enclosing and partially bisected by three elongated but reversed triangles. Small disks topped each one, lending them a resemblance to round-hilted daggers. Once it had served as the unifying insignia of the Archon Directorate and then was adopted by Overproject Excalibur, the Totality Concept's division devoted to genetic engineering. Now it was the insignia of the imperator, as was the black uniform.

Baron Beausoleil maintained the smile as she gave the woman a swift but surreptitious visual inspection. In some ways, looking at Erica van Sloan was like looking at herself, an incarnation of pure human DNA, not leavened by Archon genetic material. She always experienced a moment of disorientation when she saw the imperial mother. It was difficult to reconcile the memory of the withered old hag hunched over in a wheelchair with the reality of the tall, vibrant, superbly built beauty standing before her.

Like a handful of other predarkers, Erica van Sloan had been revived from cryostasis when the Program of Unification reached a certain stage of development. She was only one of several preholocaust humans, known as "freezies," who had been resurrected to serve the baronies. Beausoleil had seen Sloan a number of times over the years, particularly during baronial councils, and she had grown accustomed to seeing the craggy, seamed face, thin, straggly hair and small and scrawny frame. Only her black eyes ever seemed to show any life.

The imperator had not only restored her youth, but he had also put life back in her legs. He also gave her purpose beyond acting as an adviser to the baronial oligarchy. Sloan dedicated her life to building a new, productive society on the framework of the ville system. As a cyberneticist, she applied those same principles to management and organizational theory. Just as everything that occurred in the universe could be analyzed into cause-and-effect chains, the chains themselves could be used to build organizational models. Now, months after the overthrow of Baron Cobalt, a new model was being constructed, and Erica van Sloan rebuilt Cobaltville so it would serve as the template for all the others.

"I didn't expect you until later today," Baron Beausoleil went on. "I presumed your duties in Cobaltville would detain you."

"I haven't been in Cobaltville in weeks." Sloan said flatly, "I've been at the Uluru installation, making sure all is in readiness."

"Is the imperator so positive that events will unfold as he has foreseen?"

"It's not so much a matter of foreseeing," Sloan answered. "It's a matter of extrapolating. I don't question him any longer. I have limited time to fulfill the imperator's wishes."

At first, the baron wasn't sure of her meaning, then she saw the wide strip of gray running like a bleached-out ribbon through the left side of her dark tresses. She couldn't help but notice how tense the woman seemed to be, as well.

"As per his wishes and conveyed through you," Beausoleil said, "the pregnant female was allowed to escape the facility in order to join the exiles. She is now in place, a trump card to play whenever you or the imperator chooses."

Erica van Sloan seemed unmoved by her declaration. "I would prefer to see this 'trump card' and know her name. She's too unique and valuable a resource to be referred to in that casual manner."

Baron Beausoleil nodded. "Of course." She crossed the room to the computer terminal and turned it on. As the monitor screen flickered, she slid a gleaming compact disc into the port. "Her name, Imperial Mother, is Quavell."

The screen flashed and the image of a hybrid female appeared on it. She was excessively slender and small of stature, but perfectly proportioned. White-blond hair topped her high, domed skull, brushed back from her unlined brow and falling almost to her shoulders, to curl slightly inward at the ends. The texture seemed to be a cross between feathery down and silk. Above prominent cheekbones, huge, up-slanting eyes very nearly as big in proportion to her high-planed face as those of a cat, were the clear crystal blue of mountain meltwater. They looked haunted, gleaming with a flicker of emotion that was uncharacteristic of her kind.

Sloan studied her features keenly and the column of copy scrolling along the right-hand side of the screen. "So she is the one...the sole female out of dozens who actually conceived by a human male. Is there something about her that makes her special?"

"As you can see," Baron Beausoleil said crisply, "she is of the Quad-Vee genotype, first grown from existing Quadro cultures over sixty years ago. She is among the first generation."

Sloan put her hands on her hips and frowned at the image of Quavell. "Was she the only representative of that genotype who participated in the experiment?"

"As far as the records indicate," the baron replied, "yes."

"Where are the other Quad-Vees?"

"We think that the female members perished in the destruction of the Archuleta Mesa installation. Quavell herself was outside the facility at the time. The other Quad-Vees are male."

The baron smiled wryly. "Hardly suitable for the purposes Baron Cobalt had in mind. As in Nature, it is always the female of the species who is charged with the responsibility of saving a race."

Erica van Sloan smiled, too, a quick twitching of the lips. "What makes the Quad-Vee females so compatible with humans?"

"At this juncture, our medical techs have no true idea. They are working on finding an answer, or at least a theory." Baron Beausoleil paused and added,

"However, I submit it has less to do with the genotype than the individual…and more to do to with a
psychological component than a biological."

Arching an eyebrow, Sloan said, "Explain."

The baron reached out to the console and touched
a button. "Visuals will support my hypothesis in a
more satisfactory way than a dissertation."

The screen filled with a pattern of pixels, then re-
formed to show a high-angle view of a dimly lit room.
It was little more than a cube, the only furnishings a
bed and a small table holding a carafe of water and
a pair of folded towels. Sloan caught her breath in
surprise at the images.

A tall, dark-haired man, his pale eyes glazed, his
naked muscular torso sheened with a glossy sub-
stance, stood behind Quavell. He held her nude and
kneeling body up by his sinewy arms as his hips
thrust rhythmically back and forth.

"That is Kane," Baron Beausoleil stated crisply.
"Have you ever met him face-to-face?"

Sloan's eyes never left the screen. "Once…briefly.
Months ago when my son—the imperator—attempted
to recruit him."

"You are aware of the uses Baron Cobalt put him
to here, are you not? His methods?"

Sloan didn't reply, her attention totally fixed on the
monitor. Kane's pelvis surged back and forth, the
sound of wet flesh smacking wet flesh filtering
through the speaker. Despite the violent way her fragile body was being jarred by the steady thrusting,

Quavell's elfin face was a blank mask, her eyes closed.

"Kane and a companion—a little albino creature named Domi—penetrated this facility and were captured," the baron continued. "Kane was sentenced by Baron Cobalt to what amounted to stud service. During his two weeks of captivity, he was fed a steady diet of protein to speed sperm production and laced with a stimulant to provide him with hours of high energy. Since he was forced to achieve erection and ejaculation six times a day every two days, his energy and sperm count had to be preternaturally high."

In a tremulous voice, Erica van Sloan said, "I understand that Baron Cobalt held a grudge against Kane. Was this also a form of punishment?"

"To a point. The baron determined that inasmuch as Kane was responsible for the crisis, then he would contribute to its alleviation. However, the main reason he was chosen to impregnate the female hybrids was due to the fact that other human males pressed into service had performed unsatisfactorily due to their terror of our kind. At first the females selected for the process put on wigs and wore cosmetics in order to appear more human to the sperm donors. But the men had to be strapped down, and even after the application of an aphrodisiac gel, had difficulty maintaining an erection."

She nodded to the images on the screen. "As you can see, Kane did not suffer that problem. The gel's effectiveness on him was close to one hundred percent. He was a very adaptable man, something Baron Cobalt seemed to be aware of. Quavell also displayed exceptionally adaptive traits.''

Sloan glanced at her curiously. "How so?"

"Watch," Baron Beausoleil said.

On the screen, Quavell suddenly uttered a high-pitched sob and tried to suppress another one bubbling up her throat. She brought her small hands up under her and pressed their palms to the bed. With her head up and her back bowed, she pushed herself backward, meeting Kane's thrusts stroke for stroke with a growing frenzy. Her small, berry-tipped breasts trembled. She began crying out, her huge eyes wide open and aglitter with passion.

Matter-of-factly, the baron declared, "As you can see, Quavell's responses correspond with those of human females undergoing the same kind of sexual stimulation. Rather unprecedented for one of our kind, although I have heard reports that a few of our females began to enjoy such activities. Even accounting for the novelty factor, I find it puzzling."

Sloan pulled her gaze from the screen long enough to cast a challenging glance at the woman. "How so?"

Baron Beausoleil shrugged. "The concept of sexual, physical pleasure is not something we of the oligarchy understand as a general rule. There were rumors that the late Baron Ragnar liked to experiment in such a fashion with human women, but inasmuch as he was—as all our males are—inadequately equipped to indulge those desires, he resorted to artificial enhancements.''

The baron didn't remind Erica van Sloan that since the male hybrids did not reproduce, their sexual organs were vestigial, tiny reminders of the human biological material that composed perhaps a tenth of their metabolisms.

She shrugged again. ''Or so the rumors said. It matters not now, since he's dead.''

A sharp cry from the screen commanded Erica van Sloan's attention again. Quavell stiffened her small body, and she writhed as a torrent of little gasps spilled from her open mouth. Her gasps blurred into a broken, aspirated scream as her body locked in a spasming contraction of release.

Still maintaining a clinical, almost detached tone of voice, the baron said, ''Here, apparently, Quavell undergoes what is called an orgasm, a peaking of various and sundry stimuli.''

Kane pounded harder, faster, gripping the thrashing Quavell by the waist to keep her from being driven across the bed. His hands completely spanned her lower back. Throwing his shoulders and head back, he cried out and slammed his lower belly against her upturned buttocks. His hips jerked back and forth in an explosion of orgasmic energy.

Gasping, Quavell sagged beneath him, collapsing facedown on the bed. Kane fell forward, supporting himself above her by quivering arms, straining briefly against her backside, as if unwilling to accept he had spent himself within her. After a few moments he slowly withdrew from her, stumbling back half a pace.

"Oh my," Sloan murmured faintly.

Kane was still in a high state of sexual arousal, and his glistening erection looked as muscular and sinewy as the rest of his body. Quavell, her hair damp with sweat, shifted around on the bed, reaching out for him. Her hand closed around Kane's shaft, and she lovingly and shamelessly laved the crown of his manhood with her tongue. Then the images faded from the screen.

"Judging by the time Quavell exhibited the first signs of pregnancy," Baron Beausoleil said, "this was the session during which she conceived. Apparently she shifted the schedule around in order to arrange a number of trysts with Kane."

Erica frowned toward her, but the baron noticed the faint dew of perspiration at her temples—and the peaks of her breasts straining at the satiny fabric of her tunic. "Why did you show me this?" she demanded.

"It's a historic record in a way," the baron answered. "The first new human impregnated by an old human. A hybrid of a hybrid."

Sloan nodded, veiling her eyes with half-lowered lashes. Almost to herself, she murmured, "Don't you know hybrids take on all the positive attributes of their parents, becoming the most exceptional specimens?"

Baron Beausoleil assumed the question was rhetorical, more in the way of a quote, so she said nothing. Sloan gazed at her steadily, a sour smile tugging at the corners of her mouth. "Historical record? In my day we would've called it pornography or voyeurism."

The baron regarded her with wide, innocent eyes. "Indeed? If the images disturbed the imperial mother, I apologize."

Erica van Sloan gestured impatiently. "I didn't find them disturbing…it's just that I don't have your level of detachment while watching—never mind."

Beausoleil said, "I admit I found them interesting, particularly the revelation that Quad-Vees—or one of them—possessed such a reservoir of passion. Nor can I deny that the images awakened a faint spark of sexual energy in me, as well."

Sloan's eyebrows knitted at the bridge of her nose. "For Kane?"

Baron Beausoleil snorted delicately. "That hunching, slouchy brute? No, I am intrigued by Quavell's responses and the fact that at her first opportunity she fled from here to be with him, just as you predicted. She is the mystery, not Kane."

Sloan favored her with a quizzical stare. Her smile became one of pity. "You really don't know, do you?"

"I confess I do not know the touch of a man," the baron retorted defensively. "Nor do I ever care to be victimized by the kind of ministrations performed by Kane.''

With a calculated boldness, Baron Beausoleil flicked her eyes up and down the taller woman's lissome figure. In a soft, husky whisper, she said, ''But the beauty of womankind is always arousing.''

Erica van Sloan's eyes widened in surprise, and a pulse suddenly beat in her throat. ''What do you mean?''

The baron sidled up close to her, just as she had done to Maddock only minutes before. ''I mean we can be a great deal of help to each other, Imperial Mother. We are engaged in a mutually beneficial plan. You need me to fulfill the imperator's wishes in the matter he pursues. As his intermediary, you need one of the oligarchy whom you can trust implicitly.''

''And you are that one?'' Sloan asked, striving for a haughty tone, although her breath came fast and shallow.

''Who else? We are women of status in a male-dominated society. We should have no secrets from each other. We are an empire unto ourselves, far from the petty ambitions of my brother barons.'' As she spoke, Baron Beausoleil, with slow, sinuous movements undid the sash of her robe and let it slide from her body. ''I bare myself before you.''

Sloan only stared at her. The baron caught her gaze and held it unblinkingly, violet eye to violet eye. Softly she said, ''You and I are alike, utterly beyond the laws and protocols of this society. For us to make love would be like making love to ourselves. That prospect fills me with desire.''

In a breathless whisper, Erica van Sloan said, ''This isn't proper.''

Baron Beausoleil pressed herself against the taller woman's body, rising up on the balls of her feet in order to push her nipples against Sloan's. ''*We* make the rules, *we* decide what is proper.''

Cupping Sloan's face between her hands, the baron stated huskily, ''And we decide the fate of our females and their issue.''

Moaning softly, Erica van Sloan closed her eyes, lowered her head and kissed Baron Beausoleil's upturned mouth. The corners were curved in a faint, triumphant smile.

Chapter 9

The late-afternoon sun flooded the broad plateau with a golden radiance, striking highlights from the scraps of the chain link enclosing the perimeter. The breeze smelled fresh, rich with the hint of spring growth wafting up from the foothills far below. As he stepped through the open sec door, Philboyd inhaled gratefully, deeply.

"Not a trace of fluorocarbons," he declared. "I guess there's an upside to everything, even a nuclear war."

Brigid Baptiste couldn't help but laugh. "Was the atmosphere so saturated with pollutants before the nuke you could smell them even at this altitude?"

"To be honest," he admitted, "I wouldn't know. I wasn't much into mountain climbing." He gave her a slightly abashed smile. "I was just trying to make conversation."

Philboyd was a tall man, a little over six feet, long limbed and lanky. He wore a white, zippered coverall, the unofficial duty uniform of Cerberus personnel. Blond-white hair was swept back from a receding hairline. He wore black-rimmed eyeglasses, and his cheeks appeared to be pitted with the sort of scars associated with chronic teenage acne. The red weal of a healing gash showed starkly against the pale flesh of his forehead.

Brigid nodded in understanding. "Well, the air is pure enough up here...unless we get a chem storm, which isn't very likely at this time of year."

The breeze ruffled Brigid's red-gold mane of thick, wavy hair, arranging it artlessly over her shoulders and upper back. Her fair complexion was lightly dusted with freckles across her nose and cheeks. Her big feline-slanted eyes beneath the rectangular lenses of her wire-framed spectacles weren't just green; they were a deep, clear emerald. She wore a white bodysuit identical to Philboyd's, which showed off her willowy figure to full advantage. It was slender but rounded and taut, long in the leg, her arms rippling with hard, toned muscle.

"Chem storms," Philboyd repeated musingly. "It's been a long time since I saw any kind of storm."

"You were lucky to have missed out on those," Brigid replied dryly, feeling a little strange to be discussing the weather with the man. But then, weather was still something of a novelty for him.

Philboyd nodded in comprehension. "I read a little about the nuclear winter in the database here. You call it skydark, right?"

"Right," answered Brigid. "Ratio-wise, it killed more people than the actual nuke."

Two centuries before, the hundreds of very nearly

simultaneous nuclear explosions had propelled massive quantities of pulverized rubble into the atmosphere, clogging the sky and blanketing the planet in a thick cloud of dust, debris, smoke and fallout.

For nearly twenty years, it was as if the very elements were trying to purge Earth of the few survivors of the atomic megacull. The exchange of nuclear missiles did more than slaughter most of Earth's inhabitants—it distorted the ecosystems that weren't completely obliterated. The entire atmosphere of the planet had been hideously polluted by the nukecaust, producing all manners of deadly side effects in the ecosphere.

After eight generations, the lingering effects of the nukecaust and the skydark were more subtle, an underlying texture to a world struggling to heal itself, but the consequences of the war still let themselves be known from time to time, like a grim reminder to humanity to never take the permanence of the species for granted again.

One of the worst and most frequent side effects were the chem storms, showers of acid-tainted rain that could scorch the flesh off any mammal caught in the open. They were lingering examples of the freakish weather effects common after the holocaust and the nuclear winter. Chem storms were dangerous partly because of their intensity, but mainly because of the acids, heavy metals and other chemical compounds that fell with the rain.

In the immediate aftermath of the nukecaust, chem

storms could strip flesh from bone in less than a minute. As the environment recovered, the passage of time diluted their potency, but the lethal acid rain could still melt flesh from the bones during long exposure.

Fortunately, chem storms were no longer as frequent as they had been even a century before, but the peculiar geothermals of hellzones seemed to attract them. Although fewer hellzones existed now, there were still a number of places where the geological or meteorological effects of the nukecaust prevented a full recovery. The passage of time could not completely cleanse the zones of hideous, invisible plagues.

The west coast of the United States was one such zone, where most of California was under water. The best-known zone was the mile-long D.C./New Jersey/New York corridor, a vast stretch of abandoned factory complexes, warehouses and overgrown ruins. D.C., otherwise known as Washington Hole, was still the most active hot spot in the country.

Brigid still retained vivid and unpleasant memories of her one visit to the Hole. Only a vast sea of fused black glass occupied the tract of land that once held the seat of American government. Seen from a distance, the crater lent the region the name by which it had been known for nearly two centuries. Washington Hole was the hellzone of hellzones, a great wilderness of radioactive dirt and debris, where no life remained.

Even so, Philboyd had expressed an interest in seeing the place for himself. Brigid guessed that since he had spent most of his adult life cloistered in an artificial environment, breathing recycled air, the past month he had spent at the Cerberus redoubt was almost as disorienting as visiting an alien planet. He had spent the past two-hundred-plus years on the Moon, so Earth did indeed seem alien to him, as did the installation built deep inside a Montana mountain peak.

Constructed in the mid-1990s, no expense had been spared to make the redoubt—the seat of Project Cerberus—a masterpiece of concealment and impenetrability. The redoubt had housed the Cerberus process, a subdivision of Overproject Whisper, which in turn had been a primary component of the Totality Concept. The researches to which Project Cerberus and its personnel had been devoted were locating and traveling hyperdimensional pathways through the quantum stream. Once that had been accomplished, the redoubt became, from the end of one millennium to the beginning of another, a manufacturing facility. The quantum interphase mat-trans inducers, known colloquially as "gateways," were built in modular form and shipped to other redoubts.

The thirty acre, three-level installation had come through the nukecaust with its operating systems and radiation shielding in good condition. When Mohandas Lakesh Singh had reactivated the installation some thirty years earlier, the repairs he made had been minor, primarily cosmetic in nature. Over a period of time, he had added an elaborate system of heat-sensing warning devices, night-vision vid cameras and motion-trigger alarms to the surrounding plateau. He had been forced to work in secret and completely alone, so the upgrades had taken several years to complete. However, the location of the redoubt in Montana's Bitterroot Range had kept his work from being discovered.

In the generations since the nukecaust, a sinister mythology had been ascribed to the mountains, with their mysteriously shadowed forests and hell-deep, dangerous ravines. The wilderness area was virtually unpopulated. The nearest settlement was nearly a hundred miles away in the flatlands, and it consisted of a small band of Indians, Sioux and Cheyenne.

Planted within rocky clefts of the mountain peak and concealed by camouflage netting were the uplinks with an orbiting Vela-class reconnaissance satellite, and a Comsat. It could be safely assumed that no one or nothing could approach Cerberus undetected by land or by air—not that anyone was expected to make the attempt, particularly overland. However, there had been a recent exception.

The road leading down from Cerberus to the foothills was little more than a cracked and twisted asphalt ribbon, skirting yawning chasms and cliffs. Acres of the mountainsides had collapsed during the nuke-triggered earthquakes nearly two centuries ago. It was almost impossible for anyone to reach the plateau by foot or by vehicle, and Lakesh had seen to it that the facility was listed as irretrievably unsalvageable on all ville records.

Philboyd and Brigid walked across the broad, tarmac-topped plateau to where Kane's Manta ship rested on its landing gear. He was busy inspecting the battle damage inflicted on it and so affected not to notice the approach of the two people.

Brigid knew his apparent preoccupation was a pose. Kane's senses were so finely honed that not even a sparrow flitting overhead could have escaped his notice. He had arrived back at Cerberus less than ten minutes before, trans-comming to the redoubt a very brief overview of the events at Dreamland and Grant's decision to take a lengthy detour.

When Philboyd saw the depressions and dents scarring the Manta's hull, he whistled in surprised consternation. "Holy shit, Kane! You didn't tell me you took this much fire!"

Kane straightened from beneath the TAV's tail assembly and regarded him darkly. "You didn't ask, Philboyd."

The man walked around the craft, shaking his head in disbelief. "Do you know how old these crates are?"

"No," Kane retorted sharply. "And neither do you."

Repressing a smile, Brigid said, "The metallurgical analysis Bry performed on the hulls suggested they were a minimum of ten thousand years old."

"Being stored on the Moon for all those millennia

kept them in perfect working order,'' Kane commented.

Philboyd nodded. "Too bad the same couldn't be said for me."

Philboyd, like the TAVs, had been on Earth a little less than a month. Without the intervention of Brigid, Kane and Grant, both he and the Mantas would have remained on the Moon for eternity, forgotten relics of two past ages.

A mission a few months before had brought Grant, Brigid and Kane to a Totality Concept installation on a isle in the Cific Ocean, situated on one of the Santa Barbara Islands. Within the facility they had discovered a special encoded program called Parallax Points. Brigid and Lakesh made several visits to the facility, salvaging what they could. Most of the machinery was damaged beyond any reasonable expectation of repair, but the data pertaining to Parallax Points was retrieved and put to use, including the black protective garments Kane had named "shadow suits."

After weeks of study, they learned that the Parallax Points program was actually a map, a geodetic index of all the naturally occurring vortex points on the planet. That discovery spurred Lakesh to build the second version of a device he referred to as an interphaser, or to be technically precise, a quantum interphase matter-transmission inducer.

The interphaser had evolved from the Totality Concept's Project Cerberus. Before the nukecaust, the objective of Project Cerberus was essentially devoted to converting matter to energy and transmitting the energy to a receiving unit and converting it back again to matter.

Although a working teleportation device had been more or less perfected in the latter years of the twentieth century with the development of the mat-trans gateway units, Lakesh had gone even beyond that accomplishment. Two years before, he had constructed a small device on the same scientific principle as the mat-trans inducers, an interphaser designed to interact with naturally occurring quantum vortices. Theoretically, the interphaser opened dimensional rifts much like the gateways, but instead of the rifts being pathways through linear space, Lakesh had envisioned them as a method to travel through the gaps in normal space-time.

However, the interphaser was more than a miniaturized version of a gateway unit, even though it employed much of the same hardware and operating principles. The mat-trans gateways functioned by tapping into the quantum stream, the invisible pathways that crisscrossed outside of perceived physical space and terminated in wormholes. The interphaser interacted with the energy within a naturally occurring vortex and caused a temporary overlapping of two dimensions. The vortex then became an intersection point, a discontinuous quantum jump, beyond relativistic space-time.

According to Lakesh, evidence indicated there

were many vortex nodes, centers of intense energy, located in the same proximity on each of the planets of the solar system, and those points correlated to vortex centers on Earth. The power points of the planet were places that naturally generated specific types of energy possessing both positive and projective frequencies, and others that were negative and receptive. He referred to the positive energy as *prana,* which was an old Sanskrit term, meaning the world soul.

Lakesh was sure some ancient peoples were aware of these symmetrical geo-energies and constructed monuments over the vortex points in order to manipulate them. He suspected the knowledge was suppressed over the centuries. Apparently the Parallax Points program was a rediscovery of those ancient principles. Decrypting the program was laborious and time-consuming, and each newly discovered set of coordinates was fed into the interphaser's targeting computer.

But for the first time in two hundred years, the Cerberus redoubt reverted to its original purpose—not a sanctuary for exiles or the headquarters of a resistance against the tyranny of the barons, but a facility dedicated to unraveling the eternal mysteries of space and time.

Kane, Grant and Brigid had endured weeks of hard training in the use of the interphaser on short hops, selecting vortex points near the redoubt—or at least near in the sense that if they couldn't make the return trip through a quantum channel, they could conceivably walk back to the installation. Only recently had they begun making jumps farther and farther afield from Cerberus. So far, the interphaser hadn't materialized them either in a lake or an ocean or underground, a possibility that Kane privately feared. He knew an analog computer was built into the interphaser to automatically select a vortex point on solid ground.

However, everyone was nonplussed when one set of Parallax Point coordinates led to a location not just on solid ground, but off the planet itself, on the Moon. All of them knew the stories about predark space settlements, even of secret bases on the Moon, one of the largest built in the Manitius Crater region. That particular site was chosen because of its proximity to artifacts that some scientists speculated were the shattered remains of an incredibly ancient city, once protected by massive geodesic domes.

A remote probe had been dispatched first and it returned not just with evidence the Manitius Moon colony was still inhabited, but populated by a disaffected group of scientists, marauding packs of carnobots and both a flesh-and-blood devil and a machine known by the acronym DEVIL.

Philboyd was one of the scientists, as were several others who had recently arrived in the Cerberus redoubt via the more conventional gateway units, rather than the interphaser. He asked, "Do you mind if I check her over? I might find some damage you missed.''

Kane waved grandly toward the Manta. "Be my guest.''

As Philboyd strolled around the TAV to look at the rudder assembly, Brigid said quietly to Kane, "Lakesh is waiting for your full report.''

Kane shrugged. "Let him wait. I gave him all the high points over the comm.''

Brigid sighed and adjusted her glasses to examine bullet pocks on the Manta's hull. More than six months before, she had suffered a head injury serious enough to open her scalp to the bone and put her in a coma for several days. The only sign of it now was a faintly red, horizontal line on her right temple that disappeared into the roots of her hair. Although her recovery time had been little short of phenomenal, Kane noticed how she needed her glasses more and more over the past half year.

Without looking at him, she said very softly, "Quavell's not going away, Kane. It's been almost a month. You're going to have to accustom yourself to her presence here sooner or later.''

His eyebrows knitted at the bridge of his nose, but he stopped short of glaring at her. "I will when you will.''

Brigid looked at him, irritation glittering in her jade eyes. "I've come to terms with how she came to be here and the circumstances surrounding her condition. I already told you I don't blame you.''

He nodded, his lips stretched in a tight, grim line. "But that's about all you've said about it."

She combed nervous fingers through her mane of hair. "You were the one who didn't want to talk about it for the past six months. I respected your privacy. Besides, I remember what you told me when I first asked about what happened to you in Dreamland. 'Baptiste, if I told you about it, you'd be very sorry that I did.' You gave me fair warning and I accepted that."

As the self-proclaimed possessor of an eidetic memory, she couldn't claim to have forgotten what Kane told her all those months ago on New Edo. Brigid Baptiste remembered everything she read, heard or saw, and that was how and why she ended up as an exile like Kane and Grant.

Kane replied, "So I did. But what you don't say is if you've accepted the reasons she gave for being here."

"She feared for the safety of her child," Brigid replied. She paused and added in a voice so low it was almost a whisper, "*Your* child."

Kane grimaced. "You don't know that. I don't know that. She's never made that claim, either."

Brigid smiled, but it had little humor or warmth in it. "Only because you've refused to undergo genetic testing."

Kane didn't respond to her rejoinder. "She's a hybrid. And her being here is some kind of baronial ruse...or a trap concocted by the imperator."

Although he hadn't told either Grant or Brigid about his experiences in Dreamland, he hadn't known why he wanted to keep it a secret. He hadn't volunteered for stud service, after all. And it wasn't shame that kept him mute on the topic—at least, it hadn't been.

"Her being here has more to do with you or Domi," Brigid pointed out. "You claim you don't recall telling Quavell about the redoubt, but you were drugged much of the time—"

"So was Domi," he broke in harshly.

"So was Domi," she conceded. "So she might have been the one who spilled the beans on our location. But Quavell has been watched constantly since she arrived, and she's shown no indication of trying to get a message out."

Kane made a dismissive gesture. "That doesn't prove a goddamn thing, Baptiste. Do you really buy her story that Maddock helped her escape?"

"Why not? Domi buys it, since he helped her and you escape. And if he seemed to be in love with Quavell like you said, then it stands to reason he would do what he could to smuggle her out of Dreamland…even if it meant sending her to you."

Kane refused to be swayed by her reasonable tone. He said bitterly, "You know how cunning the barons, all the hybrids are. She could be a component in a long-range plan hatched by the barons. For example, why would she fear for the safety of her baby, since it was by Baron Cobalt's edict that she even conceived?''

Brigid nodded in agreement, but she replied, ''That was Cobalt's plan only, and it was apparently not condoned by the entire oligarchy. But the answer is obvious—if female hybrids can conceive offspring by human males, then a continued division between the so-called old and new human is pretty much without merit. And without a division, then the barons can no longer rule. To them, Quavell's child represents a future wherein they are no longer unique or superior.''

Her lips quirked in a wry smile. ''The other possibility is one you've refused to consider since the day we came back from the Moon and found her here. That she simply wants to be with the father of her child when her time comes to give birth.''

Kane jerked slightly in reaction to her words. His mouth twisted as if he tasted something exceptionally sour. ''Quavell has barely spoken twenty words to me since I came back.''

''No,'' Brigid said firmly. ''You've barely spoken twenty words to her. You've found some excuse or another to keep as far away from her as you can. It used to be called avoidance behavior. But now it's getting a little ridiculous, particularly since she's going to require more pre- and postnatal medical aid than our infirmary can provide—''

She broke off when she saw Kane stiffen, his eyes narrowing as he looked past her. He muttered disgustedly, ''Ah, shit.''

Brigid turned to see Domi strolling across the plateau from the direction of the sec door. She was a small, curvaceous white wraith, barely a shade over five feet tall. Her flesh was the color of a beautiful pearl, and her ragged mop of hair the hue of bone. Though petite to the point of being childlike, she was exquisitely formed. Eyes like drops of freshly spilled blood gleamed on either side of her thin-bridged nose. She wore a black T-shirt and a pair of red, high-cut shorts that showed off her pale, gamin-slim legs. She was barefoot, as usual.

"Am I interrupting something?" Domi asked when she reached the TAV.

Brigid shook her head ruefully. "Not really. It's just the same topic of conversation Kane and I have beaten to death for the past few weeks. Quavell's reasons for being here."

Domi acknowledged the comment with a playful smile directed at Kane. "Nothing to be suspicious about. From what I heard, you got a .30-30 between your legs and she's only a .22 cal."

Kane winced at the vulgar comparison, but decided to let the observation pass without comment. Due to her upbringing in the Outlands, Domi was always forthright and freewheeling in her manner. Months ago he had sworn her to secrecy about the details of his captivity, and the albino girl had kept her word, in spite of being confused by his reluctance to tell anyone about it. To his surprise, Brigid Baptiste didn't seem to be discomfited by her crude remark.

"I seriously doubt sexual attraction is a motivating factor among the hybrids," she stated dryly. "They're intellectuals first and foremost. The most mentally inferior of them probably have quadruple-digit IQs."

Kane didn't respond to her opinion. Addressing Domi, he demanded, "Is there a reason you came out here, other than to harass me?"

Domi's playful smile widened into a grin. "The topic of your conversation wants to see you—both of you. I volunteered to fetch you, since her condition keeps her from getting around too much."

Kane scowled down at her. "You're really enjoying this, aren't you?"

The grin fled from Domi's face, and she regarded him gravely for a silent moment. Then the grin returned and she intoned, "Yes. Yes, I am."

Chapter 10

The Cerberus redoubt was built inside the mountain peak. The multiton sec door opened like an accordion, folding to one side, operated by a punched-in code on a keypad and a lever control. Nothing short of an antitank shell could even dent it.

A large illustration of a three-headed, froth-mouthed black hound was rendered in garish pigment on the wall near the control lever. Underneath the image, in an ornately overdone Gothic script, was written the single word Cerberus.

According to Lakesh, the artist had been one of the enlisted men assigned to the redoubt toward the end of the twentieth century. Lakesh hadn't bothered to remove the illustration, partly because the paint was indelible and partly because the ferocious guardian of the gateway to Hades seemed an appropriate totem and code name for the project devoted to ripping open gates in the quantum field.

The main corridor, twenty feet wide, was made of softly gleaming vanadium alloy and shaped like a square with an arch on top. Great curving ribs of metal and massive girders supported the high rock roof.

From the main corridor, side passages and elevators led to a well-equipped armory, bunk rooms, a cafeteria, a decontamination center, an infirmary, a gymnasium with a pool and even a detention area.

The redoubt had been constructed to provide a comfortable home for well over a hundred people. Although there were far fewer than that now, there were still more than there had been in the past two centuries. Just as Kane wasn't used to Quavell's presence in the Cerberus redoubt, he had yet to grow accustomed to seeing more than one or two people in the corridors.

When he, Grant, Domi and Brigid had arrived at the installation two years before, there were only a dozen permanent residents. They were all exiles from the villes, although they had been brought there by Lakesh because of their training and abilities. For a long time, the Cerberus personnel were outnumbered by shadowed corridors, empty rooms and sepulchral silences.

Over the past three and half weeks, the corridors had bustled with life, the empty rooms filled and the silences replaced by conversation and laughter. The immigrants from the Manitius base had been arriving on a fairly regular basis ever since the destination-lock code to the Luna gateway unit had been discovered. Kane had stopped counting the new arrivals when he reached a dozen. Whether they intended to remain in the installation or tried to make separate lives for themselves in the Outlands was still an open question.

In any event, as more women arrived from the Moon colony, the redoubt's permanent male population was for the first time in the minority. Bry, Banks, Farrell, Auerbach and even the misanthropic Wegmann acted either like shy schoolboys or Mags in a gaudy house after a long patrol.

As Kane and Brigid strode along the passageway, he noticed heads of men and women turning toward him, and he heard his name whispered. Glamour, that's what I've got, he reflected sourly.

Kane couldn't really blame the people for staring, not just at him but at Brigid, too. If Grant had been present, they would've gaped at him, as well. The actions performed by the three of them had freed the Manitius base inhabitants from lives of unending terror and offered them an alternative to dying unknown and unmourned on the Moon. But Kane's status among the Manitius émigrés sprang more from the fact he had faced the fearsome Maccan and imprisoned the crazed Tuatha de Danaan in a stasis chamber, than from freeing them from a lunar tomb.

Kane recalled what Brigid had said to him after Tibetan bandits had bestowed upon him the title of Tsyanis Khan-po, the King of Fear. "You're earning quite the reputation in the far corners of the world," she had wryly commented.

Less than a month afterward, when Sky Dog's warriors had bestowed upon him the name of Unktomi

Shunkaha, or Trickster Wolf, he had realized that he was crossing over the road from flesh-and-blood man to enter the realm of legend. He wasn't pleased by the prospect.

Kane, Domi and Brigid entered the central operations complex, the brain of the installation. A long room with high, vaulted ceilings, it was lined by consoles of dials and switches divided by an aisle of computer stations. A huge Mercator relief map of the world spanned one wall. Pinpoints of light shone steadily in almost every country, connected by a thin pattern of glowing lines. They represented the Cerberus network, the locations of all indexed functioning gateway units across the planet.

On the far side of the center was an anteroom, and on the far side of that stood a mat-trans unit, the first fully functional, debugged gateway in the Project Cerberus network. The jump chamber itself, elevated on a circular metal platform, was enclosed on all sides by eight-foot-high slabs of translucent, brown-tinted armaglass.

Bry sat at the biolink telemetric monitor, and he nodded his copper-curled head in a greeting as Kane and Brigid entered. A round-shouldered man of small stature, his white bodysuit bagged on him. He served as something of Lakesh's apprentice.

The biolink medical monitor was electronically tied into the subcutaneous transponders every person in the redoubt carried within their bodies. The transponders were nonharmful radioactive chemicals that fit themselves into the human body, and allowed the monitoring of heart rates, brain-wave patterns and blood counts. Lakesh had ordered all of the Cerberus redoubt personnel to be injected with them. Based on organic nanotechnology developed by Overproject Excalibur, the transponders fed information through the Comsat relay satellite when personnel were out in the field.

The signal was relayed to the redoubt by the Comsat. The computer systems recorded every byte of data sent to the Comsat, and directed it down to the redoubt's hidden antennae array. Sophisticated scanning filters combed through the telemetry using special human biological encoding. The digital data stream was then routed to the console before which Bry sat and was run through the locational program to precisely isolate the team's present position in time and space.

Quavell sat at the master ops console. Reba DeFore and Lakesh stood on either side of her, gazing at the images flashing across the big VGA monitor screen. The hybrid female was small, smaller even than Domi. Her huge, up-slanting eyes of a clear crystal blue gave Kane a silent appraisal. White-blond hair the texture of silk threads fell from her domed-skull and curled inward at her slender shoulders. Her tiny form was encased in a silver-gray, skintight bodysuit. It only accentuated the distended condition of her belly and the slenderness of her limbs.

Lakesh turned toward them when they approached, fixing his intense blue gaze on Kane. They glinted with an angry impatience. By way of a greeting he declared, "I cannot comprehend how Grant could be so irresponsible as to fly one of the craft we have on loan from our Manitius friends to New Edo without asking permission."

Kane stared challengingly into Lakesh's bright-blue gaze, but the man never flinched. He still hadn't grown accustomed to dealing with a robust—relatively speaking—Lakesh, whose eyes weren't covered by thick lenses, whose voice no longer sounded like a reedy rasp and who didn't look like a hunched-over, spindly old man who appeared to be fighting the grave for every hour he remained on the planet.

The Lakesh he had first met was a wizened apparition of a man who looked exceptionally old, but nowhere near his true chronological age of 250 years. He had spent a century and a half of those years in cryogenic stasis, and after his resurrection fifty years ago, he had undergone several operations to further prolong his life. His malfunctioning heart had been traded for a healthy one, his glaucoma-afflicted brown eyes exchanged for bright, albeit myopic blue ones, his weak lungs changed out for a strong new pair.

Calcified, arthritic joints in his shoulders and legs were removed and replaced with ones made of polyethylene. None of the reconstructive surgeries or physiological enhancements had been performed out of Samaritan impulses. His life and health had been prolonged so he could serve the Program of Unification and the baronies. When he finally understood the full magnitude of the horrors the unification program had wrought on humanity, he determined to fight the barons secretly. For decades he served as chief archivist in the Cobaltville Historical Division.

Now Lakesh was a well-built man of medium height, with thick, glossy black hair, an unlined, dark olive complexion and a toothy grin. He looked no older than forty-five, despite a few strands of gray streaking through his temples. Kane recognized only the blue eyes and the long, aquiline nose as belonging to the Lakesh he had known these past two years.

Lakesh attributed his restored vitality to Sam, the imperator, who claimed he had increased Lakesh's production of two antioxidant enzymes, catalase and superoxide dismutase and boosted up his alkyglycerol level to the point where the aging process was for all intents and purposes reversed.

Kane recalled that for the first few weeks following Sam's treatment, Lakesh's hair had continue to darken and more and more of his wrinkles disappeared. But then the entire process reached a certain point and came to a halt. He didn't try to convince anyone that his condition was permanent. He had no idea how long his vitality would last. Whether it would vanish overnight like the fabulous One Horse Shay and leave him a doddering old scarecrow again, or whether he would simply begin to age normally from that point onward, he couldn't be certain.

Nobody, not even Brigid Baptiste with her seemingly endless font of encyclopedic information, knew who One Horse Shay had been or what was so fabulous about him. Kane suspected that Lakesh was taking full advantage of his restored middle-age. The glances he caught Domi and Lakesh exchanging from time to time told him that. He was also increasingly assertive and challenging—confrontational behavior that Kane attributed to his restored youth.

Still, Kane was no more inclined to tolerate highhandedness from a middle-aged Lakesh than an elderly one, so he responded to this accusatory statement with a taunting smile. "Yes, it *was* irresponsible, wasn't it? I mean, he acted like a man who essentially saved the solar system a few weeks back and who makes his own decisions without calling home to ask if it's all right if he misses dinner." He shook his head in mock disbelief. "Shocking."

"Worse," Lakesh said harshly, not in the least mollified by Kane's sarcasm. "He acted like you."

Kane glared at him, lips compressing. He fought down the anger rising in him. At the moment, with Quavell within arm's length, he didn't feel like continuing the feud that had begun on the very first day he and Lakesh exchanged words. Displacing the man from his position of total authority hadn't improved their relationship much.

Over a year before, Kane, Brigid and Grant had staged a minicoup. Lakesh hadn't been completely unseated from his position of authority, but he was now answerable to a more democratic process. At first he bitterly resented what he construed as the usurping of his power by ingrates, but over a period of time he accepted sharing his command with the other Cerberus exiles. It was the only fair tactic to take, since the majority of them were exiles due to his covert actions.

Almost every person in the redoubt had arrived as a convicted criminal—after Lakesh had set them up, framing them for crimes against their respective villes. He admitted it was a cruel, heartless plan, with a barely acceptable risk factor, but it was the only way to spirit them out of their villes, turn them against the barons and make them feel indebted to him.

This bit of explosive and potentially fatal knowledge hadn't been shared with the other exiles. Only Kane, Grant and Brigid were aware of it.

Exhaling noisily and wearily, Kane said, "Give it a rest, Lakesh." Gesturing to the biolink monitor that displayed icons representing heart rate and blood pressure, he declared, "Grant is fine—you can see that. He'll be back here before you know it."

Lakesh glowered at him. "It's not his health I'm concerned about."

"Then what has you so wired up?"

"I am the cause," Quavell said calmly in her musical yet childlike voice.

Repressing the urge to say "Why am I not surprised?" Kane turned to face her. To his relief she wasn't looking at him, but at the images on the monitor screen.

"And why," he inquired in a carefully calculated tone of neutrality, "is that?"

Her big eyes shifted toward him, and not for the first time Kane felt a strange sensation, almost physical, like a warm hand stroking the base of his spine. During the first few months following his captivity, Kane had successfully managed to keep from dwelling on memories of his forced fornications. But even when he gained a certain degree of emotional distance from those experiences, he found himself thinking of Quavell.

When he first saw her in Area 51, he recognized her immediately. During his escape from ruins of the Archuleta Mesa, he had kept Domi from killing Quavell. He had never let on he knew her, and she behaved like the encounter never happened. He knew, however, that hybrids forgot nothing, no matter how trivial.

Images of Quavell seemed to insinuate themselves into his mind during the hazy period between wakefulness and sleep. When he drowsed, he fancied he could feel her silky blond hair between his fingers, or he saw eyes of a clear crystal blue gleaming with emotions that were uncharacteristic of her kind.

Kane easily recalled other ways in which Quavell was different from the other females he had serviced. Almost all of them mounted him and rode him mechanically, not even looking at him. It was obvious they would have never engaged in intercourse with any human male but for Baron Cobalt's orders.

Although his memories were fragmented due to the aphrodisiac gel that induced a blind rutting fever, he retained a hazy recollection of her crying out in wild abandon during their last coupling. Her image would waver in his mind, then it would change and he would see her with a belly grown large with child, her long fingers clasped protectively over it, her delicate face displaying her determination to keep safe the life growing in her womb.

Kane would jerk back awake at this point in the imagery, consumed by a bewildering blizzard of unfamiliar and disturbing emotions. He was never sure if the mental pictures were examples of free association, or if Quavell was telepathically transmitting a message when he was the most susceptible.

Or, he reflected again, everything he had gone through could have been part of a complicated ruse. It certainly wouldn't have been the first time the hybrids tricked and lied to their human allies—or pawns.

He also remembered how Quavell had reacted when he questioned her in Dreamland if it were truly possible for humans and hybrids to procreate. Although she claimed they were chromosomally compatible, she had admitted the procedure was still experimental.

Then Quavell had smiled at him in a way he could only interpret as coquettish. One of her long fingers traced the faint scar on his left cheek and she whispered, "But some of us here—me, at least—find the process of trial and error very enjoyable."

The most recent memory of Quavell was not hazy in the least, though he wished it were. He still recalled with shocking clarity his first sight of her sitting in Lakesh's office when he entered to brief him about the events that had occurred on the Moon. He would have imbibed battery acid before admitting the closest he had ever come to fainting dead away was that very moment. As it was, his knees had almost buckled, but he was able to attribute his weakness to the injuries inflicted upon him by Maccan.

DeFore answered Kane's question. "Quavell's pregnancy may be endangered."

Stocky and buxom with deep bronze skin that contrasted starkly with her intricately braided ash-blond hair, the medic's brown eyes glinted with frustration and anger. "The irregularities in the genetic sequencing of the fetus have grown more pronounced. I don't know whether it's a temporary condition or something that might result in either a birth defect or a miscarriage."

Kane kept his expression composed, even though he felt the anger DeFore directed at him. The medic had never disguised her antipathy toward him—or rather what he represented. In her eyes, as a former Magistrate, he was the embodiment of the totalitarianism of the villes, glorying in his baron-sanctioned powers to dispense justice and death. At one time she had believed that due to his Mag conditioning he was psychologically conflicted and therefore couldn't be trusted.

Although her attitude toward him had softened somewhat over the past few months, the earlier resentment now flashed in her dark eyes.

In a way he didn't blame her, since he had steadfastly refused to cooperate in ascertaining whether he was the father of Quavell's child. During one of the arguments he had with her about his stubbornness, DeFore mentioned that the DNA specimen she had taken from the fetus defied every familiar pattern— even those the computer was programmed to recognize.

"Well," he ventured, "what can we do about it?"

"Us?" Lakesh inquired, gesturing to everyone in the control complex but Kane. "Nothing." His finger jabbed toward him. "But *you* can do something."

Kane felt a flush of anger and shame warming the back of his neck. His eyebrows curved down to meet at the bridge of his nose, and he opened his mouth to voice a profane repetition of the reasons he would not submit to genetic testing. Before he could speak, Quavell said softly, "You can travel to the Moon with me."

Chapter 11

Shizuka lay limp and satiated over Grant, her panting breath hot on the side of his neck. He breathed heavily himself, cradling her in his arms. *"Sugo kanjiru,"* she crooned dreamily.

Grant didn't know the exact meaning of her words, but he didn't really need a translation, not with the wild way the pulse beat at the base of her neck. Shizuka raked her tangled screen of luxuriant blue-black hair from her face. The lines of aristocratic authority had been sponged away, her mouth half-open, the lips swollen by passionate kisses.

She gently tongued away a bead of perspiration gleaming on his forehead. Even with the sea breeze wafting in from the open balcony, the air in the palace room was humid and warm.

"I should be drilling my troops," Shizuka murmured. A teasing grin creased her face. "Not being drilled myself." She kissed his chin. "You are a bellyfull, my black tiger."

Grant chuckled, but it sounded forced and self-conscious. She gazed searchingly into his eyes for a long moment. Her tumbles of glossy black hair framed a smoothly sculpted face of extraordinary beauty. Her complexion was a very pale gold with roses and milk for an accent. The dark, almond-shaped eyes that usually held the fierce, proud gleam of a young eagle, were liquid pools of pleasure and satisfaction.

Then with a sigh of disappointment, she eased herself off his softening shaft, so big and dark, so unlike those of the men of New Edo. Grant started to speak, but no words came out. Instead, he pulled her down alongside him and they lay together on the futon, their limbs loosely entwined. Absently he stroked her hair.

"Something upsets you?" Shizuka asked quietly.

He took her right hand and gently pressed it between his own and kissed her fingertips. "Not upset exactly," he said haltingly. "It's just…"

His words trailed away. Shizuka waited for him to continue, then propped her head on his shoulder. "Grant-san. Tell me what disturbs you."

Grant made a deep, rumbling noise of impatience and asked, "When was the last time we saw each other, the last time we held each other like this?"

A tiny line of consternation appeared on Shizuka's smooth forehead. "A little more than three months, by my count. When you rescued me from Sindri, on Thunder Isle."

"Is being with each other once every three months enough for you?"

In a small, sad voice she answered, "We both have our duties, our responsibilities. As much as I wish otherwise, they cannot be shirked. The time we have together, no matter how scattered or brief, is always enough for me. We must live for the moment."

A little bitterly he demanded, "Is that part of the *otoko ni michi*, the ancient and honorable samurai code?"

She didn't respond for a long, tense moment. When she did, her tone was stiff and cold. "You know it is."

In one lithe movement, Shizuka pulled her hand away and stood, reaching for a silk kimono hanging from a hook on the wall. All the walls were made of opaque squares of oiled paper and wooden lathwork. "Are you dissatisfied with our arrangement?"

Grant frowned at her frostily formal tone. "I'm afraid I am."

Shizuka gazed at him silently, then ducked her head in a short, brusque nod. "*Ah so deska.* I understand."

She whirled and crossed the room to the small balcony, exuding an air of wounded dignity. Grant waited for a long moment, then rose and joined her, wrapping a sheet around his waist.

"No," he said firmly, "I don't think you do."

Shizuka leaned on the rail and looked out over the palace grounds. "Perhaps I only understand this place. I have seen very little else of the world."

Grant followed her gaze. From their position, they could see much of New Edo. From the harbor, a cobblestoned road wound up and over a series of gently rolling hills, all with green, rich grass. Cattle grazed

inside split-rail fences. Cultivated fields made a patchwork pattern over the terrain. Gravel-covered foot-
paths branched off from the main thoroughfare, leading to modest single-level homes made primarily of
carpentered driftwood.

Not for the first time Grant was impressed by the
overall cleanliness of the village. He saw no litter
anywhere, and all the shrubbery and undergrowth
were trimmed neatly back. Some of the hedgerows
had been clipped into shapes resembling cranes and
snakes.

The fortress of New Edo's *daimyo,* Lord Takaun,
dominated the settlement, like a huge animal slumbering among gardened terraces. It was a sprawling
structure with many windows, balconies and carved
frames. The columns supporting the many porches
and loggias were made of lengths of thick bamboo,
bent into unusual shapes. The curving roof arches and
interlocking shingles all seemed to be made of lacquered wood. It was well laid out with deep moats
on three sides and cliffs that faced the sea on the
other. At the top of the walls were parapets and protected positions for archers and blastermen.

Grant never failed to feel awed, not just by the
fortress and the village, but by the fact that Shizuka's
people had accomplished so much in only eight years.
New Edo was a living testament to the strength of
human will not just to survive, but to transcend any
and all hardships. Hacking a little storybook civilization out of the rock of one of the Western Isles was

more than just difficult; it had been damn near impossible.

New Edo and its companion islet, known as Thunder Isle, were part of the Santa Barbara, or Channel, Islands. The primary Operation Chronos installation, code-named Redoubt Yankee, had been built on the small island, disguised as a satellite campus of the University of California.

As Grant had reason to know, many of the other Western Isles were overrun by pirates and Asian criminal organizations known as Tongs. The people of New Edo gave these a wide berth, but established a friendly relationship with a coastal ville called Port Morninglight. The little island empire traded with them for several years, until it was wiped out by a force of Magistrates dispatched by Baron Cobalt. When a contingent of samurai tracked the murderous Mags, their paths intersected with those of Grant, Kane, Brigid and Domi, who were engaged in the same enterprise.

"The manner by which you arrived here has only added to the luster of your legend, Grant-san," Shizuka said quietly.

She smiled up at him wanly and gestured to the left. Following her hand wave, he saw his Manta ship, surrounded by murmuring palace retainers. It was guarded by a contingent of Tigers of Heaven, New Edo's army. The Tigers of Heaven were attired in suits of segmented armor, made from wafers of metal held together by small, delicate chain. Overlaid with a dark-brown lacquer, the interlocked and overlapping plates were trimmed in scarlet and gold. Between flaring shoulder epaulets, war helmets fanned out with sweeping curves of metal. Some resembled wings, others horns. The face guards, wrought of a semitransparent material, presented the inhuman visage of a snarling tiger.

Quivers of arrows dangled from their shoulders, and long bows made of lacquered wood were strapped to their backs. Each samurai carried two longswords in black scabbards swinging back from each hip. None of them carried firearms, but their skill with *katanas* and the bows was such that they didn't really need them. Grant had been told that ammunition was hard to come by, nor did New Edo have the natural resources to manufacture it themselves. Grant had offered to supply the Tigers with guns and ammunition from the Cerberus armory, but he had been politely refused. The samurai code practiced by the Tigers considered firearms unmanly weapons, despite the fact they did have a few old World War II–vintage carbines in storage.

Looking at the grim, armored sentinels guarding his ship, Grant couldn't help but chuckle. "I don't think they have to worry about anyone stealing it and taking it for a joyride."

Shizuka regarded him with eyes that glimmered with unshed tears. "They posted themselves there as a way to honor you, not to safeguard that machine."

She turned toward him, looking up into his face.

In a low, unsteady tone, she asked, "Will you be leaving before sunset?"

"Not me," he answered. "Us."

He enjoyed the expression of first puzzlement, then astonishment that crossed her face. She stared at him uncomprehendingly, then swung her head around to gaze wide-eyed at the Manta, then back to him. "Us?" she repeated incredulously. "Me and you in that thing?"

He nodded. "You and me."

"I thought there was only one seat."

The corner of his mouth quirked in a half grin. "You can sit on my lap."

She continued to stare at him. Grant guessed she was reviewing his tale of how the ship came to be in his possession. Shizuka's dark eyes suddenly glinted with the sparks of a warrior's inner fire, not the tears of a woman. They were but dim reflections of the ferocious strength of will that had allowed her to defeat a rebellion and command the forces that beat back an invasion of New Edo, all in a single night.

"I can't go with you!" she exclaimed. "I lead the Tigers of Heaven—you know that. My place is here, to make sure my people don't factionalize again."

Grant recalled the attempted insurrection orchestrated by the Black Dragon society. According to Lord Takaun, the roots of the society stretched back three or more centuries to the last days of Japan's old feudal system. A group of *soshi,* disenfranchised and rabidly xenophobic samurai, formed an underground organization to fight the spread of Western influence. In reality, they were terrorists and later they became Nippon's pioneers of organized crime.

The Black Dragon society was revived in New Edo, hiding in plain sight, since most of them were recruited from the ranks of the Tiger trainees. They didn't want any commerce or contact with the mainland at all and were particularly incensed when Grant, Kane and Brigid arrived on the island.

Because he feared alienating the samurai, Lord Takaun didn't take action against the Dragons. He claimed that even offering hospitality to the three guests was risking a rebellion, perhaps even a coup. The *daimyo*'s fears proved to be grounded in terrifying reality. The open, grassy courtyard that the balcony overlooked had been the scene of a bloody battle six months before between the Black Dragons and the Tigers of Heaven.

Lord Takaun was grievously injured and the former captain of the Tigers, Kiyomasa, was slain. It fell upon Shizuka's slender shoulders to end the insurrection, and she did it in the only way that would satisfy the honor of both factions—by killing the Dragon leader in single combat, literally slicing him in two with her *katana*.

The rebellious Black Dragons saw only two options—to continue to press their coup and die to a man, or to swear loyalty to the samurai who had slain their leader. They decided to swear loyalty and live. Ironically, many of them didn't live long after making their oaths. They perished repulsing the invaders dispatched from Baron Snakefish. Despite the losses both the Tigers and the Dragons suffered, it was Shizuka who had led both factions to victory.

After that, they had obeyed her every command, appeased her every whim with a kind of devotion different, yet more powerful, than that they would have given to a man.

Putting his big hands on her shoulders, Grant said earnestly, "I'm not asking you to elope with me, to desert your people."

She eyed him quizzically. "What then?"

"I want us to be together."

"Here? In New Edo?" Her tone of voice vibrated with surprise.

He nodded slowly.

A frown tugged at the corners of her mouth. "You would leave your friends…your home in Cerberus to be with me?"

Grant gave careful thought and consideration to his answer. The notion of remaining on the little island monarchy had grown in appeal over the past few months, but Shizuka had never extended an invitation to him. Grant hadn't felt it was his place to raise the issue with her until the past few weeks, after the op to the Moon and the arrival of the Manitius base personnel.

Even with influx of new people to Cerberus, Grant was fairly certain Kane would accuse him of desertion, despite the fact he had taken no vows or sworn an oath of service to battle the barons. Kane was his partner, true enough, and it was a matter of Mag policy never to desert a partner regardless of the circumstances, but they weren't Mags any longer. Kane had more of a personal interest in seeing the barons overthrown than he did. It was Kane's vendetta, his vengeance trail, not Grant's. His primary contribution was to cover Kane's back. But now there were other people who could be trained to perform that function just as well.

And if Quavell really did carry Kane's child, then the entire dynamic of the struggle against the tyranny of the barons was different. In the baronies, children were a necessity for the continuation of ville society, but only those passing stringent tests were allowed to bear them. Genetics, moral values and social standing were the most important criteria. Generally, a man and a woman were bound together for a term of time stipulated in a contract.

A number of years before, Grant and a woman named Olivia had submitted a formal mating application. Both of them had entertained high hopes of the application being approved and they managed to convince themselves that it would be. After all, babies still needed to be born, but only the right kind of babies. A faceless council determined that he and Olivia could not produce the type of offspring who made desirable ville citizens.

Once their application was rejected, he and Olivia had drawn attention to themselves. Their relationship became officially unsanctioned and could not continue lawfully. In the years since Olivia, he had never given much thought to kids, at least, not having any of his own. But lately, he'd started thinking about it a bit more seriously. He wondered if creating a new life might not be a way to balance out the ones he had taken over the years.

Shizuka's puzzled "Grant-san?" drew him out of his reverie.

Taking a deep breath, he declared, "Shizuka, I want you to go with me to Cerberus. It's only an hour's flight time, even at half throttle."

"Why?"

"I want you to see the place. You asked me about it often enough. New Edo can spare you for a day or two."

"I'd like to see your home, too," Shizuka replied. "But there's more to the invitation than simply inviting me to look around."

Grant smiled, but it didn't reach his eyes. "Yes, there is. I'd like you to be with me when I tell Lakesh, Kane, Brigid and the others that I'm leaving them—and coming back here, to be with you."

Chapter 12

"The Moon, my ass," Kane snapped.

"You've said that before," Lakesh told him severely. "About a month ago."

Kane glared at him. "Yeah, well, I'm saying it again." He turned toward Quavell, forcing himself to meet her steady gaze unblinkingly. "Why do you want me to go there with you?"

DeFore leaned over the hybrid woman's shoulder and tapped the VGA monitor screen with a forefinger. "Because of those. Medical equipment and a fully stocked laboratory that's a hell of a lot more advanced than what we have here. If it's necessary to begin a regimen of gene therapy on Quavell's fetus, I'm going to need everything I can get my hands on."

"Wouldn't amniotic-fluid analysis detect a potential birth defect?" Brigid asked.

DeFore shook her head. "In some cases, yes. But that process has its limitations, and I'm limited by the equipment I have here to make a definitive prenatal diagnosis. I need a way to determine a course of treatment whether it's utilizing viral vectors or germ line therapy."

Kane squinted at the images. His eyes took in at a

glance the heavy tables loaded down with a complicated network of glass tubes, beakers and retorts, consoles with glass-covered gauges and computer terminals. A sterile maze of equipment glittered beneath the cold neon tubes on the ceiling.

Over the past couple of years, Kane had seen enough genetic engineering and medical facilities to recognize the large-scale fermentation tanks, a purification system and the massive electron microscope standing on a separate table. In one corner, he saw an oscilloscope, a fluoroscope and a stainless-steel liquid-nitrogen tank. The lid was open, revealing the honeycomb pattern of individual containers that had once held fertilized embryos.

At the bottom of the screen flashed a time and a date. The images had been recorded only ten days before, during one of the inspection tours Philboyd had conducted once the gateway transit line had been opened from the Cerberus mat-trans unit to the one on Manitius.

"You think that equipment can help Quavell?" he asked.

Quavell made a diffident motion with one long-fingered hand. He had seen Balam perform the same gesture, and he guessed it was the equivalent of a shrug. "That remains to be seen. They should be examined."

"They're at least two hundred years old," Kane argued. "Older, even, since the Manitius base was fully operational by the 1980s."

"They were in use at some point during the last two centuries," said a new voice.

Kane turned as Nora entered the operations center. Another émigré from the Moon base, she looked nothing like the woman he had met in the DEVIL control nexus weeks before. Then, she looked undernourished, her long, dark hair a tangle of Medusa snarls. Since her arrival in the Cerberus redoubt, she had been dipping into the supply of cosmetics left there by the female personnel of the installation before it had been abandoned in the days preceding the nukecaust.

The white bodysuit she wore clung to her trim, small-waisted figure. Her hair was coifed, neatly trimmed, and the makeup she had applied to her face caused Bry to stare at her hungrily as she passed him by.

"Why do you say that?" Kane asked.

In a surprisingly genial tone, Lakesh said, "Actually, friend Kane, *you* said it."

Kane swiveled his head toward him. "When?" His tone was sharp to cover his momentary confusion. He didn't like the feeling.

"You opined that Megaera's Furies were hybrids, remember?"

The mystery of Megaera and her shadow-suited Furies was the factor that had drawn Kane, Grant and Brigid to the Moon a few months before.

In ancient Greek mythology, Megaera was a Fury, one of three sisters charged by the gods to pursue sinners on Earth. They were inexorable and relentless in their dispensation of justice.

Kane had unmasked a dead Fury in Chicago and he'd recognized the facial type—long jawed, narrow chinned, with high cheekbones. The man was a hybrid. If not a full-fledged one, then certainly some traces of Archon genetic material were buried in his familial woodpile. He had been much taller than the average hybrid, and his eyes hadn't possessed the prominent supraorbital ridge arches, either. His genitals were also of normal size.

Kane nodded reluctantly. "It did seem like some form of genetic manipulation was going on up there. Maccan pretty much confirmed it." In a stern voice, he added, "But that doesn't mean that Furies and carnobots aren't still crawling around up there. Not to mention what was left of Saladin's boys. Not all of them came in once the DEVIL platform was destroyed."

Kane recalled how Philboyd claimed the deadly carnobots had been manufactured back before the holocaust and field-tested on the Moon. The killer machines were powered by a stomach that broke down food using Escherichia coli bacteria, converting the chemical energy from the digestive process into electricity. The microbes from the bacteria decomposed the carbohydrates supplied by the food, which released electrons. The robots possessed sensor chips that were programmed to detect perspiration and even pheromones. Sometime during the astrophysicist's long period in stasis, their programming was altered so they stalked and fed on humans.

Some of the humans they preyed upon were members of a paramilitary cadre led by a man called Saladin, who swore allegiance to Maccan. Saladin had died when he was exposed to the hard vacuum of the Moon's surface.

"Megaera is dead," Brigid pointed out. "Maccan is in stasis where you put him. And Enki is—well, Enki is gone."

"The medical section has been secured," Nora announced, "by Mariah and Eduardo."

"Then why do you need me to go back up there?" Kane demanded. He inclined his head toward DeFore. "You ought to be able to look over the equipment and decide what's useful and what isn't. I don't see why Quavell should go at all."

"I am more familiar with the type of apparatus I might require," Quavell said mildly.

Kane assumed she was making an oblique reference to the annual biochemical treatments every hybrid had to undergo in order to stay healthy.

"What about all the stuff in Balam's old holding cell?" Kane demanded. "The equipment there synthesized all the food—if you could call it that—he needed to stay alive. I don't remember him complaining. Or if he did, we didn't care."

Nobody laughed. Kane's comment about Balam, the only so-called Archon on Earth, evoked a variety of emotions within Lakesh, DeFore and Brigid. After three years of imprisonment in the Cerberus redoubt, Balam finally revealed the truth behind the Archons and the hybridization program initiated centuries before. Balam claimed that the Archons and their ruling council, the Directorate, existed only as myths created by the predark government agencies as control mechanisms.

Lakesh referred to it as the Oz Effect, wherein a single vulnerable entity created the illusion of being the representative of an all-powerful body. Balam himself may have even coined the term *Archon* to describe his people. In ancient Gnostic texts, "Archon" was applied to a parahuman world-governing force that imprisoned the divine spark in human souls. Kane had often wondered over the past few months if Balam had indeed created that appellation as a cryptic code to warn future generations.

Even more shocking was Balam's assertion that he and his ancient folk were of human stock, not alien, but alienated. Regardless of scraping away the myth and exposing the truth, the barons, the half-human hybrids spawned from Balam's DNA, still ruled. Lakesh had learned that the DNA of Balam's folk was infinitely adaptable, malleable, its segments able to achieve a near seamless sequencing pattern with whatever biological material was spliced into it. In some ways, it acted like a virus, overwriting other genetic codes, picking and choosing the best human qualities to enhance. Their DNA could be tinkered with to create endless variations, adjusted and fine-tuned.

"Balam wasn't a hybrid," Lakesh stated stolidly. "The material we made and he ingested sustained him, but it is not food that we're talking about."

"I thought finding the proper kind of food here was a problem for you," Kane said to Quavell.

"If you spoke to her more often," DeFore said with some asperity, "you'd know we dealt with that issue weeks ago."

When she first arrived, Quavell had difficulty finding food that was easily digestible for her simplified intestinal tract. She claimed she and her kind ingested microorganisms that consisted primarily of single-cell proteins.

"I was able to synthesize a passable version from the samples I brought with me," Quavell told him. "Fortunately, you had the raw materials here in storage."

Kane didn't know what to say, so he opted for an inane "That's nice."

"At any rate," Nora said, "the medical equipment would be of great use down here, even if it doesn't help Quavell."

"That still doesn't answer my first question," replied Kane. "Why do you need me? There are plenty of other people here just as qualified to gate to the Moon and back."

Out of the corner of his eye, he saw Bry lower his head behind the environmental ops console. The man had never been on a field mission and he had often expressed his desire to keep it that way.

The ten permanent residents of the Cerberus redoubt, regardless of their skills, acted in the capacity of support personnel. They worked rotating shifts, eight hours a day, seven days a week. For the most part, their work was the routine maintenance and monitoring of the installation's environmental systems, the satellite data feed, the security network.

However, everyone was given at least a superficial understanding of all the redoubt's systems so they could pinch-hit in times of emergency. Grant and Kane were exempt from this cross-training inasmuch as they served as the enforcement arm of Cerberus and undertook far and away the lion's share of the risks. On their downtime between missions, they made sure all the ordnance in the armory was in good condition and occasionally tuned up the vehicles in the depot.

Brigid Baptiste, due to her eidetic memory, was the most exemplary member of the redoubt's permanent staff since she could step into any vacancy. However, her gifts were a two-edged sword inasmuch as those same skills made her an indispensable addition to away missions.

''If the medical section is secure like you say—'' Kane began.

''It may not be,'' Lakesh broke in. ''Until we have an accurate head count of everyone on the Moon base, we shouldn't become overconfident. Certainly not so confident that we would risk an unborn child.''

''Besides,'' DeFore declared with a lopsided smile, ''a lot of that equipment is heavy.''

Kane stared at her, too surprised to be angry—at first. Then he growled, ''You mean you need my blaster *and* my strong back?''

''Essentially,'' Quavell answered.

Kane managed to bite back the profane retort that leaped unbidden to his tongue. Staring at Lakesh, he said, ''Why don't you go, then? You're spry and strong enough now. And you know how to use a gun. I've made two trips up there over the past three weeks. Don't you want to look around?''

Lakesh didn't appear to be shamed by the unmistakable hint of challenge in Kane's tone. ''I would indeed,'' he replied. ''However, there is a very good reason why I don't. I fear to use the gateway or the interphaser.''

Kane felt his eyebrows crawling toward his hairline. ''You created both of the damn things! You were the first human subject of the gateways.''

''I don't need to be reminded of my own past,'' Lakesh said coldly.

''I really think you do,'' Kane grated. ''Otherwise, you'd repeat the same mistakes over and over, hoping one day you'd beat the odds and get it right. Of course, the world wouldn't survive all the attempts, but you'd have another success to add to your résumé.''

Lakesh's eyes glittered with anger, then he cast his eyes downward. Lakesh tended to blame himself for many things, and for a long time, Kane gleefully helped him do so. As a project overseer for Project Cerberus, then as an adviser and even something of an architect of the unification program, he had helped to bring about the tyranny of the barons.

Much later—far too late, as far as Kane was concerned—he turned against the barons, betraying them and even stealing from them, to build his resistance movement. Lakesh found no true sin in betraying betrayers or stealing from thieves. He couldn't think of the hybrid barons in any other way, despite their own preference for the term *new human.*

Lakesh then tried his hand at creating his own new humans. Some forty years before, when he first decided to resist the baronies, he rifled the genetic records on file to find the qualifications he deemed the most desirable. He used the unification program's own fixation with genetic purity against them. By his own confession, he was a physicist cast in the role of an archivist, pretending to be a geneticist, manipulating a political system that was still in a state of flux.

Kane was one such example of that political and genetic manipulation, and when he learned about Lakesh's involvement in his birth, he had very nearly killed him.

"Why are you afraid?" Kane demanded.

Lakesh took a deep breath. "I fear that the carrier

wave will be intercepted by Sam…as happened to you."

Both Kane and Brigid regarded him in surprise, their thoughts flying back to the incident he described, nearly six months in the past. Even though Lakesh had explained the event to her, Brigid wasn't certain of what happened on that day. According to Lakesh, Sam, the self-proclaimed imperator, could manipulate the energies of what he called the Heart of the World, an encapsulated packet of the quantum field.

Buried beneath the Xian pyramid in China, the Heart was described as containing the energies released in the first picoseconds following the Big Bang, channeling the matrix of protoparticles that swirled through the universe before physical, relativistic laws fully stabilized. It existed slightly out of phase with the third dimension, with the human concept of space-time. From this central core extended a web of electromagnetic and geophysical energy that covered the entire planet. Sam himself claimed he had transported Kane, Brigid and Grant from Thunder Isle to Xian by opening a localized wormhole in the energy web at the moment they activated the mat-trans gateway in the Operation Chronos installation.

"It's possible that Sam marked me in some fashion when I was with him," Lakesh continued. "Perhaps when he turned back the hands of my metabolic clock. As you may recall, he wanted to enlist me to his cause. There's no reason why he would've changed his mind."

"So you think Sam may have the means to know when you're in a gateway or interphaser transit?" Brigid's voice was neutral, but her eyebrows were quirked at a skeptical angle. "And somehow redirect the matter stream?"

Lakesh nodded. "Yes. I have no idea of the extent of his abilities."

He stared at Kane. "You may call me a coward if you wish, friend Kane, but my fear has little to do with my own safety. If I fall into the hands of Sam again, I will not be able to escape a second time. It was a very close thing the first time, as you may recall."

Kane waved away Lakesh's explanation. "I understand, Lakesh. You're a lot of things, most of them irritating, but you're not a coward."

Lakesh smiled sourly. "I thank you for that, at least."

After a moment of awkward silence, Kane said grimly, "All right. I agree to the jump under one condition."

No one spoke. The five people looked at him expectantly.

"I want Grant to go with us. His back is stronger than mine, and two blasters are always better than one."

Lakesh frowned. "We don't know when friend Grant will return. You could take Bry."

Kane glanced toward the environmental station. Bry was nowhere to be seen. Kane figured he was crouched under the desk, or crawling on all fours toward the exit.

"You'll be making contact with Eduardo and Mariah once you're there," Nora said helpfully. "They'll show you around."

Kane snorted. "If you expect me to escort a pregnant women through a place that might be lousy with flesh-eating robots and fused-out Furies, I want Grant to cover my back—not a tech or a pair of astrophysicists."

He shot a questioning look at DeFore. "Besides, the situation isn't critical, is it?"

DeFore pursed her lips. "No, it's not that time sensitive. But if any of that equipment is functional, I'd like to know as soon as possible, so we can gate it here and set it up."

Kane nodded in agreement.

"If Grant's not back by noon tomorrow," Brigid said, "I'll go with you. I'm used to watching your back after all this time."

He threw her a fleeting, appreciative grin. "Thanks, Baptiste. I might take you up on it. But Grant will be here, and we'll do what we always do."

"Club, shoot or strangle any problem that comes your way?" she inquired with a mock innocence.

Kane turned toward the door. "You know me so well."

Brigid waited until he had crossed the threshold and into the main corridor before murmuring, almost to herself, "Not half as well some people in this place."

Chapter 13

Within a minute of Kane's departure, Brigid, Nora and DeFore all found pretexts to drift away, leaving Lakesh alone with Quavell. Bry reappeared at the far side of the command center, pretending to run a diagnostic on the Comsat eavesdropping system.

A few months before, Lakesh and Bry had created a communications scanner with ville radio frequencies and channels, involving the redoubt's satellite uplinks. They hadn't heard much about the reaction of the rank-and-file ville citizen to the rule of the imperator—most probably knew very little about it, but they had picked up signals confirming Quavell's report of civil unrest in some of the baronies.

For the majority of the ville-bred citizens, the concept of living outside a narrow, structured channel would be akin to insanity. Lakesh knew the people of the baronies wouldn't be as resilient as Kane, Grant and Brigid Baptiste, when their entire belief system collapsed into the rubble of lost dreams and meaningless dogma.

Bry sensed Lakesh looking his way, and turned his attention to the mainframe output ports. The central control complex of Cerberus had five dedicated and eight shared subprocessors, all linked to the mainframe behind the far wall. Two hundred years ago, it had been the most advanced model ever built, carrying experimental, error-correcting microchips of such a tiny size that they even reacted to quantum fluctuations. Biochip technology had been employed when it was built, protein molecules sandwiched between microscopic glass-and-metal circuits.

The information contained in the main database may not have been the sum total of all humankind's knowledge, but not for lack of trying. Any bit, byte or shred of information that had ever been digitized was only a few keystrokes and mouse clicks away.

Lakesh continued to stand beside Quavell, groping for something to say. She stared at the vid images on the monitor screen, as if she found them utterly enthralling. He tried to put his hands in his pockets, remembered his white bodysuit didn't have pockets, just flapped pouches, and settled for drumming his fingers atop a nearby computer terminal.

Quavell suddenly spoke, her voice so soft it was almost inaudible over the hum of drive units. "Do not feel compelled to remain in my presence, Dr. Singh. I understand the discomfiture I cause."

Lakesh was startled into smiling. "You don't make everyone uncomfortable, madam. Darlingest Domi, for example, often seeks out your company."

"Yes." The word issued from her small mouth in a sardonic whisper. "The novelty of a pregnant hybrid has yet to wane with her."

"I'm sure it's more than that," Lakesh assured her.

Quavell shifted around in her chair, looking up into his face. Her crystal blue eyes were as placid as the surface of a frozen-over lake. "Perhaps so. Perhaps the sight of the dying babies in the nursery at Area 51 is still strong in her memory, and she associates my condition with that tragedy."

Lakesh tugged at his long nose contemplatively, an absentminded habit that hadn't changed since his age reversal. He remembered Domi's tale of being captured in Area 51 by the insurrectionist fifth column made up of humans and hybrids, led by Quavell. Domi told Lakesh that over a period of nights and days, she realized that her hatred of the hybrids and barons was derived primarily from what Quavell referred to as "negative conditioning." In order to end the war between human and hybrid, Quavell explained, the conditioning had to be faced and overcome by both factions.

Domi had remembered conversations between Lakesh and Brigid Baptiste about how the similarity between Balam's folk and the hybrids, and the traditional myth images of demons, accounted for the instant enmity that sprang up between humans and the so-called Archon.

Lakesh opined that since ancient depictions of imps, elves and jinn were more than likely based on early encounters between Balam's people and primitive man, humans weren't capable of reaching an accord with creatures who resembled archetypal figures of evil.

Even by crossbreeding with humanity, the hybrids were still markedly different from humankind. But as Quavell pointed out, different was not the same as alien. She herself confessed that her own race viewed humans as savages, little more than apes who were incapable of transcending their roots as killers. When Kane spared her life when he could have just as easily taken it, during their escape from the Archuleta Mesa, Quavell was forced to question her own point of view. She had experienced, she claimed, something of an epiphany.

Domi wasn't familiar with the term, but as she stood and watched one of the hybrid infants, who seemed all ribs and swollen belly blindly groping for her with its tiny, spindly fingers, she experienced an epiphany of such soul-shaking impact, she was never the same again. Quavell told her the destruction of the Archuleta Mesa had done more than smash the barons' ability to sustain their lives. It had also taken away their future by destroying the incubation chambers. Only twenty-three infants remained out of two thousand. The war between old and new human, Quavell declared, was over. The old humans had won simply by killing the babies of the new humans.

The Domi who had suspiciously followed Quavell into the nursery was not the same Domi who was led out.

"Or," Quavell went on, "as an outlander, an outcast herself, she relates to my position here. At worst, I am a pariah. At best, an unwanted guest.''

Lakesh started to voice a denial, then smiled ruefully. ''You may have a point, madam.''

He employed that particular form of address rather than ''young lady'' because at her age, despite her appearance, it would have seemed rather foolish, since Quavell claimed to be sixty-seven years old.

Quavell nodded. ''I usually do. If an alternate destination had been available to me other than this one, I certainly would have attempted to reach it.''

According to Quavell, she had made the long overland trip in a stolen Sandcat, all alone. She traveled as far as the foothills of the Bitterroot Range to the permanent encampment of Sky Dog's band of Lakota and Cheyenne. They were allies of the Cerberus exiles.

Sky Dog brought Quavell the rest of the way to the mountain peak on horseback. Lakesh was still skeptical of certain details of her story, particularly how she knew the location of the redoubt. She offered only a vague explantion about learning of it from either Kane or Domi during their period of imprisonment in Dreamland. She had refused to name which one of them actually made the revelation. Neither Kane nor Domi admitted to telling her, or anyone else, about Cerberus.

Still and all, Quavell had provided Lakesh with information about the current state of the baronies, even though none of it could be confirmed. Ever since he had been forced to abandon his role as chief archivist, personal adviser to Baron Cobalt and high-ranking member of the Cobaltville Trust, his means of gathering intelligence had been extremely limited.

"Where is everybody?" a female voice demanded.

Lakesh turned to see Domi strolling into the command center. She walked between the aisles of computer terminals and up to Quavell, smiling at her warmly. To Lakesh's surprise—and disquiet—Quavell returned the smile. Laying a gentle hand on her swollen stomach, Domi asked cheerily, "What's he up to today?"

"Not as active as usual," Quavell replied. "And why do you insist on referring to the child as 'he'? You know I never underwent a sonogram to determine its gender."

Domi's smile broadened, and she carefully caressed Quavell's belly. "Feels like a he, that's all."

Quavell sighed. "That's a very illogical statement."

Lakesh gritted his teeth to keep an angry remark from leaving his mouth. He didn't know if his shortness of temper of late was due to his rejuvenated hormone levels, or whether he had simply had a surfeit of hybrid dismissiveness and hybrid diffidence.

"And a very human statement to make," Lakesh said stiffly. "Of course, your child will be of a different strain of human, will it not? That's what you and the barons suspect, at any rate. Or fear."

Quavell seemed unperturbed by the harsh, almost

accusatory note underscoring his words. "The drive to create a new strain of humanity began long before I was born, long before the nuclear holocaust. The Third Reich's breeding farms is one example."

"They practiced selective mating to produce the human of the future," Lakesh countered. "A process that required too much time after the nukecaust. Hybridization was considered an absolute necessity, was it not?"

In a quiet, calm tone, Quavell answered, "As I recall from intelligence I studied about all the baronial advisers, you also considered it a necessity...or rather you paid lip service to it in order to maintain your status as co-conspirator in the subjugation of humanity."

Lakesh fought back a surge of guilt. It wasn't an emotion he enjoyed grappling with. Nevertheless, the guilt was neither neurotic nor misplaced. He and other twentieth-century scientists had willingly traded in their human heritage for a shockscape of planet-wide ruins. After all, they had been selected to survive in order to reshape not only Earth, but also humankind in a nonhuman image. From a technical, strictly moral point of view, Lakesh had betrayed both human and nonhumans. He couldn't think of the hybrid barons in any other way, despite their own preference for the term *new human*.

Lakesh had tried many times since his resurrection to arrest the tide of extinction threatening the human race. First had been his attempts to manipulate the human genetic samples in storage, preserved since before the nukecaust, to provide the hybridization program with a supply of the best DNA. He had hoped to create an underground resistance movement of superior human beings to oppose the barons and their hidden masters, the Archon Directorate. His only success had been Kane, and even that was arguable.

He had created a straw adversary called the Preservationists, a fictitious group of scholars-seditionists, to draw attention away from his real work at Cerberus. Lakesh used his position as adviser to Baron Cobalt to choose likely prospects to join his underground resistance movement, but he always knew his tiny enclave of exiles could never overthrow the barons by staging a guerrilla war.

Humankind, at least those who were ville-bred, had been beaten into docility long ago. In the Outlands, a fragile, disorganized freedom remained, pockets of Roamers, half-feral mutants who had survived the purges, and tribes of Amerindians who had returned to their traditional way of life.

But even taken together, they represented a tiny fraction of free humans. The population of hybrids swelled as the few truly human beings on Earth diminished, killed and bred and co-opted out of existence. He had been involved in the initial stages of that co-option, and Quavell knew it. Trying to make her feel guilty because of her own participation in the near genocide of humanity was an exercise in hypocrisy on his part. For that matter, he was almost as responsible for her pregnancy as Baron Cobalt.

Some forty years before, when Lakesh determined to build a resistance movement against the baronies, he rifled Scenario Joshua's genetic records to find the qualifications he deemed the most desirable to breed into potential warriors in his cause. Kane's family line, his genotype possessed those qualities—high intelligence, superior adaptive traits, resistance to disease and exceptionally potent sperm. Kane wasn't a superhuman, but he was a superior one, and Baron Cobalt knew that. He had access to the same records as Lakesh, and he took full advantage of them.

Therefore it was irrational and even a little cruel to put Quavell on the defensive. When she had first arrived at the redoubt, she hadn't even attempted to deny his accusations that the hybrid race was an evolutionary dead end, inasmuch as the new human depended solely on the apeling for survival.

She had freely admitted that her folk were not the ultimate in evolution, that the restrictions placed on humanity were artificial, and therefore they had no way to gauge its true potential. He mentally replayed her words, apparently her philosophy: "Old and new human alike must cease seeking power and devote themselves to the development and fulfillment of life."

Quavell continued gazing into his eyes and a smile ghosted over her lips. "Yes," she said quietly. "Fulfillment."

His shoulders jerked in surprise, but he forced an abashed smile. He knew Balam was anchored to the hybrid barons through some hyperspatial filaments of their mind energy, akin to the hive mind of certain insect species. When Baron Ragnar was assassinated, Balam had experienced an extreme reaction to the sudden absence of the baron's mind filament. Inasmuch as all of the Archon genetic material within the barons had derived from Balam, a degree of telepathic ability was to be expected.

"Our differences are trifling overall," Quavell went on. "All living things use the same basic genetic code. Just as all books in a library can be written in the same language, so too are living things the result of messages written in the same DNA language."

Domi sighed wistfully, removing her hand from Quavell's belly. "Hope to have a baby one day. More than one."

"You appear capable," Quavell said. "More than."

Domi shrugged. "Keep trying, but—"

She broke off when she saw Lakesh almost imperceptibly flinch. She cast him a dour glance, then returned her attention to Quavell. "Anything I can do for you?"

"Yes," Quavell answered, extending a hand. "Help me up, please. I can do it myself, but it's becoming a strain."

Grasping her by the arm and hand, Domi steadied Quavell as she pushed herself to her feet. As he

watched, Lakesh reflected on the irony of the present
situation. The year before, he'd arranged for Beth-Li
Rouch to be brought into the redoubt to mate with
Kane to insure that his superior abilities were passed
on to offspring.

From a clinical point of view, Lakesh's plan to turn
Cerberus from a sanctuary into a colony made sense.
To insure that Kane's superior qualities were passed
on, mating him with a woman who met the standards
of purity control was the logical course of action.
Without access to the techniques of fetal development
outside the womb, the conventional means of procreation was the only option. And that meant sex and
passion and ultimately the fury of a woman scorned.

Kane had refused to cooperate for a variety of reasons, primarily because he felt the plan was a continuation of sinister elements that had brought about the
nukecaust and the tyranny of the villes. His refusal
had tragic consequences. Only a thirst for revenge and
a conspiracy to murder had been birthed within the
walls of the redoubt, not children.

Now he was aiding and abetting the birth of a new
but distinctly different generation of humanity, perhaps a superhuman of the kind Nietzsche never
dreamed. Or, he thought darkly, a monstrosity
spawned from the womb of Hell, a sibling of the imperator rather than a threat.

With a murmured word of thanks, Quavell walked
toward the door. Despite the fact she had needed help
to rise from a chair, her movements were light and

graceful, as was characteristic of her kind. When she was out in the corridor, Domi turned toward Lakesh. Her crimson eyes glittered with anger, and she thrust out her full underlip pugnaciously.

"Why you jump like that when I mention having baby?" she demanded in a harsh whisper. Under stress, she reverted to the clipped, abbreviated mode of Outland speech.

Lakesh reached for her, but she stepped back, avoiding his touch. "It wasn't that, darlingest one," he said, striving for a soothing tone. "It was the sharing of information that Quavell doesn't need to know."

"She know about us," Domi retorted doggedly. "I can tell. I think you ashamed to tell. Or afraid."

Lakesh shook his head. "Afraid, perhaps. Ashamed? Not at all. You should know by now how I feel about you."

In truth, Lakesh did love the girl, her upbringing in the Outlands notwithstanding—or, he reflected, that upbringing was one of the reasons he loved her. Outlanders were the expendables, the free labor force, the cannon fodder, the convenient enemies of order, the useless eaters. Brigid, Grant, Kane and all of the exiles in Cerberus were outlanders by default. Only Domi was one by birth, so in the kingdom of the disenfranchised, she was the pretender to the throne.

Lakesh had been fond of her since the day they first met, and over the past couple of years that affection had grown to love. He had not been able to demonstrate his feelings for her until a few months before. It was still a source of joy to him that Domi reciprocated his feelings and had no inhibitions about acting on them, regardless of the bitterness she still harbored over her unrequited love for Grant. In any event, he had broken a fifty-year streak of celibacy and they repeated the actions of that first delirious night whenever the opportunity arose—usually when Kane, Brigid and particularly Grant were out in the field.

Lakesh didn't really understand why he felt compelled to keep his relationship with Domi secret. With Grant's heart very obviously pledged to Shizuka, even though she was more than a thousand miles away on the island of New Edo, the big man was probably too preoccupied with thoughts of her to give the more covert—and personal—activities of the redoubt more than his cursory attention.

Lakesh theorized his reluctance to let anyone know about his affair with Domi derived mainly from the habit of keeping two centuries' worth of secrets. As it was, he lived daily with the fear that he would anger Grant or Kane and they would expose his biggest secret—of how and why there were any exiles in Cerberus in the first place.

Planting her fists on her hips, Domi said, "Grant is in New Edo with Shizuka. You think he cares what we do? You think *I* care if he do care?"

Lakesh stopped himself from correcting her grammar. "Like I said to you a few weeks ago, I'd prefer to make our relationship public when matters are a little less tense.''

''And when that be?'' she shot back. She gestured sharply to the door Quavell had just passed through. ''When she have her baby, when Kane admits he the father, when everybody on the damn Moon is living down here? When?''

Lakesh swallowed a profanity-seasoned sigh and let his shoulders slump in resignation. ''Very well,'' he said lowly. ''Once Grant returns, we'll tell him about us together.''

Domi nodded curtly. A wicked smile tugged at the corners of her mouth. ''Don't worry about him. If he gets mad, I'll protect you.''

''Of course,'' Lakesh replied breezily. ''I never expected otherwise.''

Chapter 14

Levering with her legs, Brigid pushed herself off the tiled lip of the shallow end of the pool and cleaved through the water. She stroked to the opposite end, then turned over, backstroking lazily. With her long hair spreading around her head, she gazed up at the domed ceiling, at the track lighting fixtures spilling a dim illumination. The pool and adjacent exercise rooms had been built to provide the original inhabitants of Cerberus with a means of sweating off the stress of being confined for twenty-four hours a day in the installation. After the nukecaust, just staying alive was probably more exercise than they actually needed.

She luxuriated in the simple pleasure of being alone, without the clatter of keyboards or drive units filling her ears, or endless debates about the imperator or Quavell's child.

Brigid Baptiste had always led something of a solitary life. The only person she had ever considered a friend was her mother, Moira. But when she inexplicably vanished from the flat they shared in Cobaltville some fifteen years ago, she had drawn into herself. All her mother left behind as a legacy was a photo of herself taken when she was about Brigid's age, and of course, the unique sunset color of her hair. That was one reason she had never cut it.

For a while, Brigid had taken some comfort in the possibility that her mother was associated with the Preservationists and was off somewhere working to reverse the floodtide of ignorance. When she learned the Preservationists did not exist as such, but were only a straw adversary manufactured by Lakesh, even that small hope had vanished.

But after her mother disappeared, Brigid had withdrawn from what passed as a social life in the villes. However, to withdraw completely would have aroused suspicion, so she entered into shallow relationships with a few fellow archivists.

The ville-bred men were raised much like herself— ordered, fed, clothed, educated and protected from all extremes. And their colorless, limited perspectives, their solemn pronouncements regarding their ambitions, had bored her into a coma. Centuries before they would have been classified as dweebs.

It wasn't until Magistrate Kane had stumbled half-drunk into her quarters and handed her a mystery to solve that she came to realize not all ville-bred men were the same. Of course, solving that mystery had earned her a death sentence and a new status as both exile and fugitive, but she had long ago come to terms with it. She knew Kane still felt guilty about dragging her into his own private and illegal investigation, not to mention involving Grant in her rescue.

But she often wondered if that was the first time he had rescued her. She distinctly remembered the jump dream to the malfunctioning gateway unit in Russia that had suggested that they'd lived past lives, each of their souls continually intertwined with the other in some manner, never knowing romance. Morrigan, the blind telepath from the Priory of Awen, had told her that she and Kane were *anam-charas*. In the Gaelic tongue, it meant "soul friends."

Floating in the water, she tried to relax. Ever since she had returned from the Moon, strange dreams had plagued her sleep, images that sprang from her travails in the citadel of the Annunaki, and some that originated from even further back, from the time she'd first met Kane. She'd been an archivist for the baron then, and her eidetic memory had been a hidden blessing as she searched through all the files kept in Cobaltville's Historical Division. If she saw it, she remembered it.

As a trained archivist, though, she knew misinformation often began with half-truths, then grew into speculative transitions as someone worked to record the event. No information was sometimes better than half information. The primary duty of archivists was not to record predark history, but to revise, rewrite and often times completely disguise it. The political causes leading to the nukecaust were well-known. They were major parts of the dogma, the doctrine, the articles of faith, and they had to be accurately recorded for posterity. The Cerberus database contained unedited and unexpurgated data, and having access to it was one of the few perks Brigid found in her life as an exile.

Life in Cobaltville had been predictable, and she sometimes missed the monotony of routine. She knew Grant and Kane often longed for it, as well. Their whole lives, from conception to death, were ordered for them, both at work and at home. Ville dogma, ville upbringing, convinced them how lucky they were to live on the bounty of the baron and not to have to scratch out a starvation existence in the Outlands. As long as they obeyed the maddening and contradictory volume of rules, they had security, medical and even retirement benefits.

It was the life Brigid had led, Kane and Grant had led, the only life they had known. Now they were forced to live with prices on their heads, which any so-called citizen could collect just by giving information about them. All because they had sinned by trying to learn a truth and develop a concept of a larger destiny.

An aspect of that larger destiny had been their forays to the so-called Lost Earths, a multitude of parallel realities coexisting with their own. On their first two jumps to parallel casements, the minds of Brigid and Kane had fused with those of their alternate selves. But for a while, they had been lost to themselves, subsumed by the consciousnesses of their doubles.

Their counterparts had been drawn to each other,

and they'd ended up making love. Or rutting like crazed weasels. Brigid still wasn't sure what to call it exactly. She remembered plainly that it had been at once smoldering and erotic, somehow steely and tender. And it had been performed in a wild, hot rush.

As she floated on the water, she remembered how Kane's hands had roved over her body, touching her jawline, her breasts, his fingers reaching into her deepest recesses and setting fire to every desire she thought she'd set aside when she'd been accepted as an archivist at Cobaltville. The head ruled the body; thinking came before emotions. There could be no other way in her chosen line of work.

Even through her closed eyes, she saw the dim glow of the light fixtures above her, but she felt her nipples swelling in erotic tension, felt her loins blossoming at the memory. Her gift of total recall was a curse, as well as a boon. She never forgot a fear or a love, never lost the panic or the joy of a given incident.

Her pulse throbbed inside her head, picking up speed as she recalled Kane's hot, steely length burning against her lower belly, then sliding lower to position the thick crown between her moist nether lips. She remembered how loudly she had cried out as she absorbed the girth of his spearing shaft, filling her as she had never been filled before. The memory of how his bruising thrusts pushed her to orgasm was deliriously vivid.

Brigid's body tightened in its desire, blindly seeking release. Her hand slid along her thigh, knowing it would be so easy to trigger the memory into a sensation that would sweep her away now.

With the single-minded discipline that had pushed her up in the ranks of the Cobaltville archivists, she resisted. She drove the burning desire to the back of her mind, walling it away, telling herself that it was actually being eradicated. The emotion she felt was too confusing. Self-gratification wasn't taboo to her way of thinking, but involving Kane in it—even his parallel-world counterpart—crossed the line of propriety.

She stood up in the waist-deep water and stretched, taking a certain pride in the fact that her body was leaner and harder than it had ever been. Another memory flashed through her mind, of Kane's lean and hard naked body—and of an equally naked Ambika kneeling before him, her silver-tressed head bobbing back and forth along his length.

She felt a flush of near homicidal fury, then almost immediately a twinge of shame. As far as she knew, Ambika was dead, her mutagenic regenerative abilities notwithstanding. If the wounds she had incurred during the final bloody battle aboard her flagship hadn't been fatal, then the warrior queen had drowned when she pitched over the side.

Regardless, she wasn't convinced of Ambika's death and although he hadn't spoken of it, Brigid was sure Kane wasn't, either. Nor was she at all certain that the possibility she had survived didn't intrigue him more than just a bit.

Brigid swallowed a sigh, trying to drive the memory of that beautiful, merciless face from her mind. Due to her eidetic memory, she knew she would never forget it, nor how Ambika had humiliated her—by binding, gagging and caging her, forcing her to watch as she and Kane made love. Or least, that had been Ambika's plan before Kane improvised one of his own.

She shook her head, disturbed by the sexual imagery that seemed to be at the forefront of her dreams. Most of the memories she retained of the three lost earths were but disconnected fragments. Suddenly being able to draw upon the recollections of what Kane's counterpart did to her willing doppelgänger— and vice versa—with such clarity was so strange she shivered, despite the heated water.

The dreams had become more frequent and more vivid over the past few weeks, beginning after the op to the Moon. She couldn't see a connection between the two. The only other factor was the presence of Quavell, but she couldn't even begin to theorize what one had to do with another.

Reaching the shallow end of the pool, Brigid waded toward the steps where her towel and bodysuit hung over the handrail. As she threw her long, water-soaked hair down her back, she saw a tall, indistinct figure standing there, extending the towel toward her.

She felt a sudden surge of apprehension, but she knew the man wasn't Kane.

She dried her face quickly then looked up at Philboyd, who smiled down at her uneasily. All she could think of to say was "Thanks."

The man's smile reflected her own sudden unease, not simply because he had barged in on her but because she became instantly, sharply aware of her near naked body. The brief brassiere and panties she wore didn't really leave much to the imagination, not with the way her taut nipples strained at the fabric of her bra, or how the wet cloth of her panties was plastered to the soft, honey-blond triangle at the juncture of her thighs.

Lack of proper dress wasn't much of an issue in Cerberus. During Domi's first couple of months at the redoubt, she had to continually be coaxed to wear something other than stockings when she strolled through the corridors.

In a husky voice, Philboyd said, "My God, you're beautiful. You look like you stepped out of the *Sports Illustrated* Swimsuit Edition."

Brigid squinted at him. "I don't know if I should take that as a compliment, or if I should be satisfied with being mystified."

"Never mind." With obvious effort, Philboyd tore his gaze away from Brigid and glanced around the pool. "It's been a long time since I went swimming."

Trying to break the net of tension that stretched

between them, Brigid playfully splashed a handful of water toward him. "Come on in, then."

He stepped back, grinning bleakly. "It's been a long time because I never learned how."

Brigid laughed and after a moment, so did he. She found something very appealing about the lanky, myopic astrophysicist. Whether it was his self-deprecating sense of humor or his intellect, she wasn't sure. He wasn't a man of action, but he wasn't a coward, either. Both of them had faced Enki, the last of the legendary dragon kings, in his lunar citadel. Philboyd's courage, although it had cracked, hadn't completely crumbled, and Brigid had been glad to have a solid bulwark at her side on that terrifying night.

As she climbed out of the pool and vigorously toweled her hair dry, Philboyd asked quietly, "Do you mind if I ask you something?"

"Go ahead."

"Something personal," he said hesitantly.

She stopped drying her hair, paused and replied, "I suppose it depends on how personal."

Philboyd cast his eyes downward. He appeared so uncomfortable Brigid half expected him to shuffle his feet. He took a deep breath and said in a rush, "Are you and Kane an item?"

Brigid blinked at him in surprise. "Why do you ask that?"

"Well…" He coughed self-consciously. "I guess I ask because I need to know."

"And why," she pressed, "do you need to know?"

"Because it seems like I'll be here for a while. And if you two aren't a couple—and I don't see how you can be with that alien chick he knocked up hanging around—I'd sort of like to…you know, get to know you better."

His final few words came out as mumble. It took Brigid a couple of seconds to place his twentieth-century phrase in the proper context. She recalled what he had said to her in Enki's citadel: "I'm a tough geek. Tough geek with a tough babe. I like the dynamics."

She tried very hard to repress a smile as she said, "First of all, Quavell isn't an alien. She was born on Earth and has spent the last sixty-seven years here on terra firma, which is more than you can say."

He nodded. "I can't argue with you about that."

"Secondarily," she continued, "Kane and I are partners. We're colleagues."

"So you're not involved?"

"No." Brigid noticed the slight hesitation preceding her one-word response. She wondered if Philboyd had caught it.

"I wondered about that," he said. "And if you aren't, why not?"

If Brigid Baptiste wondered the same thing, she never put her suspicions into words. When she and Kane were first thrown together, their relationship had been volatile, marked by frequent quarrels, jealousies and resentments. The world in which she came of age was primarily quiet, focused on scholarly pursuits.

Kane's was a world wherein he became accustomed to daily violence, supported by a belief system that demanded a ruthless single-mindedness to enforce baronial authority.

Both people had their gifts. Most of what was important to people in the twenty-second century came easily to Kane—survival skills, prevailing in the face of adversity and cunning against enemies. But he could also be reckless, high strung to the point of instability and given to fits of rage.

Brigid, on the other hand, was compulsively tidy and ordered, with a brilliant analytical mind. However, her clinical nature, the cool scientific detachment upon which she prided herself sometimes blocked an understanding of the obvious human factor in any given situation.

Regardless of their contrasting personalities, Kane and Brigid worked very well as a team, playing on each other's strengths rather than compounding their individual weaknesses. Despite their differences, or perhaps because of them, the two people managed to forge the chains of partnership that linked them through mutual respect and trust.

Only once had the links of that chain been stretched to the breaking point. Almost a year before Kane had shot and killed a woman, a distant relative of Brigid's, whom he perceived as a threat to her life. It took her some time to realize that under the confusing circumstances, Kane had had no choice but to make a snap judgment call. Making split-second life-and-death decisions was part of his conditioning, his training in the Magistrate Division, as deeply ingrained as breathing.

What conflicted her during that time was not the slow process of forgiving him, but coming to terms with what he really was and accepting the reality rather than an illusion. He was a soldier, not an explorer, not an academic, not an intellectual.

When she finally understood that about him, the two people achieved a synthesis of attitudes and styles where they functioned as colleagues and parts of a team, extending to the other professional courtesies and respect.

"The 'why not' doesn't enter into this discussion," she retorted, reaching for her bodysuit.

Philboyd gave her a jittery smile. "Good. I'd just hate to piss him off. I—all of us of Manitius—owe him a debt we can never repay. I wouldn't want him to think I was disrespecting him." After a second, he added, "Besides, he scares the hell out of me."

Brigid laughed again. "After everything you went through on the Moon, everything you witnessed, squaring off against a Sumerian god, even—one man scares you?"

"That particular man does," he answered flatly. "He's a killer, isn't he?"

Thrusting her arms into the sleeves of the bodysuit, she admitted, "He's killed some."

Philboyd frowned, absently seating his glasses more firmly on the bridge of his nose. "He went one-on-one with Maccan, which was completely insane. And he won. Since then, he gives me the feeling that he's like two steps from going completely psycho.''

Kane's voice suddenly floated through the room. ''Most people would say it's one step. And a baby step at that.''

Kane stepped through the double doors and sauntered toward the pool side. Philboyd swallowed hard at the sight of him. He was still wearing the shadow suit, which lent him a sinister resemblance to the faceless Furies Philboyd and his Manitius Base colleagues had so feared.

Feeling a little self-conscious and annoyed because of it, Brigid zipped up her bodysuit. Kane eyed her curiously, then cast his gaze over to Philboyd. ''What are you doing here, Moon-boy?''

Philboyd swallowed hard, then lifted his chin at a defiant angle. ''I was getting ready to tell Brigid about the extent of the damage on the Manta you flew.''

''Why her? I'm the pilot.''

''I couldn't find you.''

Kane glanced at Brigid, as if expecting her to confirm or deny the man's story. During her years as an archivist, Brigid had perfected a poker face and she wore it now. ''Just why are you here, Kane?''

He jerked a thumb upward. ''Grant just landed, so we can have another briefing. But I doubt he'll be very anxious to gate to the Moon. So, I may take you up on your offer to guard my back.''

''Why?''

"He's got Shizuka with him."

Brigid's eyes widened. "Does Domi know?"

"She probably does by now."

Making a wordless utterance of irritation, Brigid pushed past Kane and made quickly for the door. "What difference does it make if she knows or not?" Philboyd called after her.

Before she went through the double doors, Brigid said over her shoulder, "It may not make any difference at all. But it may make a big—and ugly—one to Shizuka."

Philboyd turned toward Kane, mouth open to ask him a question. He closed it when he saw the icy gleam in Kane's pale eyes. Squaring his shoulders, he asked, "Is there some problem?"

"Not yet," Kane intoned in a low, deadly voice. "But there very well might be if you overstay your welcome."

"Is that a threat?"

Kane turned away. "When you get to know me better, Philboyd, you'll learn that I don't waste my time making threats."

Chapter 15

"The Moon, my ass," Grant growled.

"I said the very same thing," Kane stated with a mock ebullience. "The very thing."

He turned to Brigid. "Didn't I, Baptiste?"

Brigid sighed wearily. "Yes, Kane, you did indeed."

Grant glared across the table at him. "Then why are you going?"

Kane shrugged and lifted the cup of coffee to his lips. "They asked me nicely."

The Cerberus redoubt had an officially designated briefing room on the third level. Big and blue walled, it came equipped with ten rows of theater-type chairs facing a raised speaking dais and a rear-projection screen. It was built to accommodate the majority of the installation's personnel, back before the nuke-caust, when military and scientific advisers visited.

Now, because the briefings rarely involved more than a handful of people, they were always convened in the more intimate dining hall. Lakesh, Grant, Brigid, Shizuka, Neukirk and Kane sat around a table, sharing a pot of coffee. Access to genuine coffee was one of the inarguable benefits of living as an exile in the redoubt. Real coffee had virtually vanished after the skydark, since all of the plantations in South and Central America had been destroyed.

An unsatisfactory, synthetic gruel known as ''sub'' replaced it. Cerberus literally had tons of freeze-dried packages of the authentic article in storage, as well as sugar and powdered milk.

Domi had elected not to join in the briefing, and nobody was particularly surprised, certainly not Grant and Shizuka. During their first meeting, months before, Domi had challenged Shizuka to a duel. The female samurai had easily defeated her, and since that time, Domi's hostility toward Shizuka had been so thinly disguised as to be little less than spitting on her.

Domi's temper was on a hair trigger at the best of times. Memories of the six degrading months she spent in sexual servitude to Guana Teague floated very near to the surface of her mind. She tended to overreact to any situation, no matter how trivial, that reminded her of that time.

She viewed Grant as her savior, her gallant black knight who had rescued her from the depraved lusts of the man-mountain, but in point of fact, the reverse was true. Of course, if Teague hadn't been preoccupied with crushing the life out of Grant, Domi would have never been able to get the drop on him and cut his throat. She kept the knife that had done the deed as her most treasured memento.

Regardless of the facts, Domi had attached herself

to Grant and made it fiercely clear to everyone that Grant was hers and hers alone. He had fought hard to make sure there was nothing but friendship between him and Domi, citing the gap in their ages as the reason he didn't want to get sexually involved with her. He knew how lame the excuse was, since Domi was certainly no stranger to sex, not after spending six months servicing the gross lusts of Guana Teague. Nor did she know her true age. She could have been as young as sixteen or as old as twenty-six.

But more that, Domi had proved herself to be a tough and resourceful, if not altogether stable partner. At one point she had saved his, Brigid's and Kane's lives when the Cerberus mat-trans unit was sabotaged.

Even being in her debt didn't make him more understanding of her, or appreciate her uniqueness. Grant belatedly realized he had never really known her. It hadn't occurred to him that they had forged a relationship deeper than he knew or cared to admit. And he knew he had hurt Domi dreadfully when she had spied him and Shizuka locked in a passionate embrace.

A short time before, he had told Domi about his feelings for Shizuka. The little outlander girl had accepted what he said with barely a word, almost as if she were uninterested. Her reaction had both puzzled and disappointed him, but Grant hadn't pushed it. She had studiously avoided Grant since then, speaking to him only when it was absolutely necessary, and then with a minimum of words.

Neukirk, another Moon base evacuee, was a short, chunky man with seamed, weather-beaten features and a white crew cut. He had spread out a map on the table, but neither Grant or Kane had so much as glanced at it.

"I've only been back here half an hour," Grant rumbled, arms crossed over his broad chest. Like Kane, he was attired in the formfitting shadow suit. "And you've already made plans to send me into outer space again."

Shizuka, sitting beside him, tried to repress a smile. She had met Lakesh a few months before during one of his visits to the Operation Chronos facility on Thunder Isle, which adjoined New Edo. Neukirk was a stranger to her, and although Grant had already told her about Manitius Base, she eyed him with a combination of wonder and unease. She had appeared less uncomfortable when Grant introduced her to Quavell. In fact, she seemed fascinated.

"If you look at this layout," Neukirk said, his voice a gravelly rasp of impatience, "you'd see it's not that much of a distance from the gateway area to the med section."

"I don't need to look at it," Grant grunted. "The distance isn't what's bothering me."

"What is, then?" Brigid asked.

"I've got something else I'd rather do." He nodded toward Lakesh. "You said it wasn't a time-sensitive matter."

"I did," Lakesh agreed. "But I doubt you'd be

gone more than a few hours. And though timing may not be critical at this juncture, to postpone it further may endanger a life or invite tragedy.''

Grant didn't respond to Lakesh's melodrama. It was all too familiar by now. His brow furrowed, casting his deep-set eyes into little pools of shadow. Kane recognized that expression and smiled sourly. He's getting mulish, he thought. And there was nothing on Earth more intractable than a mulish Grant.

Shizuka laid a hand on his arm. ''Grant-san, I'll go with you.''

Grant cast her a surprised glance. ''You've never made a gateway transit before, not even from one terrestrial destination to another. We'll be going to the damn Moon.''

She shrugged negligently, and the stiffened shoulder of her pale-green jacket rose like the wing of a drowsy bird. She wore a billowy *kamishimo*, the formal attire of a *daimyo*'s retainer. Her glossy black hair was gathered in a tortoiseshell beret at her nape, one stray wisp dangling across her cheek. ''I would find it very interesting.''

Kane chuckled, but subsided when Grant looked his way. In a low tone he said, ''Out of the question. I'm not going to risk you.''

Neukirk declared irritably, ''It's safe enough now, according to Eduardo and Mariah.''

In the same low voice, Grant retorted, ''I don't believe the place is as locked down as they claim.''

Neukirk bristled. ''Do you think they're lying?''

"No," countered Grant. "I think they're inexperienced…too inexperienced to secure a perimeter. There are Furies, Maccan's boys and carnobots still unaccounted for. Not only is the base itself huge—there are thousands of square miles in the Wild Lands that haven't been covered."

The Wild Lands was Manitius Base vernacular for rocky wilderness of the great southwest crater region. Most of the lunar mining operations were conducted there, near the Great Chasm, an enormous, yawning canyon that was eight hundred miles long and nearly fifty miles wide. Within were tunnels and catacombs that led to the crypts of the Serpent Kings, the Annunaki—and a vast lost knowledge that was old when Sumeria was new, that was ancient when the pyramids were built in Egypt.

"In that case," Shizuka said, "there is all the more reason to accompany Kane there."

"I've already committed to the trip," commented Kane. "I don't blame you for not wanting to go. You can stand down and sit this one out. Baptiste volunteered to take your place."

Grant rolled his eyes ceilingward in exasperation. "Don't play that tired old game with me."

"What tired old game?" Kane asked innocently.

Grant just shook his head in weary disgust, refusing to be baited. Almost everybody around the table knew to what game he referred—both Kane and Grant had been partners for nearly fifteen years, and it was part and parcel of Magistrate conditioning to always back a partner's play.

The Magistrate Divisions were formed as a complex police machine that demanded instant obedience to its edicts and to which there was no possible protest. Magistrates were a highly conservative, duty-bound group. The customs of enforcing the law and obeying orders were ingrained almost from birth. The Magistrates submitted themselves to a grim and unyielding discipline, because they believed it was necessary to reverse the floodtide of chaos and restore order to postholocaust America. As Magistrates, the courses their lives followed had been charted before their births. They had exchanged personal hopes, dreams and desires for a life of service. They were destined to live, fight and die, usually violently.

All Magistrates followed a patrilineal tradition, assuming the duties and positions of their fathers. They did not have given names, each taking the surname of the father, as though the first Magistrate to bear the name were the same man as the last.

The originators of the Magistrate Divisions had believed that only surnames, family names, engendered a sense of obligation to the duties of their ancestors' office, insuring that subsequent generations never lost touch with their hereditary roles as enforcers. Last names became badges of social distinction, almost titles.

Over the past ninety years, both the ogliarchy of barons and the Mags that served it had taken on a fearful, almost legendary aspect. For most of their adult lives, both Kane and Grant had been part of that legend, cogs in a merciless machine. They had been through the dehumanizing cruelty of Magistrate training, yet they had somehow, almost miraculously, managed to retain their humanity.

Now, for the past two years, they had exercised their humanity by doing their very best to not just dismantle the machine, but to utterly destroy it and scatter the pieces to the four corners of the world.

Kane's suggestion that Brigid Baptiste could easily replace Grant on the op was such a transparent ploy that Lakesh was a bit surprised that Kane would even trot it out.

Neukirk, however, interpreted Grant's reaction to another emotion entirely. "Grant, if you're afraid to go back up there—and Kane, if you're too much of a wuss to do it without him holding your hand, me and Philboyd will do it. Quavell probably doesn't care."

For a long, tense moment, both men were so nonplussed by Neukirk's effrontery they were shocked into speechlessness. Then to everyone's surprise, Lakesh roared, "Shut your mouth, sir!"

Neukirk literally jumped in his chair, his eyes going wide at the normally soft-spoken Lakesh giving vent to outrage. Neukirk, as a twentieth-century physicist, had been aware that Lakesh was the creator of the mat-trans gateways and viewed him as an equal, a scientific colleague. Judging by the astounded expression on his face, the last thing he ever expected was to be berated by the man.

"You are still a guest here, your credentials and background notwithstanding!" Lakesh's voice was a strident crash of fury. "And you will accord these two men the respect they not only deserve, but have earned! If not for their intervention, you would still be cowering in a corner of the Moon base—terrified of Maccan, of Megaera, of Enki, of the DEVIL platform."

In predark years, a number of different tests were conducted on Manitius Base, from the military application of particle-beam lasers to test flights of TransAtmospheric Vehicles.

A terra-forming project was also based there. There were only two general strategies for colonizing alien worlds—either alter humanity to fit the planet through pantropic science, or alter the planet to fit humanity. Mars was the first aim of terra-forming, but due to its rarefied atmosphere, that planet was disallowed and attention turned toward Venus.

Because that world was believed to be suffering from a runaway greenhouse effect, giving it an average surface temperature of around 470 degrees Celsius, the astrophysicists of the day suggested Venus could be terra-formed by the introduction of a planetismal device—essentially a heavy-mass projectile. The plan was to detonate planetismal projectiles at geosynchronous points around Venus and biocatalyic chemicals such as fluorocarbons, as well as a photon radiation would blanket the surface, ideally triggering a reaction to positively alter the planetary atmospheric conditions.

Only one such terra-forming device was ever constructed, in geostationary parking orbit above Manitius Base. It was called a Deep Electromotive Valence Induration Lithospherimal process, or known by the acronym DEVIL. In its original incarnation, DEVIL involved the covert assembly in low Moon orbit of a planetismal projectile, but according to the astrophysicists they met on the base, the device had been mutated into not just a travesty of the original project, but into a genocidal monster.

Neukirk opened and closed his mouth twice before stammering, "I didn't mean to—"

"You meant to compensate for your own feelings of cowardice," Brigid broke in acidly, "when you lived in constant terror on Manitius. So you insinuated that what Grant and Kane accomplished for you and your people wasn't much...something you and the rest of your crew would've gotten around to dealing with eventually."

Shizuka, her eyes narrowed to slits, said in a soft voice sibilant with menace, "I do not know you, Dr. Neukirk, but I know you have cast aspersions on the honor of two men who in their own way exemplify the code of Bushido. If they do not care to seek redress for your insult, I will."

"And I'll help her," Lakesh bit out.

Kane was just as surprised as Neukirk by Lakesh's

vehement defense of him and Grant, particularly
when he remembered all the bitter disagreements he
and the man had over tactics. Most of the missions
Lakesh concocted never dealt with head-on confron-
tations. Always, they involved finding some way to
strike covertly at the Archon Directorate, not at the
plenipotentiaries who actually held the reins of power.

After Balam's revelation that the Directorate was
but a diversionary smoke screen created two centuries
ago by corrupt government officials and military men
to mask their own ruthless ambitions, an entirely new
set of strategies had to be drafted.

The earlier tactics had been hampered by their own
belief they contended with a vast, omnipotent opponent, and by Kane's way of thinking they wasted a
lot of time and energy searching for ways to fight an
enemy that didn't exist.

He couldn't really blame Lakesh, particularly in
lieu of the fact he was the man who came to the
pivotal conclusion that the Directorate was but a cun-
ningly crafted illusion. Even so, he seemed reluctant
to accept the findings of his own detective work, despite Balam essentially confirming his suspicions.
Kane wasn't sure if Lakesh's doubts sprang from a
distrust of Balam, or simply because he wasn't prepared to directly confront the barons.

Not that it really mattered at this point. Lakesh's
self-assumed position as the final authority in the redoubt was no longer absolute.

A smile tugged at the corners of Kane's mouth. It

wasn't as if he, Grant and Brigid had ever obeyed him unquestioningly in the first place, but now any proposals for action had to be agreed upon by a majority vote.

Kane knew the man bitterly resented this change in procedure, but his plans had nearly gotten them all killed—worse than killed—on a number of occasions, often due to Lakesh giving them just enough information to plunge them into serious trouble. He wondered if his sudden—and uncharacteristic—protectiveness stemmed from guilt over all those previous missions that had gone awry.

Neukirk didn't even try to meet anyone's gaze. He stared at the map on the table and murmured, "I was way out of line. I apologize."

Kane and Grant exchanged bland glances. "That good enough for you?" Kane inquired.

Grant shrugged. "For the time being. Is it good enough for you?"

Kane smiled, but it had no humor or warmth to it. "For the time being. But if the manners of our Moonie guests don't improve, I think we ought to seriously consider putting them back where we found them."

Brigid shifted in her chair, not caring for the implications of the threat, but not wanting to raise objections to it, either. She tried to catch Kane's eye to show her disapproval, but he pretended not to notice.

"All right," Grant announced. "If it's this important, then let's go if we're going. But I vote we go in hard this time.''

Kane nodded. ''Why not. It's been a while.''

Turning toward Lakesh, he said, ''Ask Wegmann to put together some tools you might think we'll need if we have to dismantle anything. Tell Quavell to meet us in the gate ready room in ten minutes.''

He slid the map from the table and began folding it in quarters. To Neukirk he said casually, ''I hope this is accurate.''

The crew-cut man nodded. ''It is.''

''Good. Because you don't want to be around if we find out it isn't.''

Chapter 16

Kane, Grant and Shizuka walked from the dining hall, down the corridor and into the big square room that served as the Cerberus armory. As Kane entered, he pressed the flat toggle switch on the door frame and the overhead fluorescent fixtures flashed with a white light.

Stacked wooden crates and boxes lined the walls. Glass-fronted cases held racks of automatic assault rifles. There were many makes and models of subguns, as well as dozens of semiautomatic blasters, complete with holsters and belts. Heavy assault weaponry occupied the north wall, bazookas, tripod-mounted M-249 machine guns, mortars and rocket launchers. All of the exiles were expected to become reasonably proficient with guns, and most of them had spent some time on the firing range under Grant's tutelage. The lessons were restricted to the use of SA 80 subguns, lightweight ''point and shoot'' autoblasters that the most firearm-challenged person could learn to handle.

All the ordnance had been laid down in hermetically sealed Continuity of Government installations

before the nukecaust. Protected from the ravages of
the outraged environment, nearly every piece of mu-
nitions and hardware was as pristine as the day it was
first manufactured.

Lakesh himself put the arsenal together over several decades, envisioning it as the major supply depot
for a rebel army. The army never materialized—at
least, not in the fashion Lakesh hoped it would.
Therefore, Cerberus was blessed with a surplus of
death-dealing equipment that would turn the most
militaristic baron green with envy, or give the most
pacifistic of them heart failure—if they indeed possessed hearts.

Kane and Grant strode to the two suits of Magistrate body armor mounted on steel frameworks.

Between them hung a partial suit of samurai armor,
standing like a silent sentinel. It was the same suit
Shizuka had lent to Brigid when she served with her
on the flagship of the fleet dispatched to repulse the
invasion of New Edo. A scabberded long-bladed *katana* and shorter *tanto* sword rested on pegs inside a
glass-fronted case. The blades were almost supernat-
urally sharp, able to cleave smoothly even through the
Mag armor. Shizuka had once attributed the cutting
quality to an old technique of laser-sharpening the
edges to the thickness of only a few molecules.

Shizuka's eyes flicked from the swords to the firearms. "This Cerberus of yours is truly an amazing
place." Her voice was muted with awe. "I'm more
gratified than ever by your choice."

In the process of removing his helmet from the framework, Kane cut his eyes toward her, then to Grant. "What choice?"

"Never mind." Grant's tone was brusque. "It'll keep till we get back."

Kane arched a skeptical eyebrow. "What's wrong with here and now?"

"It's not the time," Grant replied tersely. "Let's get this Moon trip done, and when we get back we'll have a talk about choices."

Kane stared at him for a moment, then returned his attention to the armor, muttering under his breath, "Somehow, the way you put that doesn't make it seem like anything to look forward to."

He had spoken loud enough for both Shizuka and Grant to hear, but the only reaction he elicited was a wan smile from Shizuka. She watched in silence as the two men began donning the black polycarbonate armor, sensing something of a ritual in the process.

Both men conducted the procedure swiftly, their deft movements hinting at the many years they'd performed it. They dispensed with the Kevlar undersheathing, since their shadow suits covered them from toes to fingertips. The molded chest and back pieces came first, followed by the arm sheaths, locking into place magnetically. Then came the leggings and high-topped, thick-soled boots with the steel-reinforced toes. They pulled on the gauntlets, which reached to midforearm.

The close-fitting exoskeleton was molded to conform to the biceps, triceps, pectorals and abdomen. The armor was lightweight and had the ability to re-distribute kinetic shock resulting from projectile impact.

The helmet was of the same color and material, except for the slightly concave, red-tinted visor. The visor provided protection for the eyes, and the elec-trochemical polymer was connected to a passive night sight that intensified ambient light to permit one-color night vision.

Grant and Kane hammered each other on the shoul-ders to make sure the armor was fully sealed, then they buckled the holstered Sin Eaters to their right forearms and tested the spring-release mechanism. The handblasters leaped into their waiting hands, the butts unfolding and slapping into their palms. Both men made sure their index fingers were fully ex-tended, since the Sin Eaters had no trigger guard or safety. They fired immediately upon touching the crooked forefinger. Satisfied, they pushed the weap-ons back into the holsters. Sin Eaters were incredibly lethal weapons and almost impossible for a novice to manage. Recruits were never allowed live ammuni-tion until a tedious six-month-long training period was successfully completed.

"Primed?" Kane inquired.

"Primed," Grant acknowledged. "Let's get it done."

Shizuka noticed the subtle change that had come over the two men as she accompanied them out of the armory. As both men strode along, they uncon-sciously reverted to their Mag personae, with a slight swagger in their step, heads held at prideful angles, mouths drawn in grim, slightly superior smiles as if they pictured the lesser breeds scrambling out of their path.

The three people entered the operations center, crossing it to the anteroom that held the gateway unit. It was bare and unfurnished, holding only a polished table. Lakesh and Brigid stood beside it. Kane and Grant were a little surprised to see Wegmann, the redoubt's engineer, was also there. In his midthirties, Wegmann was no more than five and half feet tall and weighed in the vicinity of 150 pounds. As such he was the only man in Cerberus shorter and slighter of frame than Bry, but he always seemed to possess the self-confidence of a someone twice his height and weight.

Quavell stood at the head of the table, her body draped in a hooded, poncho-type garment. She ex-amined myriad tools clipped within an open carrying case. To Wegmann she said, "These should suffice. Thank you."

He nodded to her graciously. "You're more than welcome, ma'am."

Kane was surprised by his respectful tone. Despite the man's unprepossessing physical appearance, he was a mechanical genius. He also was something of a misanthrope, preferring the company of the nuke generators to his fellow exiles. But no one took his loner traits seriously, not after the way he risked his life to expose and to thwart a conspiracy to kill Brigid, Grant and Kane.

Shizuka gazed uneasily at the eight-foot-tall gateway chamber, peering through its open door. The floor was patterned with interlocking, hexagonal metallic disks. The pattern was repeated in the ceiling. "So you walk in there and then you walk out on the Moon?"

Lakesh laughed. "It's not quite as simple as that, my dear."

Grant grunted. "No, it isn't. And we don't have the next year to spare for you to explain how it works."

"Especially," Brigid interposed, "since even most of the people who worked on Project Cerberus barely understood it."

Lakesh regarded her a little sourly, but he said nothing. She was right, after all. He never did know exactly how many people not directly involved in Project Cerberus even knew of the existence of the gateways. He presumed the President of the United States knew, as did the Joint Chiefs of Staff. He knew secrecy was important. A device that could transport matter—like nuclear devices—was a more important weapon than the atomic weapons themselves. If a state of war existed, it was theoretically possible to invade the enemy nation and pour in troops, tanks, personnel carriers and whatever weapons tactics indicated.

Lakesh focused on the less destructive applications of the gateways. Given wide use, the mat-trans could eliminate long-haul transportation of goods and even turn international travel into no more daunting a journey than opening and closing a door. He realized, of course, that many decades, perhaps even a century, would pass before the gateway units would be accepted by the public for tourist traffic. The transit phase was so unnerving that wide public acceptance was probably an impossibility.

Eventually, Lakesh hoped, the gateways would primarily be used for space exploration, replacing cumbersome, slow-moving shuttles that were restricted to the closer planets of the solar system.

However, matter transmission had been found to be absolutely impossible to achieve by the employment of Einsteinian physics. Only quantum physics, coupled with quantum mechanics, had made it work beyond a couple of prototypes that transported steel balls only a few feet across a room. But even those crude early models could not have functioned at all without the basic components that preexisted the Totality Concept.

Lakesh, as the project's overseer, experienced the epiphany and made that breakthrough. Armed with this knowledge, under Lakesh's guidance the quantum interphase mat-transducers opened a rift in the hyperdimensional quantum stream, between a relativistic here and there.

The Cerberus technology did more than beam matter from one spot in linear space to another. It reduced organic and inorganic material to digital information and transmitted it along hyperdimensional pathways on a carrier wave.

In 1989, Lakesh himself had been the first successful long-distance matter transfer of a human subject, traveling a hundred yards from a prototype gateway chamber to a receiving booth. That initial success was replicated many times, and with the replication came the modifications and improvements of the quantum interphase mat-trans inducers, reaching the point where they were manufactured in modular form and sent to places all over the world—and, as he later learned, beyond.

The armaglass walls of the six-sided gateway chambers in the Cerberus network were color-coded so authorized jumpers could tell at a glance into which redoubt they had materialized. It seemed an inefficient method of differentiating one installation from another, but Lakesh had once explained that before the nukecaust, only personnel holding color-coded security clearances were allowed to make use of the system. Inasmuch as their use was restricted to a select few of the units, it was fairly easy for them to memorize which color designated what redoubt.

"Are we ready?" Kane asked.

Quavell nodded. "Yes." She closed the tool case and snapped the latches shut. Grasping the handle, she tugged it across the tabletop toward her. Grant saw how much effort it required and took it from her.

"Thank you," she murmured.

Grant pushed the case into Kane's arm, whose own murmured "Thank you" was hard-edged with sarcasm.

The three of them entered the chamber, Grant going in last. Right above the keypad encoding panel on the thick door hung an imprinted notice, dating back to predark days. In faded maroon lettering, it read Entry Absolutely Forbidden To All But B12 Cleared Personnel. Even after all this time, Kane still had no idea who the B12 cleared personnel might have been, or even what was so special about them.

Since the destination coordinates had already been set, the automatic jump initiator circuits would engage simply by closing the heavy, counterbalanced door. Wegmann pushed the door shut, the heavy solenoids catching with a loud click. The familiar yet still slightly unnerving hum arose, climbing in pitch to a whine.

Standing outside the jump chamber, Shizuka, her fists clenched, listened to the sound of the mat-trans unit cycling through its dematerialization program.

"Don't worry," Brigid told her soothingly. "They've done this many, many times before. There's not much that can go wrong."

Shizuka nodded. "*Hai.* It just seems like a very nerve-racking way to travel."

"Sometimes it can be," Lakesh commented. "But most of the time, it's no more frightening than closing your eyes in one place and opening them in another."

"Like magic," said Shizuka, trying to force a confident smile. "Almost like going anywhere in the world by just wishing it."

Brigid nodded. "In a way, yes. With the interphaser, the applications widen even beyond that. Jumping from any point on Earth, it might be possible to establish bases on the other planets of the solar system, if corresponding vortex nodes could be matched up within the gateway and interphaser's targeting computers."

"Vortex nodes?" she echoed.

"Yes," Lakesh said. "They are—"

The humming drone suddenly dropped to a deep, rumbling roar. Through the armaglass walls of the chamber, light pulsed, flared, bloomed.

Squinting toward it, Lakesh muttered, "What the hell is—"

The roar continued from the mat-trans chamber, rising in volume. From the control complex, Bry shouted, "I'm reading another energy signature, penetrating the matter stream!" At the near panicky note in his voice, Lakesh sprinted out of the anteroom and into the command center. Crooked fingers of energy stabbed through the gateway chamber. Shizuka and Brigid watched with awe and dread as thousands of crackling threads of light coalesced in the center of the unit.

A star seemed to go nova behind the armaglass, bringing a millisecond of eye-searing brilliance. Standing over the master mat-trans control console,

Lakesh watched indicator lights flashing madly and power gauge needles waver. He didn't even try to make sense of the spidery webwork of intersecting lines, columns of mathematical formulas, twisting geometric shapes and hatch marks glowing on the readout screen. The humming tone continued to vibrate from the gateway chamber, but it sounded different, with a strange screechy note underlying it.

"Two conflicting matter-stream carriers," Bry cried. "They're trying to cycle through the dematerialization process at the same time!"

Lakesh stared, utterly bewildered. A fail-safe device normally came online when simultaneous transits from two different units were attempted, shutting down both gateways for a twenty-minute interval. Through the armaglass shielding, he saw the blurred shapes of Kane, Grant and Quavell, their outlines fluttering. Halos of light pulsed around them, strobing in an almost hypnotic pattern.

Circuit-switching stations clicked with a castanet-like rhythm. Glancing over his shoulder, Lakesh saw the needle gauges on the boards ticking back and forth. Lights on all of the readout consoles flashed erratically. The whine of machinery climbed up out of the audible range, straining to hit an ultrasonic note. A console squirted a shower of sparks that smelled like burning rubber.

Bry moaned in disbelief and horror. "The emergency shutdown isn't working. We're losing their molecular resolution."

Lakesh rushed across the control center and through the anteroom. Facing the deep-brown-hued armaglass door of the jump chamber, he stood with Wegmann, Shizuka and Brigid, staring in terror at the swirls of light fluttering on the other side. The droning hum climbed, faltered, then tried to climb again.

Thunder pounded, surrounding the mat-trans chamber with a steady kettledrum beat that could be felt in the bones. Behind them, at the master console, Bry shouted, ''Power fluctuations across the scale!''

The sound of the mat-trans unit cycling through its jump program reached a painfully high squeal, then laboriously descended in scale. Lakesh had never heard anything like it before. The entire central control complex of Cerberus vibrated with a fierce determination to shake itself apart. The very air was like a heavy surf, pounding relentlessly against his eardrums and bones. Loose papers fluttered, pens shivered and rolled over surfaces.

Brigid shouted shrilly, ''It's a feedback pulse—another energy signature has intercepted our gateway's matter-stream output!''

Wegmann suddenly sprang forward, up onto the chamber's platform. He fumbled with the door, heaving up on the wedge-shaped handle. The door opened. He recoiled from the throbbing flare, raising his hand to shield his eyes. All of them felt the feathery touch of energy, as if they were breasting invisible waves of static electricity.

Bright skeins of plasma shimmered and a tendril of

energy whiplashed out the door, touching Wegmann's chest. A popping, pinpoint white flash at the contact point sent the slightly built man flying from the platform, arms and legs flailing. He narrowly missed colliding with Shizuka as he sprawled on the floor, arms flung wide. Smoke curled from the black scorch mark on his bodysuit.

White threads spit madly from the interior of the jump chamber, darting and stabbing. Brigid, Lakesh and Shizuka all ducked beneath the table. A crackling finger of corsucating fire stroked the corner of the table, and it shed glowing droplets of molten silver. Brigid and Shizuka recoiled, shielding their faces. The smell of hot metal and ozone filled their nostrils.

As suddenly as they began, the pulsing of sound and the display of pyrotechnics ended. Everything was calm and quiet again, except for the muffled whining of the emitter array within the jump platform.

Neither Brigid nor Shizuka hesitated. The two women rose at the same time and crossed the room. Brigid reached for the heavy chamber door, ignoring Lakesh's shout of warning. She silently endured the burning pain inflicted on her hands by the handle. Smoke and mist swirled within the chamber, so thick she could see nothing.

The mist was a byproduct of the quantum interphase, a plasma-wave form that only resembled vapor. Usually it dissipated within seconds of a successful transit, but she had never seen it so heavy before, like an ocean fog trapped within the armaglass walls. Thread-thin static-electricity discharges arced within the billowing mass.

Brigid and Shizuka hesitated only a moment, then plunged into the clouds, fanning their hands in front of their faces. They heard a faint groan from underfoot, and Brigid bent low, narrowing her eyes. She barely made out the prone figure of Kane, stirring feebly on the hexagonal floor plates.

Crackling light flashed again and she recoiled, but it limned for an instant Grant lying as motionless as a corpse. Shizuka uttered a wordless cry of horror and dropped to her knees beside him.

Over her shoulder, Brigid shouted, "Get a medical team in here, stat!"

"Already taken care of!" Lakesh's voice responded.

As the vapor dissipated, Brigid stared at the residue of oily soot covering the armor of both men. She bit back a groan of terror. A layer of soot and ashes covered them from head to toe, and she smelled the stink of burned hair.

"What happened?" Shizuka's voice was high and quavery.

Before Brigid could tell her, Lakesh appeared in the doorway. "DeFore and Auerbach are on their way." His words came out in a strangulated wheeze. Even to his own ears he sounded disturbingly like the old Lakesh.

He blinked repeatedly, trying to see through the

mist and wrinkling his nose at the oil smell and the acrid odor of charred hair. "Oh, no. Dear God—no."

In an eerily calm tone, Brigid said, "I'm afraid so. We've seen this effect before."

Shizuka fumbled with the underjaw lock guard on Grant's helmet and finally managed to pull it off. The top half of his face was of its normal deep-brown complexion while the lower part was as jet black as his mustache. The ends of it were scorched. Swiftly she looked around the chamber and asked, "Where is the woman—Quavell?"

Lakesh, in a strained, hoarse voice said, "She has been taken."

Shizuka swung her head up and around. "By whom?" she demanded.

Before Lakesh could answer, Brigid interposed, "There's only one possibility. We've been expecting a move from him for months."

Lakesh nodded mournfully. "What I feared would happen to me befell Quavell."

Horrified comprehension suddenly gleamed in Shizuka's eyes. "The imperator?"

Lakesh passed a trembling hand over his forehead. "Yes. The imperator has taken her."

"Why?" Shizuka's voice trembled with the effort to keep her emotions in check.

Brigid glanced toward her. Her one-word answer chilled the blood of both Shizuka and Lakesh. "Bait."

Chapter 17

By the time DeFore and Auerbach dragged a pair of wheeled gurneys into the ready room, Wegmann had regained consciousness. Except for a small second-degree burn on his chest, about the diameter of a poker chip, and a numbness in the extremities, he claimed he felt fine.

DeFore doubted him, so to prove it, Wegmann helped Auerbach drag the limp bodies of Grant and Kane from the gateway chamber and load them onto the gurneys.

Tight-lipped, DeFore tugged the left-hand gauntlets off Grant and Kane. She timed their pulses one by one and intoned grimly, "They're alive. God only knows why."

"The shadow suits under their armor," Brigid said, still sounding so calm as to be detached. "They're resistant to different wavelengths and intensities of electromagnetic radiation."

DeFore eyed her judgmentally. "Are you all right?"

Brigid nodded. "I think so. My hands sting a little."

DeFore frowned. "Let me see."

Brigid obligingly extended her hands, palms upward. DeFore winced at the sight of the reddened flesh that surrounded leaking blisters at the base of her fingers. "I'm not surprised. If I don't get those burns treated, they'll do more than sting a little."

DeFore glanced up toward Shizuka, who stood framed in the open door of the gateway chamber. She hugged herself, but her face was composed. "Where's Quavell?"

"She is not here," Shizuka answered, adopting the same calm, almost serene tone employed by Brigid.

DeFore's eyebrows crawled toward her hairline. "What do you mean? She's got to be in there."

Lakesh patted DeFore on the shoulder. "She should be, yet she is not."

Expression registering confusion, DeFore demanded, "Then where is she?"

"I don't know. But we may be able to find out. First take Kane and Grant to the infirmary. Brigid, friend Wegmann, you'd better go with them."

As Kane and Grant were wheeled out, Lakesh moved toward Shizuka, who still stood on the elevated platform, not moving or even appearing to breathe. Lakesh wondered if she were in a state of shock.

"You can go, too," he said to her quietly. "I assure you they'll receive the very best treatment."

Shizuka inhaled a deep breath and closed her eyes momentarily. When she opened them, Lakesh saw by their glitter she was not in shock but in a high state of rage. "Of that I have no doubt. What I want to know is what will be done about this."

Lakesh shook his head dolefully. "I don't know yet. I don't know if anything *can* be done."

He turned and walked toward the command center. When he realized he was unconsciously reverting to the shuffling gait of old, he made a conscious effort to square his shoulders and lift his chin. He grimaced at a stabbing pain in his right knee. The pain was brief, but it was familiar. He knew the symptoms of arthritis and with a sinking sensation in the pit of his stomach, he realized the imperator's gift of restored vitality was no more substantial than his own personal dogma of unity.

Shizuka followed him to the master mat-trans console. The needle gauges no longer flicked like crazed metronomes, and the lights had stopped blinking and flashing. The odor of molten circuit boards still hung fresh and sharp, only slightly less acrid due to the efficiency of the air-recycling system.

Bry looked up at him, face stricken and drained almost of all color. He murmured, "I never saw anything like this before. What the hell happened?"

As Lakesh examined the machine talk scrolling across the indicator, he said distractedly, "I told you about the imperator's abilities, Mr. Bry. He's done this before."

"According to you," Bry said doubtfully, "the imperator can open up localized wormholes."

"Yes. That's how he transported Brigid, Domi,

Grant and Kane to Thunder Isle from the Pacific to China.''

Shizuka said, "Grant told me about it...how all of their bodies had been covered by a layer of soot that smelled like hot grease. The ends of their hair had been scorched, too.''

Bry looked skeptically from Lakesh to Shizuka. Even though Lakesh had explained the event to him, the man wasn't certain of what happened on that day. Sam himself claimed he had transported Kane, Brigid, Domi and Grant to Thunder Isle to Xian by opening a localized wormhole in the energy web. However, he had transported them from a primary Operation Chronos installation while the temporal dilator was still powered up and running wild, affecting the transmissions from the mat-trans gateway there. Lakesh didn't think the two events were unconnected.

Sitting down at the main enviro-op station, Lakesh began switching the appropriate toggles and tapping the proper keys to initiate the system-wide self-diagnosis program. He wasn't overly worried about a database failure, since the control complex had five dedicated and eight shared subprocessors, which continued operations even in the event of a mainframe failure. The possibility of a hardware malfunction in the shared data link between the gateway's imaging autosequencers and the target coordinate lock concerned him the most. If that happened, no one would be going anywhere or arriving through the mat-trans unit.

As the self-diagnostic program began, the consoles of dials, switches, buttons and flickering lights that ran the length of the walls hummed. Monitor screens displayed shifting columns of numbers. Both he and Bry exhaled simultaneous sighs of relief that the systems seemed operational.

Her tone edged with impatience, Shizuka asked, "What did Brigid mean that Quavell had been abducted as bait?"

Before Lakesh could formulate even an inane response, Domi's sharp voice cut through the command center. "I want to know the same damn thing."

Lakesh's belly turned a cold flip-flop as he turned in his chair to see Domi marching purposefully down the aisle between the rows of computer stations. Her crimson eyes were fixed unblinkingly on Shizuka. "Heard Grant brought you here, tiger lady."

Shizuka's expression didn't change. She nodded and murmured, "The little ghost girl."

Domi acknowledged Shizuka's identification with a cold smile. Standing over Lakesh, she demanded, "Brigid said Sam snatched Quavell." She wasn't asking a question; she was making a statement.

Lakesh nodded. "He's the most likely culprit behind the abduction, yes."

"He take her to that same place in China he took us?"

Affecting not to have heard the girl's question, Lakesh rose from the console. "There appear to be no hardware failures."

Bry nodded, eyes fixed on the words, numbers and symbols scrolling across the different screens. "So far, most of the critical systems are functioning."

"Good," replied Lakesh. "As soon as the diagnostic is completed, activate the transponder telemetric uplink."

Bry's eyes widened in surprise, then a small smile creased his lips. "Quavell carries a transponder?"

"Standard policy, Mr. Bry." Lakesh spoke more confidently, more forcefully now that the first surge of fear and panic ebbed. "Let me know as soon as you have established a lock."

Turning on his heel, he strode out of the operations center. Shizuka and Domi followed him, taking up positions on his right and left.

"What is this business about transponders?" Shizuka asked crossly.

Domi looked across Lakesh to throw her a contemptuous glance. "So Grant didn't tell you everything about us, huh?"

The Japanese woman's lips compressed. "He told me enough. And I can see for myself that your manners have not improved since our first meeting."

Sparks of red anger flamed in Domi's eyes. Leaning forward to see past Lakesh, she spit, "You want another chance to teach me some?"

Shizuka tossed her head haughtily, not even deigning to look in her direction as she retorted dismissively, "Someone should."

Hissing between clenched teeth, Domi lunged for

the woman. Lakesh caught her by the upper arms and pulled her back, once again surprised by the steel-spring tensile strength contained in the girl's petite frame.

"Enough!" he barked sternly. "This is not the time or place to pick at old wounds."

Shizuka had instantly assumed a defensive posture, arms and legs positioned in a martial-arts stance. Lakesh knew how Domi had attacked Shizuka with a knife months before—and how the female samurai had easily disarmed her. He didn't know whether Domi's sudden surge of anger stemmed from the memories of that humiliation or whether it was due to lingering jealousy. Just wondering about Domi's motivation made him feel a pang of jealousy himself. She had a straightforward, uncomplicated manner of talking and thinking. Her passions were tempestuous, and she hated as deeply as she loved. A year or so before, Beth-Li Rouch discovered how Domi acted out her hatreds. It was the last thing she ever learned.

Nora, in the company of Philboyd, chose that moment to walk around the corner. They came to a halt when they saw the tableau. "Is everything all right?" Nora asked.

"Just fine," Lakesh told her.

Philboyd regarded him with thinly disguised suspicion. "We heard there was an accident."

"It's under control."

"Where's Brigid?" Philboyd asked.

"In the infirmary," Lakesh retorted. As Philboyd's

face registered fear, he hastened to add, "Her injuries are minor, I assure you. There's no need to clutter up the good doctor's domain with onlookers. At this juncture, damage to the essential systems of the redoubt may be more extensive than to its personnel."

Nora said hesitantly, "Maybe we can help."

"I'm sure Mr. Bry would welcome it," Lakesh replied, forcing a smile to his lips.

As the two people walked past them, Domi relaxed her tense posture within Lakesh's grasp. "Let me go."

"Will you behave?"

"If she will." Domi's tone was flat and dispassionate.

Lakesh carefully released her and the three of them continued on to the dispensary without further incident. When they entered, they saw Grant and Kane stretched out on examination tables. Both men were still unconscious, and DeFore was removing the last of Grant's body armor. Banks, another of her aides, attended to Kane, carefully sponging the film of greasy soot from the lower part of his face.

Brigid sat on the edge of a bed on the far side of the room, allowing Auerbach to use an aerosol can to apply the liquid bandage to her hands. The thin, filmlike layer contained nutrients and antibiotics that the body absorbed as the injury healed.

"Any serious damage?" asked Wegmann in his characteristic waspish tone. He was zipping up his bodysuit, and Lakesh glimpsed a patch of the liquid bandage on the center of his chest.

"We found no hardware failures," Lakesh answered. "So far. There are a few fried circuit boards, but they're not critical to operations. However, Mr. Bry is still running the diagnostic. It wouldn't hurt if you ran a similar check down in the engine room, if you feel up to it."

Wegmann nodded brusquely. "My thoughts exactly."

He turned to leave but paused in the open doorway. Without looking behind him, he intoned in a low voice, "Lakesh, do you know what happened to Quavell?"

"I believe I do, yes."

He hesitated a moment before asking, "Is she still alive?"

"I believe she is, yes."

Wegmann nodded as if the answer satisfied him, then he left the infirmary. Brigid climbed down from the bed, holding her hands out at her sides. "We're agreed that Quavell was abducted?"

"That's the only likelihood," Lakesh replied. "An accident would not have been so selective."

DeFore looked up from pulling off Grant's right boot. "How could it have been done?"

"There is only one way he could have possibly accomplished it," answered Lakesh. "He managed to lock on to the transponder signal."

A little exasperatedly, Shizuka demanded, "What is this transponder you keep talking about?"

Lakesh beckoned to Domi with a forefinger. "If I might borrow you for a moment, darlingest one?"

Shizuka followed as the two people walked into a small laboratory adjacent to the dispensary. From a black-topped trestle table, Lakesh picked up a long-handled, two-pronged device that held a small neon tube between the prongs.

Squinting at it, Shizuka inquired, "What is that thing?"

"An ultraviolet-light projector."

Lakesh thumbed a stud on the handle, and an ectoplasmic, pale purple glow shone from the tube. Stepping around Shizuka, he pushed the wall light switch and plunged the room into semidarkness.

Mystified, Shizuka watched as Lakesh placed the projector a few inches above Domi's right bicep. Tiny, dark markings were outlined against the skin, a series of symbols that resembled three downward-pointing elongated triangles, topped by circles.

"Everyone here has them." Lakesh spoke quietly.

"What are they for?" Shizuka asked.

"Standard ville ID chips are little pieces of silicon injected under the skin. They react to low-frequency sound waves emitted by scanners. Those kind of chips are relatively easy to forge. In fact, many of Kane and Grant's duties as Magistrates had revolved around apprehending counterfeiters of bogus ID chips. These markings are a new form of identity recognition, restricted to those here in Cerberus.''

Shizuka stared at the symbols. ''You sew those thing up inside of everyone?''

Lakesh shook his head. ''Not at all. They're injected. The transponder is a radioactive chemical that binds itself to the glucose in the blood and a middle layer of epidermis. It's perfectly safe. It transmits heart rate, brain-wave patterns, respiration, blood count and so forth. The signal is relayed by a Comsat satellite to the redoubt.''

''Why?''

Lakesh answered flatly, ''Part of the price of sanctuary. It's not optional. We need to know where our people are, what their physical conditions are at any given time. Quavell has one, as well. And so do most of our guests from the Moon base.''

''Do they represent anything?'' Shizuka asked.

He shrugged, turning off the projector. ''To me, they are stylized representations of the three heads of Cerberus…the watchdog of Hades. There are other interpretations.''

''Like what?''

Lakesh didn't immediately reply. In his more metaphysical moments, he often viewed the symbols as representing Brigid, Kane and Grant, a trinity, the human counterparts of the heads of Cerberus, each one symbolizing different yet related aspects of the soul. The cold reality of the matter was the sigils were the unifying insignia of the Archon Directorate, one adopted by Overproject Excalibur, the Totality Concept's division devoted to genetic engineering. It was supposed to represent some kind of pseudomystical triad functioning within a greater, all-embracing body.

Certainly Kane had never shared that view. To him, all it represented was the co-option and deliberately planned extinction of the human race.

From the doorway, Brigid announced, "It doesn't really matter. What's important is that somehow Sam had access to Quavell's signal."

Lakesh, Shizuka and Domi turned toward her. "That remains to be seen," Lakesh said a little defensively.

"I don't think so," Brigid retorted grimly. "It's apparent Sam can't open up localized wormholes through the Heart of the World without the initiation of gateway energies. We were in the process of gating out on Thunder Isle when he snatched us the first time."

Shizuka said, "That should be encouraging...he's not omnipotent, he relies on technology."

"True," agreed Lakesh. "He requires a technological enabler to facilitate his own natural abilities to tap into the quantum stream."

"How does knowing that get Quavell back?" Domi snapped.

Lakesh regarded her sadly. "Perhaps it doesn't."

"What do you mean?" Domi's tone was rich with suspicion.

"I mean we may have to accept the fact she is lost to us."

Domi shook her head vehemently. "I don't accept that."

"Me, either," Brigid stated. "If there's a way to retrieve her, we need to do it. If nothing else, as a matter of policy."

Lakesh sighed. "Dearest Brigid, you yourself said she was being used as bait."

Brigid smiled coldly. "Bait for you, Lakesh. Maybe even bait for Kane and Grant. But not for me."

"Or me," Domi spoke up.

After a moment, Shizuka said, "Or me."

Brigid surveyed the two women with appraising eyes and stated, "I think the three of us are agreed."

Lakesh opened his mouth to voice an objection, then shut it again. He stared levelly at the woman who had a memory like a computer, reflexes as quick and as dangerous as a scorpion's, and he realized there was no point in lodging an argument. He was surprised by the sensation of fear her jade-bright, jade-hard eyes awakened in him.

Bry's voice suddenly blared over the intercom. He sounded agitated, which wasn't unusual for him. "Lakesh, I established a fix on Quavell's location!"

Turning to the voice-activated trans-comm on the wall, Lakesh called, "Where is she?"

Bry took so long to respond Lakesh almost repeated the question. When the engineer spoke again, his voice was a hushed rustling. "You'd better see for yourself. I don't think you'll like it."

Chapter 18

Scowling, Lakesh reached over Bry and began tapping the keyboard. "Are you sure of this?"

Bry snorted. "How can I be?"

Lakesh punched in the sequence swiftly. A topographical map flashed onto the monitor screen, superimposing itself over the three icons that represented heart rate, blood pressure and brain-wave activity. The little symbols flashed in the midst of a computer-generated terrain.

Brigid drew in her breath sharply. "You were right, Bry. We don't like it."

"Where is she?" Domi demanded irritably.

Brigid nodded toward the monitor and the column of figures glowing at the top of the screen. "Kata Tjuta National Park, about 350 miles southwest of Alice Springs." The difficult pronunciation flowed easily from her tongue.

Shizuka shook her head in exasperation. "That doesn't tell us anything."

Lakesh straightened and blew out a long, weary breath. "Australia. Quavell is in Australia."

Standing at the engineering station, Philboyd demanded incredulously, "Why there?"

Bry swiveled in his chair to scrutinize the Mercator map spanning the wall. No lights blinked anywhere on it. "I don't see an indexed gateway in Australia."

"No," Lakesh agreed contemplatively. "But that doesn't mean much, as you know."

No one commented on his oblique reference to the number of unindexed mat-trans units that had been manufactured in Cerberus and shipped to parts unknown in modular form. Those units weren't part of the official Cerberus network, and their signals didn't register on the sensor link.

"Was there a Totality Concept–related project stationed there?" Brigid asked.

Lakesh shook his head. "None of which I'm aware."

"Does that mean there might be one?" Philboyd inquired doubtfully.

Philboyd, as well as the other members of his astrophysicist team on the Moon, had heard whispers of the Totality Concept, but by his own admission, they knew very little about it beyond the name. Brigid had explained that most Totality Concept–related redoubts were buried in subterranean military complexes mainly in the United States. There were, as they had reason to know, Concept-connected redoubts in other countries.

"A lot of the Totality Concept installations were hidden inside of national parks," Brigid told him. "Hiding in plain sight, as it were. I call it the purloined-letter approach."

A small smile of appreciation at the literary reference creased the man's lips. "I thought the Concept was strictly an American undertaking."

"Actually," responded Lakesh, "there were foreign counterparts to a few of the projects, like the Russian version of Cerberus called Szverdze. So it's not out of the realm of possibility a redoubt was built within Ayers Rock. I just never heard of one."

"Whether there is or isn't," Brigid stated matter-of-factly, "Sam certainly didn't employ a mat-trans to spirit Quavell out of here."

"Yes, it's obvious Sam activated a vortex point," Lakesh agreed, "and circumvented the need for a receiving unit altogether."

"You mentioned vortex points before," said Shizuka. "What are they?"

"Intersection points of the electromagnetic power grid of the planet," answered Lakesh. "Those points or nodes generate specific types of energy. Some have positive and projective frequencies, and others are negative and receptive in nature."

"So there's a vortex node in Australia?" Philboyd inquired.

"There are nodes all over the world," replied Lakesh. "All life and matter within our planet's gravity field are connected by an energy matrix."

Philboyd made a noise very much like a snort of derision, but Lakesh ignored it. Lakesh had learned to distrust physical scientists as a general rule. Outside of journalists, he had never met a more hide-bound, dense, play-by-the-numbers bunch. Most of them had the imaginations of tree stumps, incapable of visualizing anything unless it was within the pages of a scientific journal. He should know, since he had been just like Philboyd for many years.

Lakesh had learned the hard way the meaning of Einstein's statement that "physics had lost its walls." Einstein was obliquely calling to the attention of all physicists what philosophers had always known to be true, that the boundaries between space and time carried a large subjective element. It was only after accepting those possibilities that Lakesh had been able to make the breakthrough in Project Cerberus.

"What do you know about Australia since the war?" Philboyd asked.

"Very little," Brigid answered. "The country was a noncombatant, so the immediate physical and biological consequences were probably less prolonged and severe."

"What makes that park in Australia so special, then?" Domi wanted to know.

"Let's find out," said Lakesh. "Mr. Bry, if you run a cross-collation program with the Parallax Points data we have accrued, we'll see what we can see."

As Bry's fingers clattered over the keyboard, Brigid murmured, "There's more to this abduction than Sam interfering with the gateway dematerialization process."

Lakesh nodded. "Of course."

"How could he possibly do that?" Philboyd demanded impatiently.

Lakesh smiled slightly. "Sam practices a form of energy manipulation and interaction that once was known as geomancy. True geomancy is the art of using one's mind to tune in to the energy matrix of the planet. Sam has a natural, inborn ability to manipulate the global energy grid. The Cerberus network I so assiduously constructed over so many years is only a synthetic imitation of Sam's geomantic powers."

Philboyd favored him with a doubtful stare. "Sounds like New Age horseshit to me."

Lakesh didn't seem to be offended. "As a physicist, you should know that organic life as we define it would be impossible without electromagnetic energy. That's not New Age horseshit, it's scientific fact. I'm sure you've heard of Nikola Tesla and how he conceived of using this energy web as the basis for an entirely new principle of physics. In the late nineteenth century, Tesla built a transmitting tower on top of a Colorado mountain as an experiment to tap into the electromagnetic radiation of Earth, to provide a free energy source."

Philboyd looked to be on the verge of arguing, so Brigid interjected, "The question begs to be answered—how was Sam able to trace Quavell's transponder signal? How did he know the frequency?"

Domi's eyes flickered in startlement. "Didn't think of that. If he knows how to track us that way, he could've snatched any one of us at any time when we used the gateway.''

"Except," Brigid said, giving Lakesh a significant glance, "he didn't want just 'any one of us.'''

A bit defensively, Lakesh said, ''The interphaser has been the means of quantum stream transits for the past few months. It's a different application of a similar process.''

Brigid nodded in agreement. ''That suggests Sam had a different way of tracking Quavell. So Kane's distrust of her story about how she came to be here may have been founded in truth.''

Domi shook her head furiously. ''Don't believe she a spy. She saved my life, she helped me and Kane escape.''

Lakesh smiled at her sympathetically. ''Quavell may have been an unwitting participant in a long-range strategy.''

"Or," Philboyd put in, "she's been part of a scam all along.''

"Scam?'' Shizuka echoed in confusion.

"A scheme," Lakesh explained shortly. "It's a possibility...but it's more likely that a tracking transponder much like the ones we use here was injected into Quavell during her time at Area 51. Perhaps all the personnel there have them, human and hybrid alike.''

The computer beeped, signaling it had completed the search. Brigid and Lakesh leaned over Bry's shoulder to stare at the image dominating the screen. "I should've known," Lakesh murmured.

A huge, domed monolith of rust-red rock pushed up from a desert floor, its deeply fissured bulk washed by streaks of color. The terrain around it resembled a rad-scoured hellzone, with nothing to see but drifting plains of reddish sand, broken by a few tangled thickets. The rock rose sheer from the surrounding sands, a gigantic structure of stone with rounded sides that appeared to be unscaleable. Aeons of erosion had cut deep grooves and furrows across its base.

Brigid was irresistibly reminded of the skull of an insensible giant, with the rest of its fossilized remains buried deep underground. There was a brooding, somber magnificence to the gigantic monolith.

"A rock," Domi said, unimpressed. "So?"

"Not just *a* rock," Lakesh retorted musingly. "It's Ayers Rock, also known as Mount Uluru—the world's largest monolith and an aboriginal sacred site. In predark days, it was Australia's most famous natural landmark."

Shizuka demanded, "Why would Quavell be there?"

Lakesh shrugged. "I have no idea as to the why. But as to the how—"

"Let me guess," Philboyd ventured. "I'll bet it has something to do with this vortex nodes of yours."

"Not my vortices," Lakesh shot back. "The planet's. And yes, Ayers Rock is a focal point for electromagnetic Earth energies. Otherwise, the aboriginal peoples would not have considered it a holy spot since time immemorial.''

A column of statistics appeared on the right-hand side of the screen, and Brigid read the specifics. ''Ayers Rock is 350 meters high and nine kilometers in diameter. It's all that remains of a three-hundred-million-year-old sandstone range, which extends underground some three kilometers. It literally *is* the biggest rock in the world.''

''Why is it so red?'' Bry asked.

''It's the arkose, a coarse-grained sandstone rich in the mineral feldspar,'' answered Lakesh. ''The red color is caused by the chemical decay of minerals and simple oxydiation.''

''Rust?'' inquired Shizuka.

Lakesh nodded. ''Rust. The fresh arkose is a gray color. It actually changes color during the day, almost like a mineral chameleon. Before sunrise it's gray against the gray sky. At sunset the rock can change in color from deep red to bright orange to light purple in minutes.''

''Thank you, Mr. Wizard,'' Philboyd said snidely.

Brigid cast him an irritated look. ''Just because Kane is laid up, we don't need you to take his place as Lakesh's resident gadfly.''

She turned toward Lakesh. ''You seem to know a lot about it. Have you been there?''

Lakesh straightened, shaking his head. ''No. A couple of years back, when I was doing the initial research on naturally occurring quantum interphase points, I suspected that the Uluru, as the aborigines call it, might be a node. I did a little reading on it.''

''Why is it called Uluru?'' Shizuka asked, stepping closer to the computer station.

''Magnify the image, Mr. Bry,'' Lakesh requested.

Bry obligingly tapped the mouse, and the screen swelled with a closer view of the rock formation. Barely visible, etched across the surface, was a series of curving, twisting intertwining lines.

Lakesh pointed to them. ''Those arcs are called Uluru by the aborigines. They represent the manifestation of a single life force, how everything is related. Thus they revere all life, the Uluru.

''According to aboriginal legend, when the ancestral beings completed their work of creation, they decreed that things must remain unchanged for all time. This Dreamtime decree is the cohesive force that has kept the aborigines in harmony with the land. The concept of harmony is universal.''

''What is Dreamtime, anyway?'' Philboyd asked, sounding interested despite the scowl on his face. ''I've heard of it, of course, but I never found out what it meant exactly.''

''I doubt anyone but an aborigine would know what it meant,'' Lakesh replied. ''The Dreamtime is a difficult concept for our minds to grasp. It's both past and present and past renewed or brought into the present. It's the essence of what might be called the aboriginal religion. Dreamtime and dreaming are translations from the aboriginal words, but have little to do with dreams as we know them. Dreamtime focuses on the beginnings of life and its continuation. It is perpetuated by rituals and by ceremonies in sacred sites."

"Like Ayers Rock," Brigid commented. "Let's talk about the material world for a moment. Assuming Quavell was transported from here to there, where would she be in relation to it?"

"There are many caves in Ayers Rock," answered Lakesh. "Water dripping through the sandstone formed a number of galleries and caverns."

"Let's narrow it down, then. What's the largest cavern?"

Lakesh pursed his lips. "Mr. Bry, see if that information is available."

Bry tapped a couple of keys, and a window appeared on the screen. Framed within it was a view of the monolith's base and a dark, triangular cleft bisecting it. The shape and symmetry lent it an unmistakable resemblance to the female organs of reproduction. The resemblance was so marked that Philboyd self-consciously averted his gaze.

Sounding officiously unaffected, Bry announced, "The largest cavern is known as the Woman's Cave. Aboriginal women went there to give birth. It's also where fertility rites were conducted."

Brigid narrowed her eyes for a moment, then nodded in comprehension. "Sam just provided us with a signpost."

Lakesh tugged at his nose. "It appears so, yes."

Addressing Bry, Brigid asked, "Can you print out a map of the Ayers Rock vicinity that will pinpoint the location of the Woman's Cave?"

Bry nodded. "On it."

"I would imagine," Lakesh said thoughtfully, still tugging at his nose, "that the coordinates we feed into the interphaser's database will take you right into it."

"I'd prefer to arrive on the outside," said Brigid. "I don't want to phase right into Sam's arms."

Philboyd stepped forward, eyes shining with anxiety. "Hold on a second—are you talking about using that interphaser machine to travel there and rescue Quavell?"

Brigid smiled at him with wry amusement. "That's the general plan, yes. It's how me, Grant and Kane arrived on the Moon and met you, remember?"

Philboyd swallowed hard. "It still seems a little risky."

"I'd say it's a lot risky," Bry put in. "But they won't listen."

Lakesh smiled a little patronizingly. "Mr. Bry feels the interphaser is an unreliable and cantankerous piece of machinery. He fears it could malfunction and leave our teams stranded in the middle of the Gobi or it could do to them what the first one did—trigger a spatial and temporal anomaly and boot them all on an unscheduled trip through time."

Philboyd's jaw dropped in astonishment. "What?"

Brigid couldn't help but laugh. She didn't know if it was the almost comical expression of befuddlement on his face or the need to break the tension that had been building in her. "Lakesh's prototype of the interphaser didn't function according to its design, and Bry has never let him forget about it."

Lakesh said to Philboyd, "This latest version of the interphaser is completely retooled from the prototype. And as I have said before, the chances are very remote it will interface with the radiations of another homemade black hole."

Philboyd looked steadily at Brigid. "I honestly don't know why you're so hell-bent on going after Quavell, but why don't you and I go? We'll take one of the TAVs. You know I'm a good pilot."

Hoping she didn't sound insulting, Brigid said, "Thanks for the offer, but an op like this will require a lot more than piloting skills. And as for the reasons we're going after Quavell—"

"First and foremost," Lakesh said flatly, "she is a useful resource."

"And," Domi bit out, "me and Kane owe her our lives."

Philboyd cast his eyes downward as if ashamed. Brigid understood his objections. It had only been a few weeks since he had come to terms with the fact he would not live and die on the Moon, and he looked at Brigid as something of an anchor in his new life.

"Don't worry," Brigid stated with a confidence she didn't feel. "I'm an old hand at rescue missions."

DeFore's voice suddenly filtered over the intercom. "In case anybody is interested, Kane is conscious. Take your time about coming to see him—he sure as hell isn't going anywhere."

Chapter 19

Brigid was a little surprised and disconcerted that Domi elected to go to the armory while she and Shizuka left to check on Grant and Kane. But the Outland girl lived by her whims and impulses, and Brigid figured her fierce pride would not allow her to compete with Shizuka for Grant's attention.

When the two women entered the infirmary, they learned from DeFore that Domi's absence made little difference to the man. The medic murmured, "Grant's still unconscious. If he doesn't show signs of reviving in the next couple of hours, I'll hook him up to the EEG and see what readings I get."

Brigid looked past DeFore to the beds upon which the two men lay. Grant's eyes were closed, but his chest rose and fell steadily. An IV bag hung upside down to the left of the bed, dripping slowly into a shunt on his arm. Diagnostic scanners hummed purposefully, monitoring his heartbeat and blood pressure. The overhead lights had been dimmed, but she could still see the ashen-gray hue of his complexion.

Kane occupied the far bed. He also had an IV drip, but he was awake, staring up at the ceiling. His eyes were bagged and underlined by dark rings. His complexion was sallow. He didn't move at all.

In a whisper quavering with dread, Shizuka asked, "What's wrong with him?"

DeFore nibbled at her lower lip. "I'm afraid he's paralyzed, at least temporarily. Neuro trauma. I'm sure the same thing is affecting Grant."

"You're sure it's temporary?" Shizuka pressed.

DeFore opened her mouth to reply, then closed it with a sigh. "No, I'm not sure. I haven't told either one of them yet."

Shizuka nodded in acknowledgment of the medic's diagnosis and crossed the room to Grant's bedside. Brigid strode over to Kane. His shadow suit had been removed, and he was covered to his midsection by a sheet. Even in the dim light, she saw the crisscross pattern of old scars on his chest. His face was pale and drawn tight over the facial bones, his hair in disarray. He looked like hell warmed over and left to congeal, but she tried not to think about it.

Kane's eyes flicked toward her. In a hoarse croak, he rasped, "Grant's still out."

Brigid nodded. "I know."

"What the hell happened?" His pale, glassy eyes were confused. "DeFore says Quavell is gone."

"Yes." In a clipped, brisk, unemotional monotone, Brigid told him what had transpired and who they suspected was the power behind it all.

Kane squeezed his eyes shut. Between gritted teeth

he grunted, ''Should've killed the little son of a bitch when I had the chance.''

''You didn't have the chance, Kane,'' Brigid reminded him. ''None of us did.''

He opened his eyes again. ''You know where he took her?''

''We think so. An idea, at least. Australia.''

''Australia?'' Kane echoed incredulously. He succumbed to a coughing fit, and Brigid poured a cup of water from a carafe and placed a straw in his mouth. He drank gratefully.

Clearing his throat he demanded, ''Where in Australia?''

She told him about Ayers Rock and watched as his face became hard and cold. ''I'm going with you.''

''You're not going anywhere.'' she said calmly.

''Watch me.'' Kane strained to raise his head from the pillow, the tendons in his neck standing out in relief like ropes. He grated, ''Baptiste, get these damn straps off me—''

Brigid's eyes suddenly stung. Kane was a proud man, absurdly so sometimes. She gazed with increasing consternation at his struggle to rise, which showed none of the wolflike grace she had always silently admired.

Blinking back brimming tears, she put a hand on his forehead. ''You're not in restraints, Kane. You're paralyzed. So is Grant, more than likely.''

Kane gazed at her uncomprehendingly for a long silent moment. His face twisted into an expression she had never seen before—utter horror and a soul-freezing terror. His lips moved, and it took him two attempts before he was able to husk out, "Paralyzed?"

Hastily, soothingly, she said, "Reba is pretty sure it's a temporary condition due to trauma of the nervous system. There's no reason to believe you won't make a full recovery."

Kane's head dropped back onto the pillow, his face sheened with sweat. He asked in a barely audible whisper, "What if it isn't?"

"Nobody has thought that far ahead. There's no reason to at this juncture."

Stricken, Kane stared at her beseechingly. "Brigid—"

She felt her heart give a painful jerk. She forced himself to meet his stare. Several times over the past couple of years, Brigid had faced, then turned away from, the possibility that her soul and Kane's had been intertwined for a very long time, reincarnated over and over, destined to always find each other. Neither one of them had cared to seriously entertain such a concept. They were not and never had been romantically involved.

He had risked his life on a number of occasions for her, but only rarely had he ever addressed her by her first name. She knew that most of the time Kane shied away from scrutinizing his feelings for her, just as she did. They were as deep as they were complicated, and the unspoken bond between them was an issue neither one discussed. When she was with Kane, always her intellect and emotions rioted within her. She always feared to closely examine her feelings for him, frightened they were far too intense for her to deal with.

Their relationship was guarded, sometimes tense. Brigid tried to convince herself it was due to the fact she took pride in cool, analytical thinking, while Kane exhibited emotionalism, relying on his instincts. But she knew there were far deeper factors at work, as well.

From the very first time she met him, she was affected by the energy the man radiated, a force intangible, yet one that triggered a melancholy longing in her soul. That strange, sad longing only deepened after a bout of jump sickness both of them suffered during a mat-trans jump to Russia. The main symptoms of jump sickness were vivid, frighteningly real hallucinations.

Lakesh had postulated the so-called jump dreams might not be hallucinations at all, but inchoate glimpses into other lives and other realities triggered by the quantum channels opened by the gateway units. At the time, Brigid had refused to consider that possibility but now she wasn't so certain. At any rate, she and Kane never spoke of their shared vision, although Brigid often wondered if that spiritual bond was the primary reason he had sacrificed everything he had attained as a Magistrate to save her from execution in Cobaltville.

She knew the possibility confused him, made him feel defensive and insecure. That insecurity was one reason he almost always addressed her as "Baptiste," rarely by her first name so as to maintain a certain, formal distance between them.

Inhaling a great, shuddery breath, Kane squeezed his eyes shut and compressed his lips. Brigid knew he was processing the information. His Magistrate discipline took over now, the training that had taught him to view all situations as a matter of tactics and critical problems that could be solved by judicious strategy.

After a moment, he said flatly, "Leave her."

Brigid cocked her head at him quizzically. "What? Leave who?"

He opened his eyes and she inwardly cringed from the cold, merciless gleam in them. She had seen that gleam many times before. "Quavell. Don't risk yourself or Shizuka or Domi over her."

"Don't you owe her your life?"

"And I spared it in Dulce. We're even. But we're not talking a matter of debt. Quavell is my problem. You can't sacrifice yourself or anyone else over someone that is my responsibility."

"So," she intoned slowly, "since Quavell is your responsibility, and you can't do anything about it in your present condition, she should be sacrificed, not us?"

He nodded as best he could. "You said her abduction was bait for a trap. The most reasonable tactic when approaching a trap is not to spring it.''

''And what about Quavell and her baby?'' Brigid pitched her voice low to disguise the rising note of anger in it.

''Sam doesn't mean her harm,'' Kane replied. ''If he did, she would have never been allowed to escape Area 51, with or without help. In my estimation, she's been acting as a lure ever since she got here. Whether she knew it or not doesn't really matter.''

Brigid pondered Kane's words for a thoughtful moment. At length she said, ''You've got a point. Sam wants Lakesh swung to his side, so he's probably counting on Lakesh coming for Quavell, like a prisoner exchange.''

''Exactly. If Lakesh stays behind and if he captures you three, he's got three more hostages to use against us.''

Brigid stated smoothly, ''And if nobody comes to rescue Quavell, he still has her—and her child. It's the classic win-win.''

''And he also knows the location of Cerberus,'' Kane interjected. ''So he could stage an assault at any time. He has his own forces and those of the barons who've allied with him.''

Brigid sighed, then murmured wryly, ''I can always rely on you to pour cold water on any acts of idealism that I might entertain.''

He forced a smile. ''I've learned from the best.''

His eyes suddenly flicked to the left, and Brigid

looked up, following his gaze. Shizuka approached, her face locked in an impassive mask, but her dark eyes glittered. "Grant-san has not roused. His spirit sleeps. I fear it will not awaken."

Kane's jaw muscles knotted but he said reassuringly, "He'll pull through. He's the toughest man in the world. Compared to him, I'm made of spun sugar."

Shizuka did not smile. "*Hai.* But perhaps his spirit will awaken if we punish those who did this to him and to you."

Brigid nodded and gingerly flexed her fingers, wincing slightly at the pull of the liquid bandage on her hands. Other than that, her movements were unimpaired. "Let's get it done."

Kane raised his head, face registering equal measures of dismay and anger. "Get what done? I thought we agreed—"

"No," Brigid interrupted. "We didn't agree to anything. I listened to your input and gave it due consideration. But I'm not leaving Quavell in the hands of the imperator, either as a hostage or as a willing co-conspirator."

Anger won out over apprehension on Kane's face. "She's my responsibility, Baptiste, not yours!"

"You can't make that decision only for yourself," Brigid snapped. "That's what always infuriated you about Lakesh. Anything and everything that any one of us chooses to do affects the others—you know that."

Kane started to voice a heated rejoinder, but Brigid went on, "I'm not going to sacrifice Quavell because you're incapacitated. Nor will I allow Sam to terrorize us here without doing something to stop him. He may only be trying to prove to us that resistance against his authority is futile, but that doesn't mean we have to buy into it."

"You have no idea of the kind of defenses he might have around that place," Kane bit out.

"We have no idea if he has any, either."

"The risk is too great."

"I think it's acceptable."

"You can't do it," he said doggedly.

"It's not like you can stop me." She regretted the cruelty of her response, but she knew slapping him in the face with the cold reality of the situation was the only way to persuade him to stop badgering her.

Over the past two years Brigid had come to accept risk as a part of her way of life, taking chances so that others might find the ground beneath their feet a little more secure. She didn't consider her attitude idealism, but simple pragmatism. If she had learned anything from her association with Kane, Grant and Domi, it was to regard death as a part of the challenge of existence, a fact that every man and woman had to face eventually.

She had vowed to accept it without humiliating herself if it came as a result of her efforts to remove the yokes of the baronies from the collective neck of humanity. She never spoke of it openly, certainly not to the cynical Kane, but she had privately vowed to make the future a better, cleaner place than either the past or the present.

Kane started to speak again, then subsided, laying his head back down. For one long second, their eyes met. Kane didn't speak but his eyes were saying things he had never spoken aloud. Brigid could only return his gaze, wondering again why they were so fearful of revealing their innermost selves to each other—especially now when time and life were on the wing.

Suddenly, Brigid bent over and kissed him with a fierce, passionate possessiveness. He uttered a murmur of surprise as her tongue touched his. Then, just as suddenly, she broke the kiss and wheeled away to Shizuka and said flatly, "Let's go."

Chapter 20

Domi tested the action of her Detonics Combat Master pistol. Since the stainless-steel gun weighed only a pound and a half, it was perfectly suited for a girl of her petite build. When she had first selected it from the redoubt's armory nearly two years ago, Grant had expressed doubt she could handle the recoil. She had never experienced problems with it, except during the period when she was recovering from a bullet that shattered a bone in her right shoulder.

Before coming into the armory to pick up her weapons, Domi had dressed in whipcord pants and hiking boots. The shirtsleeves of her khaki shirt were rolled up, and a long-billed cap was on her head. Ejecting the 7-round magazine from within the pistol's checkered walnut grip, she inspected the spring mechanism, then slid the clip back in place. She slid the handgun into the shoulder holster attached to the combat harness she wore over her shirt.

Briefly, she inspected one of the tungsten-carbide pellet guns the Moon base refugees had brought. The pistol held the general configuration of a revolver, but instead of a cylinder, a small, round ammo drum was fitted into the place where there was normally a trigger guard. There wasn't a trigger, just a curving switch inset into the grip.

The barrel was unusually long, nearly ten inches in length. The weapon was made of a lightweight alloy that resembled dulled chrome. A unit of energy inside the grip moved a piston that propelled the explosive projectile. She had yet to test fire one, so she put it back in the crate where she had found it.

Reaching down, she made sure her knife with its nine-inch, wickedly serrated blade was securely sheathed to her right calf. It was her only memento of the six months she'd spent as Guana Teague's sex slave in the Tartarus Pits of Cobaltville.

She'd sold herself into slavery in an effort to get a piece of the good life available to ville dwellers, but she had never risen any further than Cobaltville's Tartarus Pits. Since ville society was strictly class- and caste-based, the higher a citizen's standing, the higher he or she might live in one of the residential towers. At the bottom level of the villes was the servant class, who lived in abject squalor in consciously designed ghettos known as the Tartarus Pits, named after the abyss below Hell where Zeus confined the Titans. They swarmed with a heterogeneous population of serfs, cheap labor and slaves like her. She ended her term of slavery by cutting the monstrous Teague's throat with the blade and saved Grant's life in the same impulsive act.

Like so many others, Guana Teague had dismissed her as a semimindless outlander. The average life expectancy of an outlander was around forty, and the few who reached that age possessed both an animal cunning and vitality. Domi was nowhere near that age—in fact she had no true idea of how old she actually was—but she possessed more than her share of cunning and vitality.

She didn't miss the short and often brutal life in the Outlands. She had quickly adapted to the comforts offered by the Cerberus redoubt—the soft bed, protection from the often toxic elements and food that was always available, without having to scavenge or kill for it.

Domi had enjoyed similar luxuries during her six months as Guana Teague's sex slave. The man-mountain of flab had been the boss of the Cobaltville Pits, and he showered her with gifts. He didn't pamper her, though, since she was forced to satisfy his gross lusts. He was obsessed with her, and that had brought about not only his downfall but also his bloody death.

Domi rarely dwelled on the past, but she often replayed how she had cut Guana's throat and how the blood had literally rivered from the deep slash in his triple chins. She always smiled in recollection of kicking his monstrous body as it twitched in postmortem spasms, just as she smiled at the memory of Grant comforting her and thanking her for saving his life.

Thinking about Grant caused her lips to twitch unconsciously in a half frown, half smile. Whenever she thought about the big man with his lion's growl of a voice, she felt a mingling of love, anger and disappointment.

She loved the man for his qualities of courage and compassion, but she experienced anger and disappointment that he never allowed that compassion to turn into passion—at least not toward her. Domi was too practical, too pragmatic to expend much energy on girlish daydreams that had already proved to be lost causes, particularly since entering into a relationship with Lakesh. A relationship, she reminded herself bleakly, that had yet to be revealed to Grant, despite his bringing his Japanese lover right into Cerberus. As angry as Shizuka's presence made her, Domi knew Grant had not done it to hurt her. He was not that petty.

Grant presented a dour, closed and private persona, rarely showing emotion. He was taciturn and slow to genuine anger, but when he was provoked, his destructive ruthlessness could be frightening. With him, slights were never forgotten, and she knew he still stung from the whip of angry words she had lashed at him months ago: "Big man, big chest, big shoulders, legs like trees. Guess they don't tell the story, huh?"

Domi regretted speaking those words almost as soon as they left her lips, but she had never apologized. When Grant rejected her love again on that day, she swore it was for the last time. Then, a month or so later, when she came across Grant and Shizuka locked in a fierce embrace, she also swore she would never forgive him. Even so, she could not bear to see him lying injured and comatose in the infirmary.

Shaking her head, Domi tried to drive the memories of that night from her mind. There were a lot of memories swimming around within the walls of her skull she would as soon have excised, and that brief glimpse of Grant showering the Japanese woman's face with passionate kisses topped the list.

Another memory she wished could be removed from her brain was her two weeks in captivity within the vast subterranean installation of Area 51. Both she and Kane had been shown the end result of their war against the barons—dying hybrid infants.

Domi still didn't know why the sight of the dying hybrid babies horrified her so profoundly, filling her with guilt and remorse. After all, she had come to the Dreamland installation in the Nevada desert for the sole purpose of killing as many hybrids as she could. The very concept of the hybrids triggered a xenophobic madness in her, the overwhelming urge to kill them, as she had killed mutie borer beetles that sometimes infested into the Outland settlement in which she had been born. But upon visiting the nursery turned morgue, she felt only shame, as if the guilt of the entire human race were laid on her small shoulders.

Kane seemed to understand her point of view. She hoped he did, but it didn't really matter. They hadn't spoken of what they had witnessed, or what they went through during their captivity. Kane was reticent to talk about it, particularly to Brigid. Domi hadn't blamed him, and she had kept her own knowledge of his experiences to herself.

At the sound of footsteps, she turned toward the door. Brigid and Shizuka swept into the armory, moving very purposefully. Brigid said, "You're ready. Good."

Domi nodded, moving to a crate of grenades. "Already told Farrell to have a survival pack waiting for us in the ready room."

In her characteristic mannish stride, Brigid crossed the room to a row of metal lockers arranged against the far wall. She opened one of the locker doors and removed a jet-black, one-piece garment from a hook. Swiftly, she stripped down to her underwear and began pulling on the shadow suit, first opening a magnetic seal on its right side. The garment had no zippers or buttons, and she put it on in one continuous piece from the hard-soled boots to the gloves. The fabric molded itself to her body, adhering like another layer of epidermis. She smoothed out the wrinkles and folds by running her hands over arms and legs.

At the same time, Shizuka shrugged out of her jacket and began donning the pieces of samurai armor over her *kamishimo*. She did so with the same smooth deftness as Kane and Grant had put on their Magistrate exoskeletons. Each segment of the armor was made from wafers of metal held together by small, delicate chains and overlaid with a dark-brown lacquer. The overlapping plates were trimmed in scarlet and gold.

Shizuka removed the two swords from the case and slid the scabbards through the wide green sash knotted around her small waist. She crossed her arms over her torso, then slid both the *katana* and *tanto* from the scabbards with lightning speed. She spun them experimentally, the flat blades cutting bright wheels in the air over her head. Then she returned the two swords to the scabbards in the same blurred motions.

Domi glanced over at her shoulder at her. Shizuka met her eyes stolidly. If Domi had been capable of blushing, she would have flushed bright red from anger. She clamped her jaws shut on the obscenity that sprang to her tongue. Shizuka's brief performance was a none too subtle reminder of the night the two of them had dueled in the California desert. Shizuka had done more than defeat her; she had humiliated her in front of Grant. The memory of that night was still like a lit match applied to the most tender part of her ego.

Brigid had paid no attention to either woman. She put on a combat harness, then removed a Copperhead from a notched wooden rack within a gun case. A chopped-down autoblaster, the Copperhead was barely two feet in length. The magazine held fifteen rounds of 4.85 mm steel-jacketed rounds, which could be fired at a rate of 700 per minute. Even with its optical image intensifier and laser autotarget scope, the Copperhead weighed less than eight pounds. Gas operated, the grip and trigger unit were placed in front of the breech in the bullpup design, allowing for one-handed use. Its low recoil allowed the Copperhead to be fired in a long, devastating full-auto burst.

From the rear of the case, Brigid took a black, six-inch-long cylinder and screwed it carefully into the blaster's bore. The two-stage sound and muzzle-flash arrestor suppressed even full-auto reports to no more than rustling whispers.

'Sorry I don't have the helmet,'' Brigid said to Shizuka.

Shizuka shrugged, as if the matter were of little importance. ''I know nothing about Australia or the aborigines Lakesh spoke of. Do they still exist?''

''That's hard to say,'' Brigid answered. ''They maintained a culture that thrived unchanged for about fifty thousand years. So, if they were half as resilient as America's own aboriginal people, then my guess is yes, they still exist.''

''Are they same as Sky Dog's tribe?'' Domi inquired.

''No. Predark anthropologists usually classified the Australian aborigine as a separate race, the Australoid, because they're so distinct from the Caucasoid, the Mongoloid and Negroid groups. But the Australian policy toward them was much the same as it was toward the American Indian.''

Domi snorted. ''Killin' them off?''

Brigid nodded dolefully. ''I'm afraid so.''

"How do you know so much about them?" Shizuka asked.

Brigid smiled wanly. She wasn't quite the ambulatory encyclopedia she appeared to be, since most of her seemingly limitless supply of knowledge was due to her eidetic memory, but her apparent familiarity with an astounding variety of topics never failed to impress—and occasionally irritate—Kane. "I don't, not really. Not even anthropologists knew everything about them. The little I know is from skimming through the database from time to time, looking for clues to Archon influence on their culture."

Shizuka lifted an eyebrow. "Were there any?"

"Not specifically. But I did find some interesting correlations with the Annunaki—"

"Grab some grens," Domi broke in impatiently.

Brigid wasn't offended. She joined Domi at the crates, picking and choosing from their lethal contents. Both of them took four grens apiece—an Alsatex flash-bang, two incends, and a high-ex. They attached them to the combat harnesses and clipped three spare magazines for their guns to the harnesses, as well.

"Primed," Domi declared.

Brigid repressed a smile at the girl's use of the Mag slang she had heard Grant and Kane employ on numerous occasions. The three women left the armory and strode down the main corridor to the command center. The lights were dimmed to simulate sunset.

Bry and Nora were the only people in the complex.

They stood in front of the medical monitor, speaking in whispers. They looked up, startled, when Domi, Shizuka and Brigid entered.

"I've got your map," Bry announced in a strained tone, extending a trifolded rectangle of paper to her. He spoke too loudly and too nervously. "But—"

Brigid took the map from his hand. "But what?"

Nora answered the question. "We've lost Quavell's life signs."

Before Brigid could request a clarification, Lakesh said from the doorway of the ready room, "There could be many reasons why we're not receiving her transponder's telemetry. We know from past experience, it doesn't necessarily mean she is dead. If we began the last rites every time the biolink signals were interrupted or blocked, we'd have sung funeral dirges for just about everybody in Cerberus."

Bry cast him an annoyed sideways glance. "I know that. But I thought they should know beforehand about the worst-case scenario."

"Thanks," Brigid said dryly. "But I always take those kind of scenarios into consideration before I do anything."

Lakesh said, "The latitudinal and longitudinal coordinates have already been programmed into the interphaser's destination buffer."

"So you found a Parallax Point in the area?"

"Actually," declared Bry, "we found about a dozen of them, some of them overlapping. It's a powerful vortex zone. We selected one that should bring you to within a couple of miles of Ayers Rock.''

Philboyd was in the ready room, leaning over the table. On it lay a square metal-and-leather case containing survival rations, such as concentrated foodstuffs and bottles of purified water, but he wasn't examining that. The man's attention was focused on a shape that resembled a very squat, broad-based pyramid made of smooth, gleaming alloy. It appeared to be only one foot in overall width, its height not exceeding ten inches. From the base protruded a small power unit and a keypad.

"You've seen the interphaser before," Brigid said, removing the power unit and pushing the keypad into a slot.

Philboyd grinned. "Yeah, but I never looked at it closely. It sure doesn't seem like it can do all the things you claim it can do. It looks like an incense burner from the sixties."

Lakesh said stiffly, "The pyramid shape is not arbitrary or aesthetic. Energy progresses by four different routes, rejoining in a single conclusionary point at the apex. The energy flows in a helix spiral pattern exactly opposite and of equal frequency. The intensity on each side of the vortex at any given point triggers a quantum induction shift by vibrational resonance."

Philboyd nodded gravely. "Oh. And I thought it would be complicated." He caught Brigid's eye and winked conspiratorially.

Lakesh frowned and tugged at his nose. "I'm wondering if this is such a good idea, after all."

"I don't recall anybody saying it was a good idea," Brigid retorted breezily, closing and latching the rations case. She handed it to Shizuka, who slung it over a shoulder by the strap.

"The mission just seems impulsive," Lakesh continued. "As Kane would say, 'half-assed,' jumping into dark territory without knowing the lay of the land."

Brigid regarded him grimly. "There's no way to know the lay of the land without making a phase transit, Lakesh. So we'll kill two scream-wings with one stone. Rescue Quavell and learn about the outback."

"Besides," said Domi cheerfully, "We didn't get dressed up for nothing."

Lakesh gave her a jittery, nervous smile. He had expected nothing else from Domi than the attitude that all life-risking escapades were grand, exhilarating larks. But Brigid's intense drive to undertake the mission disturbed him. He had always admired the way she could swiftly meld thesis, antithesis into a synthesis of diverse, sometimes contradictory concepts. Or at least, she had been capable of that until Kane's simplistic approach to life's vagaries infected her.

Picking up the interphaser, Brigid carried it into the gateway unit. When making phase transits from the redoubt, they always used the mat-trans chamber because it could be hermetically sealed. She placed it on the floor and waited for her companions to join her. Shizuka hesitated only a fraction of a second before stepping into the chamber. Domi leaned forward and planted a quick kiss on Lakesh's cheek, then climbed up to the platform, pulling the brown-tinted armaglass door closed on its counterbalanced hinges.

Brigid exchanged a long look with the two women. "Are we ready?"

Domi nodded. "Do it."

Shizuka ducked her head. *"Hai."*

Brigid knelt and touched the interphaser's inset activation toggles. As she stood, a waxy, glowing funnel of light fanned up from the metal apex of the pyramid. It looked like a diffused veil of backlit fog, with tiny shimmering stars dancing within it.

Shizuka stared in wonder, and as she stared the light expanded into a gushing borealis several feet wide, spreading out within the chamber. A thready pulse of vibration tickled their skin, and shadows crawled over the armaglass walls, moving in fitful jerks and leaps. A faint hint of a breeze brushed their faces and ruffled their hair.

"One at a time," Brigid said calmly.

"One at a time what?" Shizuka's voice was a whisper.

Brigid gestured to the shimmering fan of light. "Walk into that, over the top of the interphaser."

Shizuka eyed it uncertainly. "That's all there is to it?"

Domi smiled cruelly. "Sometimes."

Brigid swallowed a sigh. "I'll go first."

She stepped toward the pyramid and over it—then she fell headlong into infinity.

Chapter 21

Her consciousness was a confusion of speed, distortion, a plunging, spinning whirlpool that was all inside her head but seemed immense enough to encompass the entire galaxy-flecked universe. Around and around, faster, lurching, rolling, caught helplessly in a torrent of energy that somehow was not energy, of a raging flame that did not burn but chilled with a cold deeper than a gale whipping from the lifeless vacuum of space.

Always before, Brigid had experienced the interphaser transition between vortex nodes as little more than an insistent tug, the sensation lasting such an infinitesimal tick of time it couldn't be measured. What little her conscious mind retained of the phasing process from one node to another was little more than a splintered fragment of a long-ago dream.

Now she plunged like a handful of electric impulses flung out among the stars like grains of sand. All around her, suns burned with a pure, clean radiance. The clouds of nebulae glowed silver against the primal black. Constellations wheeled and glittered. She could feel the movement of the universe pulsing against her, hear the songs sung by the stars.

Then she floated alone in a void. She groped for Shizuka and Domi and couldn't find them. Brigid couldn't even sense her companions. A crushing weight of loneliness pressed down on her. She felt cut off from everything she knew as reality. The limbo in which she swam was like being trapped in a purgatory between existence and nonexistence. Somehow she knew life and death were utterly meaningless concepts in the dream in which she was caught.

Then she heard a low roar, a distant rumbling that came in gusts with whistling notes in between. She couldn't truly hear it, but sensed it as a pattern of energy in the invisible current sweeping her naked soul into a maelstrom where the past, the present and future all seemed intertwined in one vast tapestry she couldn't see but could sense nevertheless.

The roar swelled to a mourning, moaning wail and then to piping, a shrieking, overlaid with deeper notes that were like a distant, deep, throbbing drumbeat against her mind. It rolled through her like breakers on a beach, in a steady heavy rhythm or the steady beat of the invisible wings of a giant bird.

Shadow shapes flitted and swam before her, moving in jerks and whirls to the music. The shadows lengthened, shortened and then became dark figures wearing only loincloths and feathered headbands. Their deep-brown faces were decorated with swirls and strips of white clay. The figures weren't stable or stationary—they shifted, they changed, they became blendings of animal and human. Some sported fanged

muzzles, others leathery bat-wings. Colorful patterns
and figures writhed, weaving into twisting geometric
shapes. There were colors she had never before seen,
let alone imagined. The beat of the music penetrated
to the core of Brigid's soul, acting like a magnet to
pull her into the dance.

She passed from one dancer to another and sometimes the hands reaching out for her were claw-tipped
paws. A man leaped out of the shapes surrounding
her, dancing and capering in a mad dervish whirl.
Around his hips was a loincloth bearing a complex
design of intertwining curves and arcs. For some reason, Brigid saw the designs clearly, far more clearly
than anything else about the figure.

The man's otherwise naked body was painted with
alternating strips of bright yellow and red on his
chest, midriff and arms. In his right hand he held what
seemed to be a long piece of rawhide cord with a
hollow, sharp-pointed bone attached to its end.

The man danced with frenetic energy, whirling the
bone over his head. It gave off a low, ominous hum.
The hum deepened and slowly became a blend of
whispers speaking to her, as if the echoes of many
voices floated through the void. But all of the whispers held an indefinable note of sad serenity. Then
they began to sing the *inma,* the epic song cycle of
beginnings. Slowly, Brigid understood that she was
dreaming, but they were dreams someone else wanted
her to dream.

"Long, long ago before the Tjukurpa, the Dreamtime,'' the whispery voices sang, ''before time the world was soft and wobbly and had no shape. Then, at the beginning of Dreamtime, Warramurrungundii came out of the sea. A female in form, she created the land, gave birth to the people and gave them their language.

''Ginga, the giant ancestral crocodile, who got the bumps on his back when he was blistered in a fire, made the rock country. Marrawuti, the sea eagle, brought water lilies in his claws and planted them on the flood plain. When these beings finished their creations they became part of the landscape, where they remain today as our totems. Warramurrungundii is a white rock in the woodlands. Ginga is a rock outcrop, textured like a crocodile's back. These places are our sacred sites that still have the power and energy of Dreamtime.''

''Is that where I am?'' Brigid asked. ''Am I in Dreamtime?''

The voices didn't answer her question. Instead, they said, ''Our most holy of sites is Uluru, the life energy in stone form. Long ago the Kuniya, the snake people, journeyed from Paku-Paku, a waterhole near Mount Conner west of Uluru. These snake people were peaceful and nonpoisonous. They came to a large, flat sandhill in the center of which was a water hole.''

Brigid received a blurred impression of a lizard-thing walking upright on slightly bowed, powerful legs. The tough, brownish hide had a suggestion of scaliness. The narrow, elongated skull held large, almond-shaped eyes, black vertical slits centered in the golden, opalescent irises. She had seen such a creature before.

"They made their camp there and for a time life was very good. Each day the Kuniya women were able to find plenty of food, which they carried home to the camp in their curved wooden carrying dishes. They prepared their bread from seeds gathered from grasses on the plain and cooked it in the ashes of their fires. The Kuniya men, after hunting kangaroos, emus and wallabies, liked to lie resting at the edge of the sandhill as the sun set.

"This sandhill at the close of the Creation era turned to rock. The Kuniya people themselves were changed into various features of what became Mount Uluru. The women seated in their camp became large boulders in Tjukiki Gorge, while their *piti,* their carrying dish, became a tall slab of rock at the head of the gorge. A rock hole represents their campfire, and small grasses and bushes that grow in tufts in the gorge are their hairs. The sleeping Kuniya men turned into boulders, which now lie motionless in the sun on the plain beneath.

"While the Kuniya people were staying at Mount Uluru, however, life did not remain peaceful. A party of venomous snake men, the Liru, were traveling around in the Pitjantjatjara country, causing a lot of trouble. The Liru camped at Katatjuta and then decided to approach Mount Uluru to attack the Kuniya.

They were led by the great warrior Kulikudgeri, and
traveling in a large group, they crossed the sandhills
and arrived at the camp of a powerful Kuniya woman
named Pulari.

"Pulari had separated herself from the rest of her
people, as she had just given birth to a child. Enraged
by the attack and desperate to protect her child, she
sprang at the Liru with her child in her arms, spitting
out *arukwita,* the essence of disease and death. Many
of the Liru were killed, but they continued to attack.
A young Kuniya warrior challenged Kulikudgeri to a
fight to the death, and the Liru man, after an arduous
battle, fatally wounded the Kuniya man, who crawled
away over the sandhill.

"Kuniya Inkridi, the mother of the slain youth,
then rose in a fury and struck Kulikudgeri a great
blow on the nose with her digging stick. He died in
agony, his blood streaming over the surface of the
land, leaving stains on the rock that remain today.
Kuniya Inkridi mourned for her lost son. She covered
her body in red ochre and sang and wailed into the
night. She spit out *arukwita,* and any man approaching that site today will be stricken.

"Meanwhile a huge battle took place between the
Liru and the Kuniya at the water hole on the top of
the sandhill. The Liru speared a great many Kuniya
and, victorious, left the area and went back to Katatjuta. Kuniya Inkridi, the great mother snake, despaired.
Hearing of the death of her people, she sang the *arukwita* song to kill herself and the remaining Kuniya.''

Slowly, Brigid began to understand that the Anangu, the aboriginal peoples, believed the area around Mount Uluru was inhabited by their ancestral beings whose activities were recorded at many separate sites. At each site, the events that took place were to be recounted to each generation. There was a physical feature of some form at each ancestral site that represented both the activities of the ancestral being at the time of its formation, and the living presence of Tjukurpa, the Dreamtime, within that physical feature.

Whatever its form or appearance, animate or inanimate, it embodied the essence of the Tjukurpa, locked forever within it.

"At the close of the Tjukurpa period," the voices sang, "when the giant sandhill turned to stone, these epic events were enshrined in stone, also. The route of the Liru men from Katatjuta to Mount Uluru is marked by rows of desert oaks, the metamorphosed bodies of the invaders, while the tracks of the Liru men were turned into deep fissures on the southwestern face of the Rock. The spears the Liru men threw made indentations in the sand, which are now potholes on the vertical cliff face. A large split boulder was once the body of the Kuniya woman Pulari, who gave birth at this place. Within the boulder is a small cave in which her child was born.

"Near the Pulari stone is a shallow cave with stones in front, which were once Pulari and her child. Pregnant women tried to reach this cave to give birth, believing that Pulari would help them have an easier delivery.

"When the young wounded Kuniya warrior crawled away, the track he left became a watercourse. He died at a place where today there are three water holes, each of which contains the blood of the dying man transformed into water. His victor, the leader of the Liru, Kulikudgeri, became the large square boulder, while his nose—which was cut off by Kuniya Inkridi—stands out as a huge slab that has split off the main rock.

"The bodies of Kuniya Inkridi and her husband remain today as large and small boulders and rocks, the fig trees that tenaciously grip the smooth rock surface and send roots burrowing into the crevices are believed to be their hair."

The song and the pageantry of imagery went on for a long time until visions, flashes of a more recent reality rather than ancient myth, began to emerge from the shadows and penetrate Brigid's mind.

She saw from the oceans on the east and west and from the great red rock of Mount Uluru, there stood not a single building or settlement of man. It had not always been so. There had been teeming cities on the vast continent, some of them even mentioned by names in the song, but now only their memories remained, underscored by a bitter, primal resentment.

A long and vicious conflict between two starkly different ways of life dragged on for many, many years, and the memory of it, centuries later, still aroused strong emotions of hatred, sadness and rage. Invaders came, the Piranypa with white skin and rapacious appetites who tramped toward a great monolith of red rock, rising from the desert floor. She saw the council fires of the great Anangu clans, putting aside their differences, their tribal feuds to unite for a common cause. She saw spears flying, rifles belching flame, dark natives and white invaders falling and dying.

Brigid knew with the limited natural resources of the arid lands, the aborigines and the Piranypa could not live side by side in peace. The invaders fenced out the natives from their ancestral lands and tried to destroy first their way of life, then their spirits. By the time huge cities sprang up on the continent, the centuries-long genocidal warfare had reduced all but the Mutijulu people to less than memories.

The images swam faster now, flashing for only a split second in Brigid's mind. The vast backdrop of the sky turned scarlet, seeming to swell and then ripped open as if it were rotten old cloth. A bloom of distant hellfire burst open, and a sheet of flame surged outward and upward. The waves of the sea divided and the orange-yellow incandescent flare poured into Brigid and filled her to the backs of her eyeballs.

A coruscating wall of fire scorched across the ocean, riding a booming shock wave, pushing the ocean ahead of it in an overlapping series of mile-high tsunamis.

Brigid couldn't look away. A vast mushroom cloud

towered from the horizon, shot through with arcing skeins of blinding, destructive energy. A wall of smoke swept over the land. In its wake she saw ruined cities, overgrown with vegetation. Everywhere there was death. Brigid saw the whole world spread out below her, like an endless mural of horror. She passed like a phantom wind over gloomy wastes, gazing down on the legacy of the nukecaust.

The images seemed to tumble over one another in their haste to enter and exit her mind. Everywhere there was death, corpses and animated cadavers with their flesh peeled and blistered, their internal organs hanging out, boiled and burst, their empty eye sockets weeping bloody tears. Where there had once been lush and fertile fields, the desert swept in, a sea of sand lapping at the spires of half-buried skyscrapers. Instead of cities and towns, only vast, ugly craters pockmarked the ground, seething with poison.

Ungainly caricatures of human beings lurched across the wastelands, forlorn monstrosities birthed and molded by an outraged nature. Brigid tried to cringe, praying they wouldn't see her.

She soared over toxic swamps, percolating with a foul and fetid soup, and watched people desperately trying to snatch the most meager of existences from their half-dead surroundings.

She saw babies dragged cold and lifeless from rad-damaged wombs and she wanted to weep, but phantoms couldn't shed tears.

Flying up and arcing down again over bitter seas,

she plunged through a maelstrom of buffeting memory, reliving in a heartbeat all of her own suffering at the hands and bestial imaginations of the depraved men who sought to rule the ravaged ruin of the world.

Brigid understood it as the aborigines did—the apocalypse that had swept the invaders from their land, from their sacred sites. The fences had fallen down; the men who stood guard over them had sickened and died. Over a period of many years, their beloved land healed itself, renewed itself. The process was long and painful, but the Mutijulu people could afford to be patient. They had waited hundreds of years for the invaders to lose their grip on their land, on their world.

But a new group of Piranypa invaders had arrived, and they crawled and crept within the stony bosom of Mount Uluru, infesting it, infecting it, corrupting it. And if they corrupted the Uluru, they corrupted life itself.

She was flung headlong on the swirling gales, the clean, fresh wind of hope filling her lungs with an intoxicating purity. She raced upward toward the sun, exulting in its life-giving radiance.

A voice, a single one, not the mixture, spoke gruffly. "Make a choice," it said. "Dream and die or awaken and fight."

The image of the sun faded and Brigid was back in the void, a black so deep she knew she was at the far, far end of Dreamtime. She also knew she had a choice, of whether to awaken or continue to dream.

Then she felt a throbbing pain, and a moment later she became aware of her body and she knew she had decided to awaken—or that's what she fervently hoped.

Chapter 22

When Erica van Sloan finally woke up, moonlight peeped in through the polarized sheet of plastic covering the crack in the cavern ceiling. She sat up quickly, looking around the rock gallery converted to living quarters. She was quite alone. Not even Abbott and Costello, as she called her Baronial Guardsmen, were in attendance and she wondered briefly if Baron Beausoleil had ordered them away.

Sloan went to the bathroom and took a long hot shower. When she was finished, she dried herself in front of the mirrored squares glued to the stone wall and inspected her body for any sign of changes, as she did at least twice a day—particularly since she had discovered the streak of gray in her hair. As far as she could determine, it had not widened or lengthened, which was a small comfort. No new lines or wrinkles marred the sculpted smoothness of her face. She didn't murmur a thanks to Sam, as she had been wont to do before finding the sign of aging.

For over thirty years following her revival from stasis, Erica van Sloan had almost never looked at herself in a mirror. Confined to a wheelchair, she avoided her reflection with such a single-minded diligence it was almost a superstitious obsession. As far as she was concerned, her identity had died during her century and a half in cryo-suspension.

Of half-Latino and half-British extraction, Sloan had inherited her dark hair and eyes from her Brazilian mother, but she possessed her father's tall frame and long, solid legs. God only knew from which side of her family her 200 point IQ derived, but she knew she received her beautiful singing voice from her mother.

At eighteen years of age, the haughty, beautiful and more than a trifle arrogant Erica earned her Ph.D in cybernetics and computer science. She wanted to pursue a singing career, but within days of her graduation from Cal Tech she went to work for a major Silicon Valley hardware producer as a models and systems analyst.

Eight months later, she left her six-figure-a-year salary to accept a position with a government-sponsored Ultra Top Secret undertaking known as Overproject Whisper. Only much later did she realize Whisper was a major division of something called the Totality Concept, and she was assigned to one of its subdivisions, Operation Chronos. In the vast installation beneath a mesa in Dulce, New Mexico, she served as the subordinate, lover and occasional victim of a man who made her own officious personality seem mousy and shy by comparison.

Torrence Silas Burr was brilliant, stylish, waspish and nasty. He excelled at using his enormous intellect and equally enormous ego to fuel his cruel sense of humor. The word *love* had never been part of Sloan's emotional vocabulary, so she substituted for it the word *submission,* and Burr took full advantage of her devotion. He delighted in belittling and degrading not just her, but other scientists assigned to Overproject Whisper.

The one scientist he could not deride was Mohandas Lakesh Singh, the genius responsible for the final technological breakthrough of Project Cerberus, which permitted Operation Chronos to finally make some headway.

When the world blew out on noon of January 20, 2001, she ceased to think about Burr at all. Like everyone else in the Anthill installation, she prayed the safety measures would kick in like they were designed to. But despite all of their precautions, radiation still trickled in. Bomb-triggered earthquakes caused extensive damage.

Since the military and government personnel in charge had no choice but to remain in the facility, it took them a while to realize they were just as much victims of the nukecaust as those whom they referred to as the "useless eaters" of the world. Erica van Sloan couldn't help but laugh to herself over the grim irony.

Like their less educated counterparts, they had no real grasp of the scope of the global devastation. None of their painstaking calculations regarding acceptable losses, destruction ratios and the length of the nuclear winter bore any resemblance to the terrifying reality.

When this select few, this powerful elite, finally did come to terms with reality, it was too late to do much about it. They had assumed that after five years or less of waiting inside the Anthill, a new world order would be in place. Now the schedule appeared to be closer to twenty.

Sloan didn't feel she was sacrificing much when she volunteered to enter a stasis canister for a period of time, to be resurrected at some future date when the sun shone again and the world was secure.

When she awakened, more than a century had passed. During her long slumber, the Anthill installation suffered near catastrophic damage. A number of stasis units had malfunctioned, hers among them. Due to that malfunction, she was resurrected as a cripple. Worse than finding out her long, shapely legs were little more than withered, atrophied sticks, was learning the plans made for her while she slept.

Sloan was briefed on the unification program and the baronial oligarchy. She was told that to be of optimal use to the Archon Directorate and their hybrid plenipotentiaries, she needed to be as fit as it was possible for a human in her physical condition and chronological age. Moreover, Sloan was informed she was only one of several preholocaust humans, known as "freezies" in current vernacular, resurrected to serve the baronies and she should consider herself fortunate to be among their number.

In other words, she was not to grieve, mourn, weep or otherwise feel sorry for herself. She was to concentrate only on what her technological skills could contribute to the furtherance of the Program of Unification. Otherwise, she would be put out of her misery.

She learned quickly not to question. Over the years of Sloan's long life, due to the creativity and skills of her intellect, she had undergone many organ transplants, so as to extend her value to the united baronies. Despite the pain and suffering that had gone with each successive operation, Sloan never regained the use of her legs, and the neurological degeneration grew so acute she became a complete cripple.

She hadn't realized how much she loved being young, beautiful and vital, until all of it was taken from her. Then Sam, her precious son, a mixture of her in-vitro genetic material spliced with that of an Annunaki, had given it back—or at least returned the promise of it. If she could enlist Lakesh to Sam's cause, Sam would restore her youth.

Sloan ran her hands through her wet hair and tried to put the echo of Sam's words out of her mind. She was taking action, after all, putting into motion a plan that would eventually cause the imperator's path to cross that of Lakesh's again.

"Don't worry, we're still beautiful." Baron Beausoleil's soft voice startled her.

"Where have you been?" Sloan asked coolly, unwilling to show surprise by turning.

"Observing our guest." Baron Beausoleil stepped closer and her reflection slid across the mirrored squares. She was wearing the black imperial uniform, the satin tunic stretched taut across her breasts and cinched tight at her narrow waist.

"How is she?" Sloan asked.

She ran her hands over Sloan's bare shoulders. "Comfortable but confused. Not a mental state she is accustomed to feeling."

Sloan repressed a smile. Confusion was not an emotion any of the hybrids, particularly the barons, dealt with easily. She easily recalled their bewildered reactions when first they came to the realization the Archon Directorate did not exist, and then when they had first met Sam, who had been introduced to them by Balam.

At the time, Sloan could only imagine the thoughts careening and colliding within the oversized craniums of the barons. For the entirety of their artificially prolonged lives, the barons believed they served the will of the Archons—or they convinced themselves they were the Directorate's servants and therefore any action they undertook to safeguard their positions as the overlords of humankind was justified.

But their probing intelligence needed proof, and without it, doubt inevitably ate away the belief structure. Although none of the barons spoke of it, they had ceased to subscribe to the belief in the Archons. In which case, they were no longer content with their roles as the plenipotentiaries of a higher, grander authority.

They had reached this conclusion tentatively, by degrees over a period of time. When they finally did, they were as absolutely certain of it as they had been certain of the existence of the Archon Directorate. Now, dealing with the appearance of Balam, their minds were in utter turmoil, fears, desires and thoughts all crashing into each other.

Baron Beausoleil had proved to be more resilient and adaptable than the others of the oligarchy, but Erica van Sloan still wasn't sure how she felt about that. As the baron continued to caress her, her arms and belly and breasts broke out in gooseflesh, but it was not from arousal.

"Does Quavell know why she has been brought here?" she asked.

The baron laughed, a musical fluting with notes of cruel mockery within it. "She suspects. How could she not?"

"I want to speak with her." Sloan stepped away from Baron Beausoleil's touch, reaching for her uniform hanging from a hook on the wall.

The baron's role as seducer hadn't fooled her, but the woman's willingness to please her was a surprise. She had not thought it possible for a newhuman, much less a baron, to subsume her inborn arrogance and stratospheric sense of superiority to serve the needs of another—certainly not the needs of an old human.

Sloan remembered her own submission to Burr and how she had done anything necessary to stay with him, at least for a while. She had been tremendously attracted to the sheer animal dynamism of the man, but now the memory of that devotion revolted her.

Glancing into Baron Beausoleil's smiling face, she wondered how long it would take before she assessed the depth of her submissiveness to the imperial mother—and turned against her in order to add this far empire to her own holdings.

Chapter 23

Quavell was hungry. Her head had ceased throbbing, but the sharp pangs of hunger remained. She put her hands on her belly, surreptitiously examining the chrome bracelet locked tight around her right wrist. A long, slender chain was attached to the bracelet, and the other end of it was secured to an eyebolt in the wall.

Standing, Quavell started going over the area of her confinement in detail. The only furniture was a cot and a chair across the room, near the door. As she paced, she went through her memories of the past few hours, looking for anything useful that her conscious mind might have overlooked but her subconscious noticed.

She remembered the hyperdimensional transition as an onslaught of crazed sensations, wherein she felt sounds, tasted colors and smelled sights. The patchwork of experiences boiled in her mind like a caldron of pitch the size of the universe itself. Her awareness slowly returned, in bits and pieces and in no particular order. She heard a strange bass hum, as of a musical note refusing to fade, and only then did she become aware of her body again.

When Quavell opened her eyes, the first thing she saw was a rock-ribbed alcove in which she lay. Her first thought was for the safety of the child in her womb, but she sensed nothing amiss. Men in black uniforms pulled her to her feet and marched her through rocky passageways lit by naked light bulbs. Above a certain height the walls were unfinished stone, but below that they were sheathed in polished alloy. She was escorted past wooden crates, a collection of picks and shovels and other tools, and she guessed wherever she was, the installation was still a work in progress.

Quavell was brought into a cell and chained to the wall. Shortly afterward, a human male who she assumed was a medic gave her a swift, almost perfunctory examination, then she was left alone. Except for the hunger pains, she hadn't minded the isolation. She needed an undisturbed period of time to process what she had experienced, seen and overheard in order to reach a provisional hypothesis.

Judging by the uniforms the soldiers wore, she knew she was a prisoner of the imperator's forces, but she also knew she was not in the Xian pyramid. Regardless, the power that had swept her out of the Cerberus gateway unit and materialized her in the alcove fit exactly with the kind of hyperdimensional manipulation Lakesh attributed to the imperator. She was fairly certain why she had been abducted, and that knowledge allayed her anxiety to a certain degree.

Quavell stepped to the door, but the pull of the chain against her arm stopped her a foot short of it. She walked in a large half circle, examining the smooth stone of the floor, looking for loose rock. She found none, so she reached up and grabbed the chain with both hands. She threw her full weight against it, but the eyebolt held without budging even a fraction.

Returning to the cot, she sat down and took a deep breath, calming herself. She concentrated on a breathing pattern to control her hunger. Then she felt a stab of sudden fear and she swung her head up and around, toward the door. An instant later, it swung open. Two women walked in, both attired in imperial black. Quavell recognized both of them instantly.

The taller of the women smiled at her patronizingly. "Hello, Quavell. Are you comfortable?"

Quavell nodded, not speaking.

"Answer the imperial mother when she asks you a question!" the other woman snapped.

"Yes, my lord baron." Quavell's response was automatic, by rote, but Baron Beausoleil's eyes widened just a trifle in surprise.

"You know me?" she demanded.

"Yes, my lord baron. Both of you. I have seen you at Area 51."

Understanding glinted in Erica van Sloan's eyes. "Ah. I confess I was unaware of you until recently."

"That is to be expected," Quavell replied smoothly. "Until recently, I was just another drone of the Quad-Vee genotype."

Baron Beausoleil came nearer, her eyes never wavering from Quavell until she was standing right in front of her. "And what are you now?"

Quavell didn't look at her. Instead, she kept her eyes downcast as she had been conditioned to do, fixing her gaze on the baron's boots. "I appear to be a hostage, my lord baron. Or perhaps a lure would be more appropriate."

Erica van Sloan chuckled. "Or flypaper. Do you know why you are here?"

"I can only speculate."

"Please do."

In a flat, neutral monotone, Quavell stated, "Dr. Singh informed me of the imperator's desire to enlist his aid in his undertakings. He feared that if he utilized the Cerberus network, the imperator would sense it and redirect the matter stream. Apparently the imperator took this fear into account and developed a secondary choice."

Quavell paused and Sloan said, in a voice purring with amusement, "Do go on."

"Obviously I was that secondary choice, particularly after it became known I had been impregnated by a human. Due to the signals transmitted by the subdural transponder I was injected with upon my permanent reassignment to Area 51, the imperator was able to lock in on me during a mat-trans dematerialization. Now you expect Dr. Singh to come after me."

"No," Sloan said bluntly.

Quavell raised her brow arches in surprise. Erica van Sloan's smile was almost pitying when she explained, "Neither I nor my son ever envisioned Mohandas—Lakesh, I mean—gating here to the rescue, offering his services in exchange for your life and that of your child. He is not that gallant."

Quavell nodded. "I comprehend. You expected Kane to come after me. And more than likely Grant, and perhaps even Brigid Baptiste would accompany him. You would have all three of them, as well as myself. Gallantry aside, Dr. Singh would not sacrifice all of them just to save himself. Logical. Almost flawlessly so."

Erica van Sloan arched an ironic eyebrow. "Almost?"

"You overlooked one important fact—Kane wants nothing to do with me."

Baron Beausoleil frowned. "He is a human male. You carry his child. You love him. Therefore he feels responsible for you and the child in your womb."

Quavell gazed into the baron's face. "I do not love Kane. Nor does he love me, or feel responsible for me in any way. I am sure if he feels any strong emotion over my abduction, it is relief."

Baron Beausoleil's lips twisted in a sneer. "You are foolish. I saw the vid record of your seeding sessions with Kane. You were completely enamored of him. Your responses were not fabricated."

"I did what Baron Cobalt bade me to do," Quavell retorted stolidly. "Because I might have learned to take pleasure in the sessions does not mean I love him.''

The baron gazed at her in baffled anger for a long moment. Then she bent over and put both hands on either side of Quavell's face, clasping her tightly. ''Show me.''

Quavell started to struggle, then subsided. She hastily tried to empty her mind, visualizing an impregnable brick wall around her memories and store of knowledge. A drill bit of pain seemed to bore into the cranial bone at the center of her forehead. She winced.

''Your simple defenses are a waste of energy and time,'' Baron Beausoleil said. ''At best they are a temporary diversion. We are biologically and mentally linked, and you cannot hide your thoughts from me—and even if you manage to resist, I will leave your mind destroyed. You will have nothing—and we will still have you and your child as hostages.''

With a sinking sensation of resignation, Quavell realized the baron spoke the truth. She stopped erecting the mental barrier. Baron Beausoleil's eyes widened and held hers captive, peering deep, deep through them into the roots of her soul. She felt her memories being rifled, examined, weighed and judged.

''Show me,'' crooned the baron.

He helped her off with her bodysuit, peeled it down to her ankles, then lifting her out of it. Naked, they lay with their foreheads touching and he found his

*way into her. The pain was brief and gradually melted
into a delirious burning of the nerves that began in
a part of her she had always believed to be without
feeling.*

"Show me," urged the baron.

*The burning filled her entire body and she cried
out, thinking she could not bear so much pleasure
without going mad. She pulled him closer, and the
bedding beneath her turned a glorious red as her
sixty-seven years of virginity ended with a sob from
her lips and a hoarse call of release from Maddock—*

Baron Beausoleil released her, stepping back
swiftly, her face twisting in shock. "*Maddock?*"

Quavell trembled, hugging herself as the psionic
probe ended. She nodded, not speaking.

Puzzled, Erica van Sloan asked, "Who is Maddock?"

The baron gestured to her to hold off on further
questions. "It is Maddock you love?" Her voice hit
a high note of incredulity.

Again Quavell nodded.

"Is he the father of the...*thing* you carry?"

This time Quavell refused to nod or even acknowl-
edge the question. A thin, cold smile spread over
Baron Beausoleil's face. "I understand now. You
seek to protect him. Your union was unsanctioned. I
am disappointed in you, Quavell. True first love, like
any other strong drug, is addicting. And like strong,

addictive drugs, a true first love always has tragic consequences.''

Quavell stared into the baron's face, keeping her expression composed.

"You've shared memories of the man with me," Baron Beausoleil went on. "Permit me to return the favor."

An image of Maddock's face flashed into her mind, very brief, but no less horrifying—his eyes stared upward sightlessly, his mouth gaped open and his discolored tongue protruded. Blood glistened on his lips and chin. His features were frozen in a twisted mask of terror and agony. Whatever sort of death had come to him, it had been swift, but painful.

Quavell shut her eyes against the sudden wave of grief that washed over her brain. She didn't want to see anything more.

Baron Beausoleil's voice entered her ears as a taunting whisper full of savage satisfaction. "Have you nothing to say?"

Quavell opened her eyes and her pale lips stirred. Her "Yes" was barely audible.

"Speak, then," the baron commanded.

Quavell regarded her with calm, placid eyes. "I am hungry. Inasmuch as any rescue attempt is in serious doubt, will you bring me something to eat? Preferably something that won't upset my stomach?"

Chapter 24

Brigid opened her eyes, and at first she saw nothing. She felt a surge of panic, wondering if the interphaser had malfunctioned and struck her blind, but when she shifted her head, she caught a yellow glimmer of dim light. She stirred feebly, and the motion caused sweat to break out on her forehead. Her mouth was dirt dry, she felt feverish and nausea was a clawed beast trying to tear its way out of her stomach.

Gritting her teeth, she lay quietly for a long time, listening to the slow, steady thud of her heart. Then, by degrees, she turned her head and again caught the glow of light as she squinted at her surroundings. She lay inside a lean-to made of lashed-together saplings hardly large enough to accommodate the narrow, very lumpy pallet she was lying upon. It was made of woven reeds that exuded a musty vegetable odor.

The booming of drums and the incessant piping and skirling filled Brigid's ears only as a cacophonous clamor without meaning, a confusion of faraway noise and motion. The drumming was steady and regular, almost like the muffled beating of a huge heart, seeming to come from all sides at once. The sulfurous smoke of the many fires drifted around, carried on a light, eddying breeze.

Just outside the lean-to, a bonfire blazed. High flames licked from rough-hewed logs, and people danced around them, in time with the throbbing drumbeat and the eerie piping and wailing. The vibrations were like the steady beat of the wings of a great bird. Numerous figures danced near the outer ring of fires, leaping and spinning like dervishes.

There seemed to be an equal number of men and women, most of them naked but for knotted loincloths. Sweat glistened on their bare flesh. Dark skinned, slender but solid of build, and under medium height, all of them possessed the same strong features, although hair color and texture varied widely. Their painted bodies jerked in rhythm to the drums, as though the measured beats inflicted muscular convulsions.

In their hands they gripped spears and flattened pieces of wood shaped like extended Vs. With a sense of shock, she realized that the spears were called *uwas* and the V-shaped lengths of wood were *kalis,* and she watched the ceremony from inside a *wilga.*

"Tjukurpa," Domi's soft voice murmured. Brigid knew she had said "Dreamtime."

Brigid sat up quickly, gritting her teeth, silently enduring the brief spasm of vertigo. Hitching around, she saw Shizuka and Domi lying on their sides atop reed mats, breathing deeply and regularly in their sleep.

Swiping a gloved hand over her eyes to clear her vision, Brigid looked around for their weapons and the interphaser. Adrenaline flooded her system when she couldn't see her Copperhead, Domi's Combat Master or Shizuka's swords inside the *wilga.*

Brigid began to heave herself to her feet when the flickering flames struck gleaming highlights on their weapons, bound in a neat bundle just outside the open door. She didn't relax because she didn't see the interphaser. Taking a deep, steadying breath, she tried to remember what happened. Her last clear recollection was the wavering funnel of light fanning out from the apex of the interphaser. If it had been lost or confiscated, then she and her companions were stranded, thousands of miles from home.

"It's safe, do not fear," a deep male voice said.

Brigid stiffened in surprise, then put on her poker face as she tried to determine the location of the speaker.

"I'm out here."

Leaning forward, Brigid squinted toward the bonfire and saw a man sitting cross-legged directly across from the lean-to. How his voice had been projected so clearly across the many yards that separated him from her mystified Brigid.

Carefully, she eased out of the *wilga,* noting the coarse-grained red sand shifting beneath her hands. At the same time, she noted the glow of the bonfire reflected off the metal-walled pyramid resting on the man's lap. The designs on his loincloth were identical to those she had glimpsed the figure wearing in her dream. But now she could see his face.

As she moved toward him, she surreptitiously examined his face. It was broad and strong, with a splayed nose, wide, thick-lipped mouth and overhanging brows. His hair was an unruly black mass confined by a feather-bedecked headband. His near naked, sinewy body was a warm chocolate in color, underneath layers of bright yellow and red paint.

Brigid shivered involuntarily, feeling the pressure of his gaze. But she didn't feel any fear and that surprised her. "You speak English," she said blandly.

The man nodded. "Yes, the Piranypa tongue. And you learned a bit of the Anangu language while you dreamed. Enough at least so you can understand concepts, if not the precise definitions."

"What concepts are those?"

He gestured to his right, and Brigid looked toward the dancers cavorting around the bonfire. She realized with a distant sense of shock the sound she had attributed to drums were made by sticks in the hands of the musicians as they struck them together to keep a beat.

The piping, skirling notes were produced by hollow logs called didgeridoo, and the ceremonial dance was a corroboree, a plea to the spirits of the great creator heroes for help.

"My name," said the man genially, "is Yindi. I am a practitioner of the Aunquiltha."

"Magic," Brigid retorted bluntly. "That would make you a shaman or a sorcerer."

Yindi shrugged his knobby shoulders. "No less a sorcerer than you, who can fly through Dreamtime without the ritual of *raypirri,* the purification. Truly, Warramurrungundii, the Great Mother, brought you here."

Brigid didn't address his statement directly. "What about my friends?"

"They slept and dreamed as you did."

"But I woke up."

"As shall they."

As soon as the last word left Yindi's lips, Brigid heard sounds of stirring from within the lean-to, little muffled gasps of commingled surprise and fright. Within a few seconds, Shizuka and Domi crept out. Neither one of them appeared to be overly bewildered, so Brigid figured they had received the same history lesson during the interphaser transit as she had. Domi always felt an affinity for primitive people, so she seemed particularly at ease.

"What is going on?" Shizuka demanded.

Brigid gestured to Yindi. "That's what I want to know. Maybe we should all introduce ourselves first."

Names were exchanged all around, and Yindi nodded to each one respectfully. "On behalf of the Great Mother, I welcome you and thank you for heeding her call."

Facing him, Shizuka smoothly arranged her legs in

a lotus position. "What makes you so sure she brought us here?"

A smile touched Yindi's lips, and he cast his gaze skyward. "The eyes of Warramurrungundii have foretold your arrival for many days."

Brigid, Shizuka and Domi followed his upward stare, and for a long moment they saw nothing but the star-speckled tapestry of the sky, turning gray on the horizon as dawn approached. Then their breaths caught in their throats when the leathery rustling of great wings reached their ears. Dark shapes soared above them, blotting out the stars.

They could only catch glimpses of their features, but they saw long, narrow-snouted heads, the mouths full of wolfish fangs. The necks were leanly muscular. Huge wings, scalloped at the edges and stretched over bony frames, swept down to wiry legs that terminated in talon-tipped prehensile feet. Brigid guessed the wings at full extension would measure some eighteen feet from tip to tip.

Shizuka murmured a few astonished words in Japanese, and in a hushed voice Domi asked, "What are they?"

"Bats," Brigid said. "Giant mutated fruit bats. They used to be called flying foxes."

The first two or three generations of mutant animals born in the aftermath of the nukecaust had run toward polyploidism, a doubling or tripling of the chromosome complement. For a time, gargantuan species of mammal and even reptiles had roamed the world, but their increased size had greatly reduced their lifespans. Only a few of the giant varieties existed any longer. Certainly by the time Brigid was born, most of them were extinct.

Yindi didn't dispute Brigid's identification of the flying creatures. "They have been spying on the defilers of Mount Uluru, reporting to us their strength and their numbers. The woman you seek is among them."

"We know as much," Shizuka said. "How do you know that?"

A flame seemed to ignite in Yindi's eyes. "The Great Mother speaks to me—she weeps for the sacrilege done to her holy womb. She bade me curse the defilers, and so I did—I spoke the ancient words and pointed the bone. They have been dying ever since, but to complete the curse, I have been awaiting the instruments of Warramurrungundii."

"Let me guess," Brigid said dryly. "You think that's us."

"I do not think," Yindi snapped. "I know. The spirits of our ancestors are linked to Mount Uluru, and we are linked to our ancestors. The mount was ancient even in our oldest histories. Yes, much of the old way has been lost, but we do not mourn it. Instead, we have devoted our lives to preserving what survived the Pock-ee-clipse. We can do no less to honor our ancestors."

Remembering the brief vision of the snake people and their unmistakable resemblance to the Annunaki,

Brigid asked, "Where do your legends say your ancestors went?"

Yindi answered Brigid's question with a long, convoluted story of dark and mysterious matters, of Warramurrungundii conjuring magic from within Mount Uluru. Although Brigid was always interested in legend and myth, she was more impressed by the manner in which Mount Uluru still exerted a terrible elemental power over the aborigines. It filled their whole lives. The Dreamtime decree was the cohesive force that kept the aborigines in harmony with their land for over fifty thousand years. Since they were part of the land, they couldn't understand why anyone would want to defile it, particularly a sacred site like Mount Uluru. To Yindi, it was tantamount to destruction of the life force itself.

When Yindi paused for breath, Shizuka interjected, "We wish only to rescue our missing friend, not act as instruments of the Great Mother's curse."

"You cannot do one without the other," replied Yindi. "The heart of the Great Mother beats within Uluru, the life force of our people."

"Will you help us?" Domi asked.

"Of course," answered Yindi.

"How?"

"I can show you Dreamtime paths by which you will arrive within the heart of Warramurrungundii, and our enemies will be unaware of your presence."

"Actually," said Brigid, "our enemies expect

somebody to show up. So we won't exactly catch
them by surprise.''

Yindi leaned back on his haunches and a wide
smile split his face. "I think we will."

A ROSE-PINK SUN INCHED over the rim of the world,
splashing the sky with variegated scraps of color. By
the time it was a finger's width above the horizon,
Brigid figured they had walked about five miles. Vegetation sprouted from the sand, scraggly leaves moving slightly in the breeze.

She, Shizuka, Domi and Yindi strode swiftly across
the arid ground, through thickets full of shrubbery
with steely thorns. The wind-drifted sand glimmered
in long red ripples. The ground wasn't smooth, although it looked deceptively so. All of them but the
barefoot Yindi stumbled at least once on the sharp
creases of rock hidden by siftings of sand. The soles
of his feet were thickly callused.

The sun grew red and menacing as it climbed
higher. By the time it was three fingers' width above
the edge of the world, the air was heavy with radiating
waves of sheer, hellish heat. The desert hardpan
seemed to soak it up and reflect it back. There was
no shelter in sight from the rising inferno. Domi, fair
skinned and sensitive eyed, suffered the worst, but she
kept her complaints to herself. She quickly soaked her
shirt through with perspiration.

Yindi gestured for a halt at the base of a rock-
strewed dune, then motioned for them to crawl up it.

The three women did so, Domi and Brigid being careful not to get sand in the slide mechanisms of their blasters. They peered over the crest and saw pretty much what they expected. A long chain of rocky hills curved across the horizon like the fossilized vertebrae of some prehistoric monster.

The rocky hills led toward a vast, monolithic formation that shouldered the sky. The early-morning light played over its surface, splashing its domed surface with bloodred streaks. Brigid tried to estimate the size of the monstrous monolith, using the hills as a reference point, but she realized Mount Uluru was of such staggering proportions as to make its true distance from the hills difficult to gauge. She figured they were nearly a quarter of a mile away.

"Now what?" Domi muttered, shading her eyes with her hands.

"Now the eyes of the Great Mother will do more than simply observe—they will divert the attention of the defilers."

Although Yindi sounded as if he had spoken from directly behind them, when Brigid turned her head she saw him still standing at the foot of the dune, holding the interphaser in both hands.

"What do you mean by that?" Brigid asked him.

Shizuka drew in her breath sharply through her nostrils. "Look."

Brigid looked back toward Mount Uluru and glimpsed darting shapes around the domed top, the shift and blur of dark wings, black against the blue sky. Faintly, borne on the warm breeze, came the cracking reports of multiple gunshots.

A grim smile of approval tugged at the corners of Domi's lips. "Those things would divert anybody's attention."

The three women quickly backed down from the crest of the dune and clustered around Yindi. Brigid asked, "Now that we've got the diversion, what's your plan?"

Yindi hefted the interphaser. "Working in tandem with your mechanism, I will show you how to slip into the flow of Uluru through the Dreamtime paths and return safely."

"Sort of like a back alley through space-time?" Brigid inquired wryly.

Yindi frowned. "You mock my beliefs?"

"Not at all," Brigid interjected hastily. "But I have to point out that we don't know the location of our missing friend, or we could have used our 'mechanism' to deliver us right to her."

Yindi's frown turned into a patronizing smile. "I thought you understood by now—it was the will of Warramurrungundii that events unfold in this fashion. We are all caught on a wheel from which there is no release, but by grace of the Great Mother. We are whirled up into life, the light of day and carried down again into death, the darkness of night. But then another day dawns red, much like this one, and we are reborn. Death is no release from the wheel, unless the Mother should intervene."

"Will she intervene now?" Shizuka asked.

Yindi shrugged. "If you had arrived within the womb of the Great Mother in the manner you say, she would not. All of you would have died at the hands of the defilers. Now, the energy of Uluru will be with you, it will protect you and the one you seek. My belief will speed you on your way."

"Belief?" Domi echoed, her eyebrows knitting at the bridge of her nose. "What does that have to do with anything?"

Brigid knew what Yindi referred to, and she also knew neither she nor he could possibly define what he meant. It was the concept of reality as perception. Dreamtime and Uluru were powerful imprints on the minds of the aborigines, and since they didn't believe they were trapped within the parameters of a mere three dimensions, they knew the distinction between any form of existence, even past, present and future, was only an illusion. In that, the aborigines were not that far removed from theoretical physicists—they always sought symmetry.

Brigid reached for the interphaser. "I need to program in the destination coordinates."

Yindi didn't relinquish the pyramidion. His patronizing smile became outright pitying. "I thought I had myself clear...Warramurrungundii has already taken care of that."

He stepped back and placed the interphaser on the ground. Brigid stared at him, too confused to ask questions. Yindi passed the flat of his right hand over the apex of the device. Instantly, an ectoplasmic flame sprang up from the tip, stretching out, seeming to follow the movement of his hand.

With a genial smile, Yindi said, ''Now do you understand?''

Chapter 25

Although McCloy had known for weeks he was dying, none of his gloomy speculations on the manner of his death had included a blazing dawn full of inhuman howlings and the thrash of wings.

Even his field promotion to second lieutenant after the death of Yan had not alleviated his sense of foreboding. He knew some kind of doom would reach out for him, but he hadn't envisioned it stretching down from the sky.

McCloy, Cavanaugh and Franklin had been walking sentry among the crags and clefts atop Ayers Rock. With the achingly slow arrival of sunrise, they had looked forward to nothing more dangerous than being relieved and climbing down to a dining hall improvised from a cavern, having a bite to eat, then sacking out in the barracks. At the onset of the new day, none of the three men expected a swarm of winged monsters to wheel out of the sky.

Cavanaugh was the first to warn them about the attack, and he did so by shrieking in mortal agony. McCloy and Franklin were stunned by the sudden savage thundering rush of wings. They glimpsed only a horrific shape swooping away with Cavanaugh writhing within the clutch of cruel claws.

When they saw a drizzle of blood speckling the rock at their feet, McCloy and Franklin broke the chains of shock and began firing their SIG-AMTs. The first fusillade was the most effective—one of the giant bat-things howled in pain as it snapped at the crimson-leaking hole in its furred body, before plummeting from the sky.

Then the creatures dived and swooped all around them, until the soldiers were buffeted constantly by the shock of their passage. McCloy managed to press the chicken switch on his trans-comm a fraction of a second before the tip of a wing knocked the instrument from his hand. He didn't know if he had activated the alarm, since he could hear nothing but gunfire, high-pitched howls and the incessant beat of leathery wings.

Then he heard something else, a hoarse scream from Franklin. McCloy turned to see curved talons sinking into his partner's neck and wolflike fangs gorging deep in his midsection.

McCloy echoed the man's scream with one of his own, but it was filled with mindless terror as the monster flapped aloft with Franklin kicking feebly within the prison of its claws. Blue-sheened intestines trailed away from the man's torso like a ghastly banner.

When McCloy felt warm, thick drops of crimson raining onto his face, his last, tenuous grip on courage slipped. He raced toward a shelf of rock, squirmed feetfirst under it, found the ladder with his groping feet and pushed himself down into the vertical shaft.

His descent down the ladder was more of a controlled fall than a climb. His hands and feet missed several of the rungs, and when he landed at the bottom, it was flat on the soles of his boots. Sharp pains shot through his ankles, the twin impacts jacking both knees up into his lower belly. Over the whoofing explosion of violently expelled air, he heard the wail of the alarm siren.

Falling over onto his left side, McCloy tried to drag air into his emptied lungs. Troopers were pounding toward him, all of them brandishing autoblasters. They shouted questions at him, but McCloy could only gesture toward the ladder and snap at air. They tramped past him, over him, even on top of him.

Forcing himself to his elbows, breath rasping in and out of his straining lungs, McCloy dragged himself away from the ladder so he wouldn't be an obstacle. He pulled off his helmet as he crawled toward a recessed archway in the cavern wall, hoping to get out of the way of the imperial soldiers.

Before he reached it, a light sprang up from within it, seeming to sprout from the floor. It stretched upward in a column, then expanded into a shimmering fan shape. He gaped at it, wheezing, his thought processes frozen.

A yellow nova of brilliance erupted from the archway. McCloy felt a shock wave slapping his face. His eyes stung fiercely. He knuckled his eyes, and through the blurred afterimage of the flare, he saw three dark, shadowy shapes shifting in the fan of light. The shadow shapes looked distorted, as if they approached from a great distance, elongated and strangely silhouetted by a sun he couldn't see. The edges of the light seemed to peel back and fragment. A trio of human figures stepped out of nowhere and stood in the archway. Below, the glowing funnel disappeared back into the cavern floor, as if it were liquid and had been sucked down by the rock.

DOMI TOOK IN their surroundings with one swift glance, made a split-second threat assessment, then bounded forward to the kick the black-clad man in the chest with her left foot and knock his autoblaster aside with the right. The man's eyes gazed up at her, glassy and full of pain, his lips writhing over his teeth in a silent question.

By the time Shizuka and Brigid reached them, Domi's Combat Master was aligned with the soldier's head. "On your feet," the albino commanded.

Slowly and carefully, the man pushed himself erect, his eyes darting from the bore of Domi's pistol to the Copperhead in Brigid's hands to the unsheathed swords held by Shizuka.

"What's your name?" Brigid asked.

"McCloy," he husked out.

Brigid stated, flatly, "Well, McCloy, if you tell us what we want to know, you'll live through this. We're looking for a woman."

McCloy shook his head. "No women here, except for the baron and the imperial mother."

Brigid's mind raced. "Imperial mother?"

McCloy only nodded.

"Who is that?" Shizuka demanded.

"He can only mean Erica van Sloan," replied Brigid. "But who is the woman baron?"

"Baron Beausoleil," the imperial soldier answered.

"Where are they?" Domi asked, pushing the bore of her pistol against his chest.

McCloy swallowed hard. "I really don't know."

Brigid gestured with the Copperhead. "Take us to where they might be."

As McCloy started to step forward, Shizuka laid the edge of her *tanto* against the base of his neck. In a low, deadly voice she intoned, "Play us false and you die."

McCloy led them through several dimly lit rooms, seeming to pay no attention to the alarm siren.

Domi whispered nervously to Brigid, "Don't like being here without the interphaser."

Brigid nodded. "Me, either. But we have to trust that Yindi can control the vortex nodes in here like he claims."

McCloy pushed open a heavy sliding door that led into a corridor that ran in a long, gradual zigzag past another doorway, like the one they had just stepped through. Within a natural recessed niche, a little finger of glowing light danced like witchfire.

McCloy stared at it as they passed, but didn't ask

questions. The man seemed to be in a state of shock. He stepped before the next door and pushed it open. "The mess hall for the unit is down here."

Domi and Brigid looked around suspiciously, their guns at the ready, but they followed the man into a large room full of tables and benches. McCloy marched across the hall swiftly. They moved through a doorway on the far side and into a cavern that was buttressed at intervals by thick pillars. From the ceiling dangled large hooks on chains that stretched down from traveling hoists. The room was packed with crates.

Brigid repressed a shudder. "This is the Woman's Cave."

McCloy blinked at her. "Yeah, that's right. How did you know?"

Brigid only shook her head and pushed him forward. The cave went on for a hundred feet, then reached a junction point, three passages radiating off like the spokes of a wheel. At the mouth of each tunnel, numbers one through three were painted in red on the floor.

"Now what?" Domi asked irritably, her voice sounding hushed.

The alarm suddenly stopped wailing. The sudden cessation of the shriek was almost as nerve-racking as the sound itself.

"It appears the diversion has been dealt with," Shizuka muttered.

Domi grabbed a handful of McCloy's tunic and

pushed him into a passage. "We've wasted enough time," she snapped. "I'll go with him. You two take the other tunnels. Let's meet back here."

Brigid opened her mouth to voice an objection, then shrugged. Shizuka gave her a rueful smile and chose a tunnel more or less at random. Brigid watched her go, then swiftly entered a passage. She had walked less than fifty yards, when she heard the murmur of voices ahead of her and the scuff and scutter of feet.

Brigid flattened against the wall, waiting and listening. She heard a woman's voice speaking sharply and imperiously, then a male mumbling a response. In the passage between two archways, a pair of men appeared in white uniform jackets, red trousers and black, polished knee boots. Although she had never seen one, Kane had once described Baronial Guardsmen to her.

As a general rule, Magistrates held Baronial Guardsmen in contempt, because their duties consisted of strutting around, opening doors and sneering at the infrequent visitor seeking an audience with a baron. Kane had learned the hard way guardsmen were products of bioengineering and were anything but mere servants.

These two guardsmen were identically trim and blue eyed, though one had blond hair and the other black. They made up for the color difference by styling their hair the same way. Both of their faces were clear of complexion, subtly sculpted to be the epitome of male beauty.

Walking between them was a tall woman who Brigid saw was close to the epitome of female beauty. She had only seen her once before, but she recognized her instantly.

Brigid stepped out into the center of the passageway, Copperhead held in such a way that she could catch both guardsmen with a left-to-right pattern of fire with little chance of the rounds ricocheting off the rock. In a studiedly casual tone, Brigid said, "Dr. Erica van Sloan. The imperial mother."

The guardsmen came to an immediate halt, shifting position to completely block Erica van Sloan from target acquisition. Their eyes widened and slitted in unison.

Peering over the broad bulk of their shoulders, Sloan gazed at Brigid steadily. Her reaction was not what Brigid had expected. She laughed.

"Did I say something funny?" Brigid asked.

Sloan shook her head. "Not really. It's just I had pretty much convinced myself the plan to entrap Mohandas had failed. Now, here you are. Who came with you? Kane? Grant?"

"Neither," Brigid retorted.

The woman's violet eyes slitted. "You didn't come alone."

Brigid shook her head. "I didn't say I did. But Kane and Grant are safe with Lakesh."

"Oh." Sloan said the word as if she understood everything. "Then they'll be along shortly."

"I'm afraid not. They were injured by the energy backlash of Sam's wormhole. If you were hoping to hold me hostage or use me as a pawn, you'll have to come up with another strategy."

Sloan glowered at her. "I don't believe you."

"I don't care if you do or don't," Brigid retorted grimly. She waggled the noise suppressor of the Copperhead suggestively. "You know why I'm here. Take me to her."

Sloan stepped back, raising an imperious hand. "Abbott, Costello. Get rid of this arrogant bitch."

Brigid squeezed the trigger, firing a 3-round burst. The silenced shots sounded like an old emphysemic man sneezing.

The guardsmen moved swiftly, bounding toward her. Two of the three rounds caught the black-haired man on his right shoulder. Scraps of tunic exploded in a clot of blood. Erica van Sloan screamed something incoherent, but by her tone she was both outraged and frightened.

The guardsman stumbled, arms windmilling, his boot soles squeaking on the floor, seeking purchase. They found it and the man regained his balance. He and his brother guardsmen exchanged long looks. Then they rushed toward Brigid.

She had little time to think and even less to act. Swiftly, she took the flash-bang stun grenade from her combat harness, pulling the pin and slipping off the spoon all in one smooth motion. She threw the bomb toward the guardsmen, and it landed directly in their path. She squeezed her eyes shut a shaved sliver of a second before a stunning, painfully loud thunderclap battered at her ears. A blazing nova of dazzling white light accompanied the teeth-jarring concussion of compressed air.

When she opened her eyes, she saw the men reeling in agonzied shock, hands either clapped over blinded eyes or cradling hemorrhaging ears. Erica van Sloan was nowhere in sight. Brigid moved forward, sidling past the pair of guardsmen.

A hand closed around her right arm. It felt like a steel vise, painfully crushing muscle and tendon against bone. The guardsman jerked, and hammered her against the opposite wall.

Brigid managed to go with the force of the throw, cushioning the impact with forearms and hands, trying to cover the left side of her head.

Over the past two years, she had been involved in any number of life-threatening situations, and she still didn't know if she'd survived them through luck, divine intervention or simply the proper management and application of skills to circumstances. Although she had taken pains to develop survival and fighting skills, the deranged Otto Skorzeny had inflicted a serious injury to her skull. Now she found herself almost unconsciously overprotecting that side of her head.

The blond guardsman groped for her blindly,

growling deep in his bull throat. Brigid lifted her Copperhead and drove the butt forward from the shoulder in a fast, flat trajectory. The metal stock impacted like a battering ram against the bottom tip of the man's nose. There was a very faint, mushy crunch of cartilage. Like a skier catching a low branch under the chin, the man's head snapped back, his legs flying out from under him. His crushed nose spewed blood as bone splinters pushed through his sinus cavities and into his brain. The Baronial Guardsman was dead before his body settled.

The dark-haired guardsman whirled, his hands clawing empty air for her. She dropped flat on her left side, sweeping her right leg out in a slashing kick, catching the man just behind the knees. His legs buckled and he staggered, but he didn't fall.

In the short span of time it took the imperial soldier to recover his balance, Brigid had her hands on her Copperhead and she worked the trigger, firing a triburst into the man's head. Part of his scalp floated away amid a misting of blood.

As his body sagged, Brigid rolled her feet and broke into a sprint, picking up the chase for Erica van Sloan. She had barely taken three strides when her trans-comm chirped. Pulling it from her harness and opening the frequency, she heard Domi's breathless voice, "Found her. But we can't afford to overstay."

At that moment, the alarm siren began wailing again.

Chapter 26

McCloy led Domi down a corridor that was dimly lit by overhead bulbs encased in wire cages. The passageway was lined with numbered doors.

"What's this area?" Domi asked the soldier quietly.

"Private quarters," the man answered equally quietly, "for officers and important people."

Domi forced McCloy to knock on each door, and if he received a response, to identify himself by his name and rank. McCloy did as he was told, but no one called out from the rooms.

At the last door, McCloy rapped on it and already started to turn away when a feminine voice asked, "Yes?"

Domi nodded shortly and gestured with her Combat Master for McCloy to open the door. He did so, pushing it open slowly. Domi stayed out of sight, the bore of her pistol pressed against the small of his back. He stiffened and said over his shoulder, "I think this is the woman you've been looking for."

Pulling him back, Domi peered around the frame and saw Quavell sitting in a chair, calmly eating little cubes that resembled foam rubber. A plate resting on the floor beside her contained a number of crumpled paper wrappers.

A curse started up Domi's throat, then she saw the chain leading from Quavell's right wrist to an eyebolt affixed to the wall. Knowing for certain that she was a prisoner made her almost as relieved as seeing her alive.

When Domi stepped into the cell, Quavell's hand froze as it lifted a food cube to her lips. Domi enjoyed the expression of surprise that crossed her usually masklike face.

Turning back to McCloy, Domi said, "Get in here."

McCloy shook his head. "Sorry, I can't."

Domi glared at him. "What do you mean you can't?"

A slender, dark-haired woman wearing a black uniform identical to his slipped around McCloy. A short-barreled pistol was nestled in her delicate right hand, but it wasn't pointed at Domi. The barrel was on a direct line with Quavell.

"Drop your weapon," she said.

Domi didn't move or otherwise react.

Softly, Quavell said, "This is Baron Beausoleil."

Domi refused to allow the astonishment welling up in her to register on her face. A female baron wasn't a concept she had ever entertained.

"Do it," Baron Beausoleil grated, "or I'll kill Quavell and her child...and then kill you."

Domi slowly lowered her pistol, placing it on the

floor at her feet. The baron jabbed the pistol in her direction. "Turn around."

The albino girl complied. The baron stepped into the cell, and when Domi felt the cold tip of the gun touch the back of her neck, she stepped backward, stamping down hard with her foot on the woman's instep, pivoting on it with all her weight, her hand sweeping back to chop at the gun. She knocked it askew.

Baron Beausoleil uttered a half scream as Domi hooked her left fist into her body. Starting from her hip, the punch hinged the woman in the middle and her mouth and eyes flew wide. Latching on to her right forearm with both hands, Domi snapped up a knee as if the baron's arm were a stick of kindling she intended to break in two.

Baron Beausoleil uttered a gagging shriek, and the pistol fell to the floor. Domi shifted her hold, trying to get her into a hammerlock and force her facedown on the floor. She had struggled with hybrids in the past and she assumed it wouldn't require much effort to lay the woman out.

The baron surprised her, first by wriggling out of her grip, then by head-butting her in the lower belly with such force she felt bile leap up her throat. The baron's hands lashed out, sharp fingernails seeking her eyes. Domi slapped them aside, and found herself battling less of a woman than a crazed animal. The baron's hands clutched her around the throat, the thumbs seeking her larynx.

Prying on the woman's wrists, Domi managed to break Baron Beausoleil's mercilessly choking grip. The baron feinted to the left, then leaped to the right, pivoted and swung her left leg up and around in a pretty fair crescent kick.

Domi surged forward in the opposite direction. The baron's boot grazed her head, but she slammed against her, grabbing a handful of silky black hair. Both women fell heavily, the baron striking her head against the floor.

The baron struggled and heaved and gouged savagely at Domi's eyes. She grasped Domi beneath the chin, her long nails raking at her face. The albino girl sank her teeth into Baron Beausoleil's thumb, and the baron shrieked in pained fury. With a twist and sideways wrench of her whole body, Baron Beausoleil managed to shove Domi to one side. She rolled and came swiftly to her feet, planting a boot on the side of her adversary's head as she tried to rise.

Domi went with the force of the kick, back-somersaulted to her feet and rushed her. The baron rammed the crown of her head forward, trying to butt her face into the back of her skull.

Dodging, Domi kicked out with one long leg, clipping Baron Beausoleil at ankle level. The woman fell, caught herself on the flats of her hands and swiveled around, kicking Domi's already tender midsection. As she stumbled, the baron sprang to her feet and launched a left hook.

Domi shunted the blow aside with a right arm

sweep, then brought her left fist up fast, connecting with the underside of the baron's jaw.

The uppercut snapped the woman's head back. Arms windmilling, she toppled and fell almost at Quavell's feet. Quavell gathered the slack of her chain in one hand and whipped the metal links against the back of the baron's head. She crumpled to the floor in a senseless, slack-limbed heap.

Domi gave Quavell a quick smile and retrieved her pistol. She inspected the bracelet around Quavell's wrist, then visually traced the chain to the eyebolt in the wall. She raised her Combat Master and said, "Cover your ears."

Quavell barely had time to follow Domi's suggestion before she squeezed the trigger. The .45-caliber wrecking ball punched a crater in the wall, knocking loose the eyebolt with a spurt of rock dust. Quavell instantly began reeling in the loose chain.

Domi drew out her trans-comm and keyed in Brigid's and Shizuka's frequencies. "Found her," she said. "But we can't afford to overstay."

At that moment, the alarm siren began wailing again.

As THE SIREN SEEMED to scream directly in her ear, Shizuka whirled on the ball of one foot and came up with a two-handed stroke. With a faint wet sound, the blade sliced the soldier's right arm off just below the elbow. Coming up from under his armpit without ceasing her movement, she circled back, the *katana* flashing in her hands. The trooper's head fell from his shoulders, his mouth open and moving as if it had one last thing it wanted to say. The head rolled across the cavern floor like an awkward ball. The severed neck spouted a scarlet-foaming fountain from the opened arteries.

Shizuka pivoted, her *katana* and *tanto* cutting glittering wheels through the dim light of the junction. She closed on a trooper just as he raced out of a passageway. The edge of her blade sank into the man's jaw at the high collar of his tunic. It wasn't a particularly powerful blow, but sufficient to open up the man's throat in a jetting stream of crimson.

She continued to glide gracefully even as she struck, moving around him as if performing a dance step. The trooper made a peculiar croaking sound, then blood bubbled up in a precise line across his torso. The cut was from the juncture of the neck just above the seventh vertebrae, then through the collarbone, angling to the sternum, slicing through the cartilage and spinal column. The man slid wetly in two pieces to the ground.

Shizuka looked at the two dead men and tried to catch her breath. She had been waiting for Brigid, Domi and Quavell in the junction where the tunnels met for the last minute. The passageway that led back the way they had come was disgorging the black-uniformed imperial soldiers for the last thirty seconds.

Running footfalls commanded her attention and a trio of troopers sprinted out of the passage. They jolted to shocked halts when they caught sight of her. Shizuka raised her swords, crossing them to fashion an X. The three men could only goggle at her, even though they were armed with spidery-looking auto-blasters.

In that half second of confusion and disbelief, Shizuka's right-handed *tanto* sliced through a man's neck and blood spattered across the cheek of the soldier standing next to him.

As he reeled away, trying to staunch the scarlet streams squirting through his fingers, Shizuka advanced on the two black-uniformed and helmeted men, sweeping her swords in elaborate figure-eight patterns. They backed away as she approached, then they turned and ran.

Shizuka permitted herself a cold smile of satisfaction and resumed her place in the center of the junction. Within a moment, Brigid appeared, panting and wincing as if in pain. As soon as Shizuka caught sight of her, Domi and Quavell emerged from the mouth of the passageway directly opposite her.

Brigid swept her eyes over the glittering pools of blood on the floor and the maimed corpses. Half under her breath, she murmured, "You can't do one without the other. Warramurrungundii ought to be pleased."

Domi, half supporting Quavell, snapped, "I know I am. At least if we can get out of here by the way Yindi promised."

"I think we can take his word for it," Shizuka said.

Brigid eyed Quavell closely. "Are you all right?"

Quavell seemed too bewildered to speak. "I do not understand why you risked your lives to save mine."

Brigid took her by the arm and hustled her toward the tunnel. "It's not saved yet."

Eyes alight, Domi laughed. "It's a girl thing."

Quavell looked at her, her expression puzzled. "Again—I don't understand."

Brigid smiled at her. "It's what we do, Quavell. After you've been with us a couple of years, you'll get it."

Quavell gazed at her, then shook her head. Quietly, she said, "It will take more than a couple of years."

Epilogue

The chill that came with nightfall set Mammoth Mare McSween's teeth to chattering, but she walked on. The wind had veered during the day, blowing down from the north and bringing unseasonably cold breezes gusting across the hills.

Mare walked alone, having been deserted once and for all by her crew the day before. Not only had they abandoned her—they also took her beloved Mossberg rifle with them. Then they had scattered, but shortly thereafter she spied at least half a dozen Deathbirds cutting search patterns across the sky. She knew they were looking for her crew, so she didn't mind that they had left her. Most of them had stayed together and offered easy targets for the Mags.

She tramped through a gully and there was enough light from the rising Moon, peeping from behind ragged clouds, to light her way. The trail became rockier and more treacherous as it wound around steep ravines. The detonation of thunder boomed in the distance, a long, loud roll. Mare scanned the sky and saw billowing clouds massing above the jagged peaks of hills, less than a couple of miles away. The underside of the clouds bore a sickly green tinge, undershot by a salmon pink.

Fingers of dread closed about her heart at the prospect of being trapped out in the open by a chem storm. She quickened her pace, even though the footing was uncertain. There was another flash of lightning, intimidatingly close. Mare could feel her body hair tingle and stand up. The thunderclap followed almost immediately. She smelled the sharp sting of acid in the air and knew the storm would be a bad one.

Then, when lightning flashed again, she saw the dark mouth of a cave only a few yards ahead of her. Mare quickened her pace, but she didn't immediately enter. Cupping her hands around her eyes, she peered into the shapeless darkness. She sniffed the air, but didn't detect the musky scent of an animal. Cautiously she took a step forward. Then, from the blackness ahead of her, she heard a voice, taut with fear but sounding old and tired. "So, you've found me at last."

Mare halted but didn't say anything. Her eyes scanned the darkness, expecting at any instant to hear a gunshot and feel the hot hammer of lead pounding into her body. When it didn't happen, she took a couple of more steps into the cave, straining her ears and eyes, but it was too dark to make out anything.

"I'm not looking for anyone," she said. "I just want to get out of the storm."

After a moment she heard the rustle of movement. "Where are you from?"

"Nowhere in particular. Who are you?"

A note of autocratic authority entered the voice. "This is my place, I ask the questions. Do you have a name?"

Mare forced a laugh. "Of course I do. It's Mary Lou. How about you? Do you have a name?"

"Name?" The tone was a bitter, husky whisper. "I had a title, which is more important than a name."

Mare felt her nape hairs tingling. She heard the scuff of shambling feet. From the shadows limped a gaunt, man-shaped figure with unusually long arms. He appeared to be naked, his body covered with leaking sores and discolored lesions. The man's face was in dark shadow, but Mare was able to glimpse a long, narrow visage and a round, hairless skull that seemed just a bit too large.

In a hoarse voice, but with a steel edge to it, the man declared, "I was Baron Cobalt. And I command you to do one of two things—help me live or help me die."

Stony Man is deployed against an armed
invasion on American soil...

DEEP RAMPAGE

In this brand-new episode, Stony Man comes up against
the shkval—a supersonic underwater rocket with stunning
destructive capabilities. Elusive arms dealers have put it up
for sale, making it available for any terrorist group with a
cause...or a grudge. Racing against the clock, Stony Man
hunts for the elusive arms dealers selling blood and death.

STONY MAN

*Available in
December 2002
at your favorite
retail outlet.*

Take
2 explosive books
plus a
mystery bonus
FREE

DEATH LANDS®

Destiny's Truth

Available in December 2002 at your favorite retail outlet.

JAMES AXLER

DEATH LANDS

Destiny's Truth

Emerging from a gateway in New England, Ryan Cawdor and his band of wayfaring survivalists ally themselves with a group of women warriors who join their quest to locate the Illuminated Ones, a mysterious pre-dark sect who may possess secret knowledge of Deathlands. Yet their pursuit becomes treacherous, for their quarry has unleashed a deadly plague in a twisted plot to cleanse the earth. As Ryan's group falls victim, time is running out—for the intrepid survivors…and for humanity itself.